DEATH WISH

DEATH WISH

A CHARLEY SPENCER NOVEL

DIANE FANNING

Prologue

Mary Alice Monroe rubbed a heart-shaped hunk of angelite between her thumb and index finger as she stared out at the crystalline whiteness of the falling snow.Each flake descended in an artful melody, covering the ugly and the beautiful without distinction, like an act of grace and forgiveness. Despite the serenity of that moment, dark thoughts obsessed her. Fantasies of Hank's death ran on an endless loop.

She imagined him walking in on a hold-up at the convenience store where he always stopped to grab a cup of coffee and a pastry on the way to a job site. The robber turned, startled, and fired without thinking.Hank's blood flew everywhere as he dropped lifeless to the floor. And Mary Alice remained standing, staring in the window—the hapless widow.

Her dominant fantasy on this day, though, revolved around the weather. The snowflakes started falling before dawn on top of the previous night's chilly rain that formed a barrier of ice on the pavement. Since Hank's early morning departure, no one had attempted the steep hill of the road in front of their house, leaving an illusion of perfection as far as she could see from the front door. The muddy ruts Hank left in the yard when he drove home drunk last month were gone.White blankets covered the gray dormant tree branches and turned winter-naked shrubs into snowy sculptures.

And yet, Hank insisted on going up the mountain, greedy for the check payable at the completion of the current phase of construction and paranoid that if he missed the meeting, he'd never receive the money.

She imagined him driving home, hitting a treacherous sheet of ice that grabbed and pulled the wheels of his truck. Instinctively, he turned the steering wheel in the opposite direction and then remembered to turn with the slide, but it was too late. All four tires left the road, and the vehicle's creep over the rocky soil turned into a roll, gaining speed with every rotation of the axle.

He raced downhill backward, and the driver's side of the truck smashed into a tree, preventing him from making an emergency escape out the door. The back two wheels dropped over the precipice with the drive shaft balanced on a protruding boulder. For a moment, Hank thought his life was spared. Then, the rear end dropped like a seesaw, raising up the front and launching the truck into a somersault before plunging eighty feet below. The truck came to rest on the roof of the cab with Hank's lifeless body hanging upside down, restrained only by the seat belt.

"Aaaah," she sighed as a smile curled her lips. "If only it were true." She rolled the thought of Hank's death around in her mouth. It tasted as sweet and thick as honey.

There were so many ways he could end up at the bottom of the mountain. A sloppy swerve to miss a deer. Another driver losing control in bad road conditions and slamming head-on into Hank's truck. A heart attack in the middle of a bad curve. Just thinking about it made her feel as warm as if the sun were shining through glass directly on her skin, toasting her body from head to toe.

Living with him was a life she didn't want. But she had to admit that her own bad choices got her there. She was so desperate to get out of her childhood home that she embraced the first guy that showed any serious interest. Instead of attending college as she'd planned, she dropped out of high school when she got pregnant and married Hank. She was shocked when her new husband informed her that he had arranged for an abortion. When he said she'd have to raise the child on her own if she decided not to go through with it, she acquiesced.

From that day onward, she made scores of faulty decisions, going along to get along with Hank. She stood on the sidelines and watched as he destroyed all her dreams. She knew it wasn't fair to blame him for everything wrong in her life. She'd enabled him after all. She'd accepted all his criticism as if it were the gospel truth. She'd absorbed his control into her skin like osmosis. He chased away all her friends, now his friends were all she had. Her lifelong desire for a family? According to Hank, she wasn't fit to be a mother. He said, "You can't take proper care of a husband, and children are far more demanding." For the longest time, she kept trying to please him, to prove him wrong. But nothing was good enough. Nothing would ever be enough. Now, the only dream that remained in her heart was that Hank would drop dead.

She left her idle musings behind as Hank's truck descended the hill, desecrating the purity of the white covering on the road. She scurried to the kitchen to put the finishing touches on dinner. Before she could get anything on the table, the back door slapped open, stopping only after it banged into the wall.

"Where's my supper?" he said.

"Putting it on the table right now, Hank."

"About time," he muttered.

She opened her mouth to respond, then slapped it shut. If she reminded him that if she'd put everything on the table when he said he'd be home, it would all be cold by now. She held her peace, loaded the table, and took a seat.

"Where's my beer? What's wrong with you?"

"I'm getting it, Hank," She said in response to the first question. She knew better than to answer the second. She was too tense to eat now and just watched him shoveling down forkfuls of meat loaf, mashed potatoes, and green beans into his mouth. He set down his fork and took a long swallow of beer. "What the hell did you do with yourself all day? You sure didn't mop the floor. It's a mess."

"Well, I made this dinner that you're eating and…"

"It sure didn't take you long to throw this slop together."

Teeth clenched tight, Mary Alice said, "If it's slop, Hank, why are you eating it?" She knew she'd made a mistake, but it was too late to take back her words.

"You avoiding my question? Did you spend the whole day lazing around reading another book?"

"No, Hank, I didn't."

"All you want to do is read, read, read. The floor needs mopping, the tables need dusting, and I bet you haven't made the bed yet. None of your responsibilities matter to you. You just stick your nose in a book and forget it all."

For a moment, she thought about his reaction if she said that she'd spent the day thinking about the many different ways he could die, before responding to his criticism. "As I said, I didn't spend my day reading.The books I lazed around with today were your business books. I did the fourth quarter financials, the payroll tax, and started on the annual report."

"You sound resentful, Mary Alice. That business pays our bills and puts food on the table. You're a damned bookkeeper. Seems to me you'd be glad to do the paperwork for our family business instead of slaving away for someone else."

"If I slaved away for someone else, I'd get a check at the end of the damn week." She knew she was in trouble even before he rose from the chair.She could smell his rage. She tried to jerk back from his hand, but all that did was disrupt the balance of the chair.It fell over with her in it.

She wanted to jump up on his back and gouge his eyes out. She knew, though, if she tried, he'd not stop until she ended up in the emergency room again, lying to nurses and doctors. Instead, she laid there, breathing in and out, trying to subdue her anger and calm the storm of rage that made her body shake.

"Oh, for god's sake, woman. Get your lazy ass off the floor. You've got a kitchen to clean up."

He threw his napkin at her face, obscuring her view. She couldn't see, but she could still hear his footsteps going down the hall, the basement door creaking open, and his boots descending the stairwell. When she knew he was completely out of sight, Mary Alive dared to get up—furious with him and disgusted with herself.

Chapter One

The urgency in Sheriff Dwayne Hatcher's voice when he hollered my name made my feet hustle over to his side.

"We got a suspicious death—actually, three. Anyway, it's your case. Out on Old Spotswood Road. The Monroe place. You know it?"

Viewing dead bodies was not my idea of fun. Still, I was jazzed. I'd worried this moment would never come. "The one with the big red barn with a stone foundation?" I asked.

"Yep. That's the one. Whitely and Riley went out there on a wellness check. They've secured the premises and are waiting for you."

"Who called it in?"

"Daughter-in-law, it says here, a Mary Alice Monroe. Looks like a homicide-suicide." He handed me a slip of paper with the Monroe address.

"Has she been informed?"

"No. She needs to be told in person. You can take care of that after you confirm the situation."

Out in the parking lot, piles of dirty snow reminded me that a trip out into the sticks was going to be a challenge. Before I could get into my car, Lieutenant Russ Holcombe stopped me. Holcombe was a grumpy, old guy with the big ears and droopy eyes that made him look like a basset hound in a perpetual bad mood. A lot of cops didn't want to work with him, but I did. His wealth of knowledge and solid police sense added up to a great teacher.

"Listen, Spencer," he said, "they gave you this job because Whitely told the sheriff it's a murder-suicide. Figured you can't screw that up. But Riley called me. He says something doesn't look right to him. He thinks someone else was involved. Don't say anything to him in front of Whitely. Riley would get his ass chewed for going behind Whitely's back. Got it?"

"Yes, sir."

"Check and double-check everything. Don't assume anything."

"No worries, Holcombe. I learned from the best."

The main roads were easy to traverse, but I was still concerned about what I might find on unplowed secondary streets like Old Spotswood Road. The entry to the Monroe place worried me even more—I hoped the driveway wasn't a long stretch of snow-covered gravel. Whitely and Riley had gotten there, though, making it unlikely that I would have any serious problems.

On top of my apprehension about driving conditions, I felt a churning excitement over taking the lead on a homicide for the first time. I'd worked two homicide cases, but only as an assistant. I couldn't believe my luck. I knew some of the sheriff's hesitation rested in my gender. He seemed to have a hard time accepting the fact that a woman had the competence and toughness needed to crack a murder case. I knew I had a lot to prove and was determined to do it.

The electric buzz of anticipation and fear of failure ran through my middle and down the length of my arms. I needed to keep it all in check to solve this crime, while maintaining a professional façade at all times.

Old Spotswood Road had been plowed, sort of, with patches of flattened, dirty snow making it a bit of an obstacle course. Along the roadside, mountains of pushed aside scrapings made me feel like I was driving through a dirty white tunnel with a sunroof. As usual, more snow had fallen out here than in town.

Another pleasant twist of fate was the care the plow operators took to not close off the end of the Monroe driveway. That was cleared, too, though with a narrower blade than the one on the county plow, probably one hooked to a pickup truck or a tractor. I drove about a hundred yards on the snowy gravel before I reached Whitely's, and Riley's squad car pulled off to the side. I followed their example, pulling up behind them.

Stepping out of my car, I was distracted by the brilliant red of a cardinal, looking twice as bright against the white background. Undulating drifts of snow covered the ground. Mounds of it piled up on the bowed branches of barren trees like frosting on a wedding cake. Icicles hanging from the barn roof sparkled in the sun. A snapshot of serenity and beauty that made it difficult to believe I had entered a crime scene and three dead bodies rested inside that homey, two-story farmhouse in front of me.

At the front door, I kicked off my snowy boots before pulling on the latex footies and gloves. On the large, braided rug in the living room, two white teacups decorated with pink roses lay on the floor in front of two overstuffed chairs. The two matching saucers were a few feet away—one right side up, the other upside down.

Whitely said, "Spencer."

I acknowledged both men. "Whitely, Riley." Both nodded in response.

Whitely said, "There are three bodies in the bedroom. Two older folks tucked into the bed, and a younger guy sprawled over them. The guy on top of the covers has a gunshot wound in his temple—suicide most likely. Looks like a family problem."

I glanced over at Riley. His eyes were wide, and his lips pursed. I nodded my head, hoping to deliver the message that Holcombe had relayed his concerns to me.

"Let's go to the bedroom," I said. I followed Whitely, and Riley trailed after me. Riley tapped on my shoulder and mouthed, "Holcombe?" I nodded

The oak-framed bed was the only untidy object in the room. An elderly nightgown-clad woman rested on the left side, a nightshirt-wearing older man on the right. A younger man in blue jeans and ropers sprawled across the lower half of the older man's body. On one side of the room, an elaborately carved oak dresser was covered with a doily. A silver mirror, comb, and brush were arranged with precision on the right side and a small jewelry box on the left. An identical dresser sat against the adjacent wall with a similar doily on its surface, a small bowl with cufflinks and tie tacks, along with a comb sat on top of it.

"What did it look like when you entered the room?" I asked.

"Pretty much like you see it. Two heads on pillows, bed linens pulled midway up their chests, with their arms on the outside of the duvet. All very neat and tidy as if they were asleep," Whitely said. "When we moved closer, we thought they were both dead. We checked for vitals anyway and called for an investigator and an ambulance. Then, I checked the bathroom across the hall. It appeared as if someone had thrown up in there a lot."

I bent over next to the sprawled body to get a closer look at the entrance wound. The stippling tattooed the area around it, indicating that the barrel was close to the skin but not quite touching it.

"Did you find the gun?" I asked.

"Yes, right over on the other side of the bed."

I walked around and looked at it, then examined the position of the younger man where he lay on top of the older man's body. The younger man's hands were wedged beneath his body. "How do you think the gun got over here, Whitely?"

"It looks to me as if he shot himself, and as he fell forward, the gun flew out of his hand and onto the floor."

I glanced at Riley, eyes still wide, lips still pursed. "How did his arms get under his body, do you think?" I asked.

"A muscle memory jerk—pulled his arms back and tucked his hands to protect his core."

I didn't think that made much sense, but I still need to get as much feedback from him as I could to investigate all possibilities. "Which of his hands held the gun?" I asked Whitely.

"The right one, of course."

"Do you know that he's right-handed?"

"No. But most people are, and he was shot in his right temple."

"Let's take a look at the bathroom," I said.

I stepped into the small room, and Whitely and Riley waited in the hallway. Splatter covered the exterior of the toilet, and the sour, stomach-churning smell of vomit filled the air of the small room. The floor had smeared speckles on it as if someone had tried to clean it up. "Did you see any indication of the source of the vomit?" I asked the two officers.

Riley answered, "When I checked the elderly male, I noticed that his mouth smelled sour, and he had crusty stuff on his lips."

"Anything else of interest when you went through the house?" I asked Whitely.

"Back door was slightly ajar. The steps were cleared, but there are a couple of footprints beside the sidewalk—they looked distorted by the melting. Nothing else caught my eye."

"Do either of you know the Monroes?"

"A bit," Riley said. "They went to the same church as my folks. After I was grown, I stopped going regular. But I saw them there a couple of times when I went to services to make my mom happy. That was a few years back so I can't be 100%, but the two of them in the bed look like how I remember the Monroes."

"Did you recognize the third body?" I asked.

"Nope. I know they had two sons—if that's any help—but I sure can't say if it was one of them."

I heard a laboring vehicle outside. Looking out the window, I saw the four-wheel drive crime scene Jeep pulling up to the front door, followed by the medical examiner's van riding in its tracks. I went downstairs to brief the crime scene techs.

Rose Culpepper, the seasoned head of the department, walked inside with her assistant Chip Gonzales in her wake. They both carried large satchels with equipment and collection containers.

"Spencer, what we got here?" Rose asked.

"Gunshot wound and two possible poisoning or overdose victims. Because of the latter, you'll need to take samples of edibles in the kitchen or elsewhere and bottles of any medications you find. Of course, we'll need prints from all the likely places, from doorknobs to toilet handles. But before you do that, collect DNA samples of any bodily fluids, including the vomit in the bathroom across from the bedroom. And I'll need the hands of all the deceased swabbed for gunshot residue. Aside from that, put your suspicious mind to work and bring back anything to the lab that strikes you as possible evidence."

"You got it," Rose said.

With a video camera in hand, Chip backed up to the front door and recorded as he crossed the floor and went down the hall

Rose pulled out a digital camera and shot still photos of the teacups and general photos around the room before following Chuck to get multiple angles of the bodies in the bedroom.

By that time, Assistant Medical Examiner Dan Molder was in the house. He waited patiently while Rose recorded the death scene. Then, he knelt by the side of the young male on the bed. Rose turned his way and said, "Let me know when I can swab the hands." She left the room to shoot photos of the bathroom from the hallway.

"Won't be long," he said. "Spencer, the point of entry was not direct contact, but the barrel was very close to the wound."

"You think suicide?" I asked.

"Could be," Molder said, "but not definite at this point. Are you thinking murder-suicide?"

"That was the theory presented to me," I said.

"I'll have to get him on the autopsy slab before I can say one way or the other. Spencer, your skeptical tone is duly noted."

I repeated the information Whitely had passed on to me as Molder examined the other two bodies as best he could with the obstruction on top.

"Culpepper," Molder called, "come swab the deceased on top so I can get a better look at the two under the covers."

When Rose gave the all-clear, Molder bagged the hands. "Spencer, you want to check for a wallet or ID before I have him moved?"

"Yes, sir," I said. I turned the pockets inside out, pulling out a pack of gum, two screws, and a pair of leather work gloves, but didn't find anything useful for identification purposes. Molder called for his assistants to remove that body.

After looking over the other two, he said, "Just like the gunshot victim, rigor is firmly established, Spencer. I'd estimate time of death was at least ten to twelve hours ago, but no more than two days ago. I'll be able to narrow it down at autopsy. If you get any 'last seen' information for any of them, pass it along. It could be helpful."

I went downstairs and got everyone's attention. "Does anyone know the gunshot victim?"

Rose said, "Sure, I do. It's Henry Clay Monroe. His mama's maiden name was Clay. Local rumor has it that her family is related to the famous Henry Clay, who once served as a Senator from Kentucky and later as the Secretary of State."

"I didn't know you were a history buff, Rose."

Rose smiled and shrugged.

"Did you know the deceased well?"

"Knew his folks from church, but never exchanged more than a few words with him. He built a house in the Wintergreen ski resort for one of my neighbors a few years back. I talked to him a couple of times when they were away from home, and he wanted to leave a message for them."

It was now doubly important for me to visit the woman who'd called in the wellness check. She was now not only the daughter-in-law of the dead couple, but perhaps a new widow, too.

I made sure no one had questions or problems at the scene before taking my leave. By the time the second body was loaded in the medical examiner's van, I was on my way to Mary Alice Monroe's house. On the ride over, I wondered if the order of the killings was as it seemed and how that might impact the financial benefit to the widow.

Chapter Two

The Wednesday before the gruesome scene at the Monroe farmhouse, I'd confronted the sheriff about when I'd get my first homicide case, and he'd once again told me I wasn't ready.

I tried to hide my frustration with a polite "Yes, sir," but exasperation scraped its claws on the inside of my skull, desperate to escape and explode.

"I've been doing this a long time, Spencer," the sheriff told me. "When you are ready to take the lead on a homicide case, I'll know it. And I'll give you one. You're getting close, but I'm not certain you're there yet."

The sheriff looked down at his desk, shifted papers from one side to another, a clear sign that it was time for me to go.

Nonetheless, I was not finished. "Sir, Thornhill has been here six months less than I have, and you gave him the Randolph murder."

"Now, now, Spencer. You calm down. You'll get your chance sooner or later. Shut the door on your way out, please."

I wanted to rant. I wanted to demand. I wanted to play the damn "woman card." My mentor Lucinda, however, told me again and again doing that was a fatal error.

"Never, never, never play the woman card. You might win the battle you're having at that moment, but you'll never win the war. Prove to them that you are better, more competent, more dedicated, and smarter than any of the men in your position. Then, you'll get what you want, but you have to be patient."

The first time she said it, I scoffed. I did not want to believe that in this day and time, I'd face discrimination because of my gender. I hadn't in college, but then I went to the police academy and learned I was wrong the hard way. Some instructors were patronizing, some of my fellow students mocked me, and others assumed I was either a lesbian or a slut. I passed off the attitudes of my male peers as their personal immaturity or simply a product of the competitive environment. It was the higher-ranking men who stood between me and my goals that puzzled and angered me.

And, of course, rattled my cage. I've long assumed that my high anxiety level was the product of my mother's murder when I was eight years old. Maybe, though, it went back further than that. I remember multiple occasions with my mother when she assured me that I was good enough, smart enough, capable enough to do anything I wanted to do. I wonder now if she'd recognized a seed of anxiety burrowed in my core. I'd never heard her talk to my sister Ruby like that, but, then again, Ruby was only three when Mom was killed.

I shuffled over to my desk and pulled out a scene report form, knowing it wouldn't be long before I'd head out somewhere to solve a piddly crime or two. My intelligence and training seemed to be wasted here. Maybe taking this job was a mistake. Or maybe I wasn't good enough. I did what I always do when that negative thought snuck into my consciousness. I closed my eyes and envisioned my mother. With every passing year, her image grew less sharp and less comforting.

I'd had a couple of job offers in larger cities, but every one of them would have placed me in a lab doing forensic analysis. I turned them down because I wanted to be in the field investigating crimes—most of all, I wanted to be a homicide detective like Lucinda. Once a person was a lab rat, the opportunity to shift over to investigative work was rare if not impossible. I had to make the most of my opportunity here—it had more potential to help me reach my goal.

"Spencer, line two," echoed through the room, disrupting my thoughts.

I picked up the receiver, suppressing a sigh. "Sergeant Spencer. How can I help you?"

A man, spitting with fury, shouted into my ear. "This is Ryan Twisdale. I just arrived at the work site, and the place is trashed. Looks like eight thousand dollars worth of damage in the kitchen alone."

"Give me the address, and I'll be right there." My sigh erupted again as soon as I hung up. Vandalism. Crap!

I arrived at a site for about two dozen townhomes that appeared to be in their final stages of construction. A rectangular strip of road running past the residences was cleared of yesterday's snow, but piles of dirty white marked with bird tracks filled the center of a space that would probably be green in the spring. A landscaper's truck was parked just inside the property, and a man with a clipboard walked the grounds making notes. With snow still on the ground, I wondered how he could tell where pavement ended and soil began.

A scowling Twisdale stood in front of one black enamel entrance door, arms folded across a burly chest. I flashed my badge in his direction. He waved me over and said, "It's about time. This way."

I followed him inside. To my left, an open flight of stairs with hardwood steps and an intricate wrought iron railing led to the second floor.

"Not much damage upstairs," he said, "but here in the living area—well, you can see for yourself."

A wash of off-white allowed glimpses of the once-beautiful hardwood floor. The tiles around the hearth were smashed to pieces. The mantlepiece hung at an angle from one side.

More paint marred the dining area floor. In the kitchen, it looked as if someone had been doing wheelies—black skid marks were everywhere. All the cabinet doors were hanging by one screw or sprawled on top of the counters or on the tile beneath my feet.

A smashed carafe lay in the sink with a generous sprinkling of coffee grounds all over the stainless steel. The plumbing underneath was mauled to pieces as if attacked by a team of mad tigers. In front of the pantry, someone had defecated and used some of their waste to write "Dirty Boy" on the backsplash.

Above the breakfast nook in one corner, a smashed window and muddy footprints pointed to the entry point for the vandals.

"Do you have insurance?" I asked.

"Yeah, but there's a high deductible, and, after this, I'll have to hire round-the-clock guards for the duration of the project. On top of that, repairs will put me way behind schedule, and I haven't checked the other units yet."

"Have you called the insurance company?"

"They're sending an appraiser over."

"You'll need to hold him off until I can get the forensic guys in here. I'll call right away, and then you and I can check the other units and make sure they're okay."

"That's just going to take more time and…" Twisdale paused and sighed. "Never mind, the insurance company will want a thorough forensic investigation anyway. I'll have to suck it up. This disaster we walked through was our model home. We were installing finishing touches like the coffee maker and canisters to add to the home-like atmosphere. The only blessing is that the furniture was scheduled for delivery tomorrow. I'll have to change that, but at least the little bastards struck before it was here."

"Upstairs? You said there was damage?"

"Minor. Clothes racks pulled off their hardware and drawers sitting on the floor in the walk-in closet. A roll of toilet paper was unwound, put in the shower, and the water was turned on and left on—but no flooding in there, just a mess."

As we walked through the rest of the units without finding any further destruction, I asked about anyone with a grudge—a terminated employee, an unhappy subcontractor, a personal relationship gone sour, a former client angry about his completed project.

"Whenever you're doing this kind of work, you can't make everyone happy all the time, but I don't ignore problems," he said. "I always seek an equitable resolution. I can't think of any suspicious person in my business contacts. I guess it must have been kids acting stupid, ma'am. Got to drinking and daring and carrying on. Their parents should know what they are up to—then it's up to the insurance company if they want to pursue them. You think you can figure who they were?"

"I'll certainly try," I said, hoping to find a reformed teenaged troublemaker among the neighborhood adolescents who'd be willing to open a few doors for me. "Considering all the workers who have been through here, I doubt if fingerprints will be of much use, but you never know. I'll make sure the crew lifts them all."

Chapter Three

The afternoon of the townhouse vandalism case, my next assignment involved bicycle theft. Oh, please, still my heart—I don't know if I can handle the excitement. I got a search warrant for the house of the suspect I'd identified and drove off to the address with Deputy Jack Preston.

I pulled my unmarked car up to the curb in front of a neglected '60's era ranch. In the middle of the front yard, dead weeds poked up through the retreating snow that encircled an empty bird bath impersonating the leaning Tower of Pisa. One shutter was missing from a side window, and paint peeled profusely from the soffit. A chunk of concrete was missing in the middle of the third step, leaving an unattractive hole and a hazard for anyone walking to the door.

"It's a small house," Jack said.

"Yes, but I suspect you could store a lot of stolen bikes in that basement."

"True. You ready?"

"Yes, let's do it."

We walked up the sidewalk, ascended the three steps, which felt sturdy despite their need of repair. I pressed the doorbell but didn't even hear a faint echo from the interior. "Did you hear anything?"

"No. Try again."

I pressed long and hard on the bell as we both leaned forward to concentrate on hearing any sound from inside. We exchanged looks and shook our heads. I pulled open the screen door, which screeched in protest. I made a couple of polite knocks, then, still hearing nothing, I pounded on the wood with my fist.

From a distance, I heard a thready voice. "I'm a'comin'. I'm a'comin'. Don't have a conniption fit. I'm a'comin'"

The knob rattled, and the door jerked open to reveal a short, slightly stooped, gray-haired woman with swollen ankles. She wore a stained blue and white checked gingham apron over a green flower print house dress. Without raising her downcast eyes, she said, "Whatever you're sellin' I ain't buyin'."

She started to close the door, but Jack stopped it with his foot. Flipping open my badge and holding it at the woman's eye level, I said, "We aren't selling anything, ma'am. Are you Martha Ferguson?"

"Yep. What's this about?"

"Does Travis Ferguson live here with you?"

"You could say that. He's my grandson. He sleeps here. Sometimes he eats here. But I hardly ever see him. He's either upstairs or downstairs when he's here, but I can't get up and down steps no more since my knee went out."

"We're from the Sheriff's Department, Ma'am. We've got a search warrant for your house. I'm Sergeant Spencer, and this is Deputy Preston."

"Search warrant? Good Lord, that boy is gettin' as bad as his daddy. What's he done now?"

"He is a suspect in a case we're investigating."

"Let me see that warrant." She snatched it out of my hand. Squinting at it, her lips moved as she read through it. She brought up her head and glared at us. "Bicycles? Bicycle parts? Repair tools? Doesn't anybody who ever done had any kids have some of that stuff laying around?"

"I imagine so, Ma'am. I realize you can't climb any stairs, so we're going to trust you to sit down here in the house, be quiet, and not make any phone calls. Can you do that?" I asked.

"How long you gonna be?" She peered down at her watch. "I'm fixin' to make some macaroni and cheese for supper, and I need a little time to grate the cheese, cook the elbows, and so on before I pop it in the oven."

"We'll be as quick as we can. If time turns into a problem for you, just holler at us, and we'll see what we can do. Okay?"

"I reckon there's not much I can do about it. Go on 'bout your bizness."

Jack and I stopped at the basement door to pull out our weapons before making our way down. At the foot of the stairs, I turned and saw an unbelievable array of bicycles supported on their kickstands to the right and bins of used bicycle parts to the left, along with ten bicycles next to a long wooden bench.

I walked over to the latter area and examined the space. A locked attaché case lay on the surface. I slipped on latex gloves and jimmied it open. It was full of clear, sealed plastic bags of pills.

"Jack, look at this." I lifted one bag and stared at the contents. They were white, round, and scored on one side. On the other, I read, "IP 203."

"Opioids?" Jack asked.

"I'd guess Oxycodone, but I could be wrong."

"Connected to the bikes?"

"Let's take a look at this group over here," I said, pointing to the ones by the bench. We started deconstructing one of them. Jack detached the seat and broke it down to its components, but found no pills. I removed a bike pedal and did the same—no luck. Together, we took off the handlebars. After removing one handgrip, I saw cotton batting. I pulled gently on a piece of it and felt small, hard objects pressed into the filling. Setting that on the work surface, I slowly peeled it open to reveal pills cushioned in the interior.

"I admit, Jack, I was irritated about getting the lead on a case of simple bike theft, but now it looks bigger than anyone imagined. They'll probably regret assigning me to this one."

"That's why you should never give up. I know you can erode their resistance."

I rolled my eyes. He had more confidence in me than I did. Hearing a vehicle pull into the driveway on the side of the house, we both scampered behind the hot water heater with guns pointed at the door. Footsteps descended the outside steps. A key slipped into the lock. The bottom of the door scraped on the concrete as it opened.

A young man strode straight to the bikes by the bench. He reached for one and wheeled it toward the door. I stepped out with my gun raised, "Sheriff's

Department, stop right there."

He dropped the bike and took a step towards the door. "Don't try it," Jack said. "Put your hands on top of your head."

For a moment, he froze in place, his eyes darting in panic as he evaluated the situation. He raised his arms and dropped to the floor, wincing when his knees hit the concrete. Jack stepped up and cuffed him.

"Are you Travis Ferguson?" Jack asked.

"No. No, man. Who's Travis Ferguson?"

"Playing dumb won't work. You are in the basement of his residence."

"I didn't know that. Somebody told me there were a bunch of bicycles down here ripe for the picking. I admit I came here to steal them. I didn't know anything but the address."

"Do you have any identification on you?" I asked.

"In my wallet. My right rear pocket."

Jack stepped forward. "I'm not going to get stuck by anything, am I?"

The young man shook his head. With two fingers, Jack slid the billfold out of the pocket and handed it to me.

"This your driver's license?" I asked.

"Yep."

"So, Mr. Harding, you say you don't know Travis Ferguson. Tell me, then, how did you get a key to the basement?"

"I don't have no key, search my pockets."

"I know I won't find it in your pockets, Harding, because you left it in the doorknob."

"It was there when I came down them steps."

"Jack, keep an eye on him. I'm going to talk to Ms. Ferguson and call for a patrol to pick him up and get a forensic team out here."

Jack nodded, and I went upstairs. I was pleased to see Martha sitting in a rocking chair far from the phone.

"Ma'am, do you know a Sylvester Harding?"

She furrowed her brow. "Can't say that I do."

I pulled out Harding's ID. "Does he look familiar?"

She leaned forward, squinting again, pulled a pair of reading glasses from the apron pocket, and looked again. "I seed him around. Didn't know his name."

"Is he a friend of your grandson?"

"I don't know the relationship 'tween 'em, but I've seen 'em together from time to time. Is that the other voice I heard down there?"

"Yes. He used a key to get into your basement door."

"He has a key to my house? I told Travis not to give no keys to nobody."

"He won't tell us how he got the key, ma'am. Do you know what's in your basement?"

"Used to, but then my knee—I got all the things I needed moved up outta there. I sold or gave away anythin' that was left. Travis told me he wanted to do a bicycle repair business, so I 'magine there's bikes down there."

"But you didn't bother to mention that when you read the warrant, Mrs. Ferguson. I hesitate to even ask you if you are aware of any illegal substances down there?"

"Illegal substances? You mean like drugs?"

"Yes, ma'am."

"Well, if they're down there, take 'em with you. I don't have no truck with drugs."

"I'm calling for an officer to take Sylvester Harding into custody and a forensic team to gather the evidence in your basement. After that, I'm going to search upstairs."

"Do what you hafta do."

On the second floor, there were two rooms. One looked like storage for seasonal items, once worn clothing, and miscellaneous collections from a long life. Although scattered across the room, the piles of items seemed neat and tidy.

The other was Travis's bedroom, a chaotic jumble of piled up-clothing, dresser drawers spilling their contents to the floor, and an unmade bed that looked like a battle scene. In one corner, a small desk and chair stood in a circle cleared of debris. I pulled on my gloves and started there. Small spiral binders stacked in the center, to the side, an ashtray full of the tail ends of smoked joints, and two pencils and a pen lined up like soldiers in between.

I used one of the pencils to turn back the cover of the top notebook. Inside were a column of phone numbers, with figures and dates next to them. I flipped through several pages, and it appeared to me that these were possible contacts for Travis' drug business. I'd need a forensic team here, too. Engrossed in my discovery, I didn't heed the small noises behind my back, thinking them to be the creaking sounds of an old house. A louder thump, however, broke through my concentration. My right hand slipped to the holster as I started to turn.

A physical force slammed into my back, knocking me flat on my face. Stunned, I listened to pounding feet descending the stairway. I pushed up and regained my feet, grateful that I still had my gun in hand. I raced to the top of the stairs and spotted Martha at the bottom with a "who-me?" expression on her face. "My heavens, officer, what is goin' on?"

I heard a screen door slam against its frame and rushed down the steps. "Out of my way, ma'am."

Martha backed up and over to the open front door and leaned against it, pushing it closed. More steps bounded up from the basement. I pushed Martha to the side and opened the door and the screen. I heard Jack right behind me. We ran down the sidewalk, my head swiveling like the eyes in a crazy cat clock. Neither I nor Jack saw any sign of Travis.

"Harding?" I asked.

"I cuffed him to the radiator," Jack said.

"Good. We need to get him and Ms. Ferguson down to the station."

"Mrs. Ferguson's flat on the floor right now," Jack said.

"I knocked her down? I didn't mean to push her that hard."

"You didn't knock her to the floor," Jack chuckled. "She was standing after you went by, then she saw me at the top of the steps and dropped. Reminded me of watching a football player trying to get an undeserved injury foul."

At least that was good news. A harsh scrape of metal-on-metal greeted me as we went inside. I glanced at Jack. He responded with a nod and went down the stairs to check on Harding. Martha was still on the floor, rocking and whimpering. When I stood over her, she chanted, "Police brutality, police brutality, police brutality."

"Give it up, Ma'am. The other officer saw what you did. You have obstructed an investigation, and I'm going to have to take you down to the station. You should be ashamed. You are minimizing the situation of those who have been treated violently by police. I pulled Martha to her feet and guided her over to a chair. "Sit. Don't move. If you behave, I won't cuff you until we leave the house."

Martha bounced to her feet. "I have my rights."

"At this moment, you are under arrest. I will read your rights." I pressed a hand on Martha's shoulder, returning her to her seat. Pulling out the laminated card from a pocket, I read the Miranda Warning to the scowling woman.

"I ain't got nothin' to say 'cept I don't have an attorney. You need to get me one."

"Yes, ma'am. We'll do that at the station."

Chapter Four

The next morning, while waiting for Sylvester and Martha to arrive from the jail, I worked on the paperwork for the two cases from yesterday. I felt the looming presence of someone behind me. I tensed when two big hands landed on my shoulders. I lurched upwards.

"Didn't mean to scare you, Spencer," the sheriff said.

"I was engrossed in my reports, sir. Didn't hear you approach."

"No matter. Just wanted to congratulate you. Not every day I send out an investigator to arrest a bicycle thief and end up busting a drug ring. It'll look real good on TV. Press conference this afternoon at two. Put on some face paint and meet me in the briefing room. You don't need to say a word. Just give the public a glimpse of your face—show the department's diversity."

I wanted to growl but muttered, "Yes, sir."

All I knew about press conferences was what I saw on the news. Relieved that I wouldn't have to speak, I was still apprehensive about what the sheriff would say.

* * *

My phone buzzed, and a deputy let me know that Sylvester Harding and Martha Ferguson were in separate rooms with their respective attorneys. I decided to talk to Martha first. Her attorney insisted his client was innocent because she was clueless. "She can't go up and down stairs. She did not know there were bicycles or drugs in her basement."

"Is that true, Ms. Ferguson?" I asked.

"Yes, ma'am. And let me tell you, I was upset when you first got to my house and I done said that my grandson was as bad as my son. That was just from my fear at that moment."

"Ms. Ferguson," the lawyer interrupted. "You don't need to be talking about your grandson right now. Let me answer the questions."

"I gotta say my piece. My Travis is a good boy. This whole bicycle business thing was that Sylvester's idea. I'd bet my bottom dollar that Travis don't even know the bikes were stolen."

"You know, Mrs. Ferguson," I said, "the reason I arrested you is because I plan to charge you with obstruction of justice and possibly accomplice after the fact for the bicycle theft and distribution of drugs. However, if you want to tell me more about your grandson and what he was doing in your residence, I'm more than willing to listen."

"I don't want my client to make any further statements at this time," the lawyer said. "Is she under arrest or can she go home now?"

"You'll have to talk to the magistrate about whether and when she can be released."

"The charges?"

"Just obstruction for now. But others could come later."

Martha interrupted. "Wait. Wait. I'm here. Talk to me. I spent last night in that hellhole. I ain't never before been in jail in my whole life—except for visiting folks behind bars. I don't want to go back now. What can I tell you to keep that from happenin'?"

"Miss Ferguson," her lawyer said, "that is a very bad idea." Turning to me, he said, "She's elderly. She doesn't understand. Please let me have a few minutes with her."

Martha's elbow slammed hard into her lawyer's side. "Who you callin' an old lady?"

I smiled at the attorney and said, "No problem."

* * *

I went down the hall to the next interrogation room. I looked in the window before going inside. Sylvester slouched in his chair with his legs stretched under the table and beneath the chair on the opposite side. He'd folded his arms across his chest either out of defensiveness or belligerence. His facial expression indicated the latter, but it could be an attempt to look tough.

His lawyer sat upright and rigid as if her life depended on good posture. The dark grey suit she wore looked brand new and shiny. Her blonde bob was hair-sprayed to an inert helmet state. Her lips were pursed as she stared straight ahead.

I pushed open the door and introduced myself. Sylvester's attorney stood and extended her hand over the table. "Trinity Bellows," she said as I shook her hand. "My client is not your problem. Travis Ferguson is. My client was duped."

We took our seats, and the lawyer continued. "Sylvester was hired to transport bicycles to different locations. He did not know they were stolen. He thought Travis was operating a legitimate bicycle repair business. He was not aware that any illegal substances were involved."

I turned my gaze to Sylvester. "Mr. Harding, if what your lawyer said is true, then why did you lie to us about the basement key when we first saw you?"

Sylvester stared at me from under heavy lids, then turned his head to his attorney. She nodded and said, "He was scared. He panicked. You know that law enforcement often causes that instinctive response, particularly in young men of color. He also was aware that since Travis is white, police officers were more likely to believe Travis and were far more likely to pin the blame on my client."

I suppressed the surge of anger that rose in my chest whenever I was accused of racial bias by another white woman. I understood that too many cops fed into that narrative, but I wasn't one of them. I resented being lumped together with them. If Sylvester had said that directly to me, it would have been easy to blow it off as an opinion based on a previous experience with a bad cop. Coming from a snooty Caucasian female, on the other hand, rubbed me the wrong way. However, since all I wanted was the truth about this criminal enterprise, I smiled and changed the subject.

"Mr. Harding, can you explain to me, in your own words, how you were tricked by Travis?"

"No, he can't," Trinity said. "I have advised him to let me be his spokesperson in all encounters with law enforcement and prosecutors."

"That is a real shame, counselor, since I can't judge his credibility when you do all the talking. That means I must rely on the word of Martha Ferguson, who is insisting that the illegal acts committed in the name of the business were all dictated by your client, who took advantage of her grandson," I said.

"That is slander."

"Please. I'll leave you to talk to your client about his openness to a plea bargain."

"What is our negotiation point?"

"The truth about his involvement in the business and the possible whereabouts of Travis Ferguson."

Sylvester finally spoke. "Fuck you, bitch."

Trinity blanched. "Mr. Harding, please! Don't be stupid!"

I sneered at him and left the room.

After ordering both Sylvester and Martha transferred back to jail, I sent my reports up to the Commonwealth Attorney's office. I added notes to each, one saying I had no problem with Martha Ferguson being released on her own recognizance; the other requesting that, if possible, it would be helpful to our investigation if Sylvester Harding were held until his partner in crime, Travis Ferguson, was apprehended. I called it a day and fantasized about the glass of wine I'd been promising myself for hours.

* * *

Just before two p.m., I went down to the briefing room and was shocked to see every chair occupied, a few more reporters leaning against the wall, and multiple television cameras in the aisles. Standing behind and to one side of the sheriff, I relaxed a bit as he ran through the events of the bust. When he said my name, my heart pounded with anxiety.

"Our investigator, Sergeant Charlotte Spencer, is responsible for our success yesterday. Step up here, Spencer." He threw an arm around my shoulders. "We're real proud of our new and upcoming star detective."

I smiled as I thought about kneeing the sheriff in the groin.

To my horror, multiple reporters shouted, "Sergeant! Sergeant!" at me, shoving tape recorders toward me.

"Now, now, now," the sheriff chastised the gathered media. "The sergeant's never been to a press conference. Let's give her a break this time around."

I knew he didn't care about the state of my nerves. He wanted to bask in the glory I'd earned. I felt my jaw clench as I re-established my fake smile, stepped back away from the podium, and leaned against the wall.

After a few questions and non-answers from Sheriff Hatcher, the public information officer stepped in and said, "That'll be all for now." She latched onto my elbow and steered me toward the back doors. "Get on upstairs and don't stop, no matter how many journalists badger you."

I reached the secure stairs to the back and looked over my shoulder. Three reporters with notebooks in hand raced toward me. I scanned my ID card and escaped just in time.

* * *

My red brick apartment building had once been very grand with its white marble windowsills and front porch. Now, it looked old and tired. Up-close, chips in the marble and tarnish on the railing were visible. Only a fading illusion of grandeur remained. The interior of the structure, though, made me fall in love. Period light fixtures graced the hallways. Magnificent woodwork, arched doorways, and built-in shelves and cabinets filled each apartment. The downside stared me in the face as I stepped inside the foyer.

I stared at the "Out of Order" sign taped to the elevator. I willed it to disappear. Sadly, it did not cooperate. With a firm grip on the worn but elaborate walnut railing, I pulled and trudged up the three flights, one step at a time. I could hear my black and white Tuxedo cat, Flash, meowing his displeasure over my late arrival before I opened the door.

When I got inside, Flash darted through the kitchen, bounced on the back of the recliner, ran across the back of the sofa, leaped to the coffee table, then the floor, and skittered to a stop by his food bowl, where he emitted a pitiful yowl. Even at six years old, he still lived up to his name.

I checked for messages on my landline. One from Dad—the only person besides telemarketers who doesn't call my cell.

"Hi, honey! Just calling to remind you about the dinner with Ruby Saturday night. You do remember it's her twentieth birthday, right? No longer a teenager—hard to believe. We'll meet up at her favorite place as usual. Oh, and I didn't invite Lucinda to join us because I have something that I want to talk to the two of you about. Love you."

My groan earned a startled look from Flash. I suspected Dad wanted to talk about that damned memorial again. Neither I nor my sister wanted him to go through with it, and, so far, our distaste had stalled the project. Dad simply could not understand our point of view. His plan was a simple plaque in the park near where our family lived when Mom was alive. If it had only Mom's name, my sister and I would be okay with it. But he wanted to list the names of all the victims of that serial killer. Ruby and I knew that everyone would call it by the murderer's name: All his victims would be diminished and his infamy elevated.

Ruby and I couldn't understand why our father would not put it all to rest—it was nearly seventeen years ago. Even Lucinda agreed with the two of us. She argued with Dad to let it go. Lucinda was my mentor and the homicide detective who'd caught the serial killer.

I knew, as uncomfortable as it was, I could get through listening to Dad talk about the memorial one more time. Ruby could survive it, too. If my sister showed signs that it was getting too heavy, I'd remind Dad that it was Ruby's birthday and he needed to lighten up.

It would be so much easier if he would stop, but that was not how my father operated. Right after Mom's death, he was all forget-about-it-and-move-on. Then, he realized the folly of that approach and turned into Mr. Talk-About-It-All-the-Time. No middle ground for him. Nonetheless, he was a good dad, a loving dad, and he gave us girls all he had to give. We knew that. We loved him. And we would put up with his obsession the same way we tolerated his over-protectiveness. It was irritating when we were younger, struggling for independence, but now, I think we both realized it was just human. The only way to grow up was to accept that your parents weren't perfect—that no one's parents were.

I felt the rumble of anxiety filling my chest and churning my stomach acid. I had a bottle of Xanax that my doctor prescribed, and I grabbed a pill, sat back in the recliner, and waited for the soothing to begin. I longed for my college days when I could pull out a pipe and enjoy some weed. Two tokes were all it took to settle my hackles. I can still see that small carved wooden box where I stored my stash. Those were the days. Sure, the Xanax worked, but it was slow-acting, compared to my drug of choice, and addictive, too. One day, pot would be legal. I could see the ads now—Marijuana, more effective than pharmaceuticals, fewer calories than alcohol—anxiety never met a better foe.

Chapter Five

I had thought the drug bust earlier this week might have elevated me enough to get the lead on a homicide, but I didn't expect it to happen this quickly. I found it hard to believe and more than a little overwhelming. Here I had three active cases, and one of them was a triple homicide—or maybe, like the sheriff said, a murder-suicide. I had too many doubts about that to sign off on his opinion on Whitely's conclusions alone. I feared I was not good enough to meet the challenge.

Leaving the crime scene, I drove to the Henry Monroe home to deliver the death notification and ask a few questions. I parked in front of an older, white Cape Cod with a cottage green metal roof, shutters on the windows, and a white picket fence encircling a yard of melting snow. I followed the shoveled sidewalk up to the front door.

Pressing the doorbell, I listened to the house, hearing the drone of a vacuum from deep inside. The sound ended. Since I didn't hear footsteps, I knocked on the door. Then, I heard someone approaching. The door was opened by a woman in her late twenties or early thirties wearing blue jeans and a Willie Nelson tee-shirt. Her long blonde hair was pulled back in a ponytail, putting emphasis on her attractive facial features—high cheekbones, full lips, and eyes the soft blue of cornflowers.

"May I help you?" she asked.

"Are you Mrs. Henry Clay Monroe?"

She stared at me for a moment as if she were not used to the sound of her formal name. "Yes. Who are you?"

"Sergeant Spencer with the county sheriff's department. May I come in?"

"What has Hank done?" she asked.

An interesting reaction, but was it relevant to the investigation? "We need to talk. May I come in?"

"Oh, yes. Certainly. Come in," she said, spreading an arm wide. "Please have a seat." She gestured to the furniture in the living room.

Inside, the house looked cozy with its unrenovated post-World War Two style. Small rooms with broad, arched entries that connected the living and dining rooms to the kitchen, but not with the wide-open concept that is so popular today—a nostalgic layout that spoke of families gathered around the radio with a mug of hot chocolate in everyone's hands.

I sat down on a comfortable chair with a high back and padded, broad arms. The moment I had sunk into the cushion, I worried that it might be too comfortable, making it a challenge to rise from it with dignity. The presumed widow took a seat on a three-cushion sofa at the end closest to my chair.

"Mrs. Monroe, I regret to inform you that your husband has passed away," I said. For a moment, I thought a smile threatened to erupt on her lips, and a twinkle flashed in her eyes. It was gone in a nanosecond. Did I imagine it?

"Did he run off the road? Or was another vehicle involved?" she asked.

"Ma'am, at this point, we are not sure if your husband's death was murder or suicide. He was found in his parents' home—deceased."

Mary Alice clutched her hands together at her neckline. Her eyes grew huge. "What?" Her eyes shifted to her right toward the small dining room and kitchen.

"Mrs. Monroe, is there anyone you can think of who wished your husband or in-laws harm?" I asked, wondering what concerned her in the room out of my sight line. Was there another person in the house?

She sharply pulled the focus of her eyes back to me. "Murder? You think it's murder?"

"It's one of the avenues of our investigation, Mrs. Monroe. Do you know of anyone?"

"Please, call me Mary Alice—no one calls me Mrs. Monroe—that's Hank's mother. I don't think anyone had any hard feelings toward my in-laws. In

Hank's line of work, though, there was always somebody ticked off at him. Either an employee or subcontractor he chewed out for substandard work. He sometimes had me hold payment on a bill until whatever was wrong was made right—unless it was really poor quality, then he'd get someone else to fix it and deduct the cost from the submitted invoice. Some of those subcontractors got right pissed over that. Or then there's clients who insist on things a certain way, and then when they get it, don't like it, and break bad on Hank—even to the point of lawsuits. They never amounted to much since my husband is very good at what he does. That enraged some of them. But enough to murder? I wouldn't think so."

She turned her gaze in the direction of the kitchen again. Odd. Was she hiding something in there?

"Mary Alice, is there someone else in the house?"

She jerked her head back to face me as a pale pink suffused her cheeks. "No. No, it's just me and the vacuum." She made a half-hearted laugh that sounded as if she'd rather cry.

Her response made me edgy. I wasn't certain I believed her. "Okay. I have to ask you an uncomfortable question. Where were you yesterday evening and overnight last night?"

"Right here," she said without hesitation. "Hank was here with me in the evening until Pops called just before ten. I haven't seen him since he left."

"And he never returned?" I asked.

"I don't think so. If he did, he was super-quiet and left before I woke up. I called and called. I called Hank's cell phone, his folks' landline. I used my iPhone to make those calls, so you can look at it if you need some sort of timeline or alibi or something. But they never answered. That's why I requested a wellness check this morning."

"Why did his father call?"

"I don't know. Hank didn't know. Hank said that Pops just said, 'Help' a couple of times before the line went dead, and Hank rushed out of here to see what the problem was. Told me to stay home in case Pops called again. Does Pops know Hank is dead?"

"I don't know if—" I began to answer.

Mary Alice cut me off, her voice rising in pitch as well as in volume. "Well, why not? Shouldn't he know first? He's Hank's dad—he's known him for more than thirty years. I've only known him for a dozen. He's more next of kin than I am."

"Did you get along with your father-in-law?"

"Get along? I adore him. And I worry how he'll take the news of Hank's death. I should be with him right now." Mary Alice started to rise.

"No, ma'am, you can't. I have more bad news for you."

"Oh no. No, no, no, no, no. Not Pops. No." She slumped back down on the sofa and shook her head vigorously.

Is her reaction an accumulative effect? If not, why is she more upset by an in-law's death than her husband's?

I said, "Your father-in-law has passed away. I'm sorry for your loss, ma'am. It's too early in the investigation to determine the sequence of the injuries; as such, I can't tell you if your father-in-law knew about his son's death before he lost consciousness."

"Ohmigod! Did they get into a fight?" Mary Alice asked.

"Why would you think they'd do that?" I wondered if she was about to tell me something that would make me lean toward murder-suicide.

"They've been having a huge disagreement. It was all about Momma Monroe."

"Why do you say it was all about your mother-in-law?"

"She suffers from dementia—I don't know if it's Alzheimer's or something else—and it's been getting difficult for Pops to care for her at home. He was going to have her admitted to a lockdown unit, and he'd chosen a rather expensive one. Pops said Hank didn't want him to waste money sending her any place nice since she didn't know where she was most of the time anyway."

"Did your husband tell you that?"

"Not a word. I learned about it from Pops. What a minute—what have you done with Momma Monroe? You didn't leave her out there alone, did you?"

A big sigh rushed from my lungs. "She did not survive the incident in the home either."

"Oh, that poor, poor woman. I hope she didn't understand what was happening. If she was murdered, I would bet on my life that Pops did not do it."

"What about Hank?"

"I don't know."

Now that was interesting. "Mary Alice, because of the circumstances, I'll need to secure your husband's computer as well as his business papers and any firearms and ammunition in the house. I'll also need to search for incriminating evidence. Do I need to get a search warrant before I start? If you want, I'll sit here with you until one is brought to me. Otherwise, I'll call and have someone handle the paperwork while I get started." I studied the reaction on her face.

Her complexion paled as she swallowed in rapid succession. Indication of guilt? Her eyes would not stay still; neither would the lids. They seemed to blink out Morse Code in a foreign language I could not translate. She scraped her upper teeth across her lower lip, shook her head, and said, "Oh, of course. Take whatever you need. At some point, sooner rather than later, I'll need to get the laptop and business records back to get uncompleted projects finished by others and close the books on his company."

"Did your husband leave his wallet and phone at home?"

"I know he didn't leave the cell here, or I would have heard it ringing when I tried to call him. I can look around for his wallet. I guess you checked his pants' pockets."

I nodded.

"What about his truck?"

"The only truck at the farm was green, had a plow attached to the front of it, and is registered to your father-in-law. Are you talking about that one?"

"Pops drove that old green one. He probably used it after the snow to plow his driveway. Hank had a bright red, crew cab with tool chests in the truck bed. If he was there, then his truck should have been there with him."

"It's not there, Mary Alice, and we don't know where it is," I said. "Are you sure he drove the red truck over to his parents' house?"

"We only have two vehicles—mine is here, his is not."

"Do you know the license plate number on Hank's truck?"

"No, I'm sorry, I don't."

I called the station and got someone working on the tag number and putting out the BOLO on the vehicle. "Was your husband right-handed?"

"No," she said, furrowing her brow. "Why does it matter?"

It certainly did, but I wasn't going to explain it to her. Instead, I changed the subject. "Where do you keep your firearms?"

"Firearms? Why would you ask about them? Were they shot?"'

"I'm sorry. I can't discuss the manner of death at this time."

She rose to her feet and put her hands on her hips. "This is my husband you're talking about—and the only real parents I've ever had. It's wrong for you to keep this information from me. I would like to talk to whoever is in charge of this investigation."

"I'm sorry, Mary Alice. I'm the lead on this investigation."

Mary Alice's eyes and nostrils flared. "Fine. But I will file a complaint with the sheriff after you leave. C'mon down the hall. I'll unlock the gun cabinet for you.

Mary Alice stepped into the spare bedroom and over to the gun safe. Her hand trembled as she struggled to slip the key in the lock. She forced a smile on her face that looked more like a grimace and said, "There you go. I'll leave you to it." She turned sharply and quick-stepped out of the room.

I removed two handguns from holders mounted under the top shelf—one .38 caliber, the other 9 mm—and set them down atop the baby blue chenille spread on the guest bed. The clash between the homey and the lethal was a bit unsettling. The three rifles were next—one single-shot, two bolt-action. There was also a shotgun that looked older than the woman of the house and rarely used, if ever, in recent years. I checked all the weapons for live rounds. Ignoring the cleaning kits and vises, I gathered all the boxed ammunition in the gun safe—when it was all out on the bed, I had what was needed to fire any one of the weapons except the shotgun, not a shell in the bunch.

I left the bedroom when I heard a small clink coming from the direction of the kitchen. I entered that room as Mary Alice dropped the lid on a slow cooker. She turned bright red from her hairline down to her collarbones.

She stammered, "Just checking on my dinner. Were they poisoned?"

Why did she ask that as she was checking on her crockpot? "As I said, Mary Alice, I cannot discuss the cause of death until after the autopsy."

Her whole body shook as if a chill passed from head to toe. She smiled weakly in my direction and shuffled into the dining area, where she took a seat in a Windsor chair by a round oak kitchen table.

"You need to stay out of the room with the gun safe for a while," I said. "I laid all the weapons and ammunition on the bed for the forensic staff to secure and remove. And by the way, I didn't see any shotgun shells."

"Oh, no," she said with another nervous laugh. "That was Hank's grandfather's gun. My husband has a sentimental attachment to it, so he can't dispose of it even though he doesn't use it. I think Hank wants to just let it *rust* in peace." A soft smile twinkled on her lips, then vanished.

The doorbell rang, and Mary Alice rose to her feet. I gestured her down with an arm wave and a nod. I opened the door and stepped out on the porch to speak to the evidence collectors before they entered the house. I was pleased to find Randy and Chad standing outside. Both were thorough, willing to act on their own initiative, and had worked together often. I allowed them to decide which one would handle each particular task, knowing they were more familiar with each other's strengths than I could be.

Inside, Chad went straight to the spare bedroom, Randy to the kitchen. For a few minutes, I stood still behind Mary Alice, watching her observe Randy. As he explored the kitchen cabinets and their contents, Mary Alice drummed her fingers on the table. She seemed to notice her nervous reaction and folded her hands together. Almost immediately, her foot started tapping on the floor. She looked down at it and wrapped both feet around the chair rungs. Her eyes focused on Randy videotaping every shelf with its jars of spice, boxes of Rice-a-Roni, home-canned tomatoes. Her hands ran amok again, this time making random motions in the air and shaking like leaves buffeted by a breeze. She shoved them both in her armpits to still them.

I sat down across the table from the new widow. "I have a couple more questions for you, ma'am."

Mary Alice nodded and said, "Sure."

"You seemed more distressed by your father-in-law's death than your husband's. Did I misinterpret your feelings? Or, if I am correct, why is that?"

Mary Alice's mouth drew in tight as she bit her upper lip. Her eyes darted around as if she could find the right answer hiding in a dark corner of the room.

"I can't deny it," she said.

"Why is that, Mary Alice?"

"Because I hated that son of a bitch I married," she answered. "My only regret is that I didn't run far away the day I first laid eyes on Henry Clay Monroe."

Chapter Six

I certainly did not see that coming. Mary Alice jumped up. "I need to go to the bathroom." She rushed down the hall and out of sight. When she returned, her face and the edges of her hair were damp. "I didn't mean to say that. He's just been a difficult man to live with."

"In what way?" I asked.

Mary Alice rolled up a sleeve and displayed an arm that bore a patchwork of bruises—some vivid, others nearly faded. "That way." She hung her head, and her face turned hot chili pepper red.

"Did he hit you often?"

"Often enough, but only when I ticked him off. A lot of times, I ended up in the emergency room lying to the doctors and nurses about how I cracked a rib or dislocated a shoulder."

"Why didn't you leave him?" I said, realizing the question was insensitive, as soon as it crossed my lips.

The acid burn of bitterness scratched across Mary Alice's laugh. "You think I didn't try?"

"No, ma'am," I said, looking away from her hard glare.

Mary Alice blew a hard breath that made her lips vibrate. "I did try. The first time, I went to my parents' house with a black eye and a swollen wrist. Mom acted so sweet—leaning me back on the recliner, putting a bag of frozen peas on my eye, taping a pack of mixed vegetables on each side of my wrist, asking what happened to upset me so.

"I cried my heart out about Hank and how he treated me. I told Mom I wanted a divorce. She made all the comforting responses, patted my hand, made me feel loved. I was sitting there realizing that I'd been wrong when I thought girlfriends who moved back into their parents' home were trading one bad situation for another. At that moment, I thought it wouldn't be bad as a stopgap measure. Then, I saw Hank's truck pull into the driveway out front. I pushed up on the recliner, stunned. 'He should be at work. How does he know I'm here?' I asked.

"My dad said, 'I called him.' I staggered at that revelation and turned to my mother for support. But she clearly was not there for me. 'You promised to love, honor, and obey, Mary Alice. You need to stop making him angry and remember he's the head of the household,' she said. I hated them both—maybe more than I loathed Hank.

"They turned their backs on me—literally—as Hank screamed in my face. They said nothing as he grabbed a hank of my hair and pulled me out of the chair."

I wanted to find Mary Alice's parents, punch them both in the nose, and arrest them for being uncaring jerks. Unfortunately, that was not a crime. Instead, I asked another question, a bit apprehensive about the answer she'd give.

"Did you try again?"

"Oh yeah. I thought I could outsmart him. I planned it all out, for all the good it did me. I scrimped on groceries and incidentals for months until I'd saved enough to rent a small studio apartment in the city. I gave my address to no one. I found a job using my maiden name. For six weeks, I was free." She rested her chin on the palm of her hand and gazed out the window. A soft dreaminess filled her eyes. She sighed. "I stopped looking over my shoulder when I walked down the street. I no longer jumped when the phone rang. It was glorious," she said as her eyes closed, and a smile brightened her face.

"One morning when I was at work, the boss stomped out of his office with a letter curled up in his fist. 'You are fired,' he said. 'Gather your personal belongings and get out of here. You will get your final paycheck after the books are audited.' He turned to my co-worker and ordered her to stand beside me and make sure I did not steal anything belonging to the business—'not one pencil, not one paperclip,' he said.

"He walked back towards his office, and I followed him, asking, 'Why? What have I done?' He spun around and said, 'If you are not out of here in five minutes, I'm calling the police.' He slammed the door in my face after that. My co-worker asked what I did, but I couldn't give her an answer because I didn't know. I made her promise to call me if she figured it out.

"Returning to my apartment, I found Hank waiting for me. He waved a letter in my face and told me to read it. Addressed to my boss, on Hank's business letterhead, the writer informed my current employer that I'd embezzled one hundred thousand dollars when I worked at my previous job. I looked up at Hank. He had to have seen the hatred in my eyes. He laughed as he bent towards me. 'I settled up with your landlord. Pack up your things. We're going home. Try this again, and you won't live long enough to pack.' I was angrier at myself than him. I should have known that I needed to move far away to get out of his grasp." Her shoulders slumped, and her head hung down.

For a few moments, overwhelmed by her experience, I said nothing. Then I asked, "Was that the last time you tried to leave him?"

"It wasn't the last time I thought about it. I was planning." She jumped up and walked over to the large oak cabinet where the television rested. Beneath were shelves of books and electronic equipment. She pulled out a fat volume and reached behind it.

"Look," she said, flourishing a large pouch. Unzipping it, she pulled out a wad of bills. "I have a whole three hundred and thirty-seven dollars." She fanned the bundle of bills in front of my face. "It took me a year to slip that much out of Hank's wallet while he was in the shower. I needed a lot more than that to get far away from that man. And I finally figured out how to get it."

"What about your paycheck? Couldn't you save any of that?" I asked.

Mary Alice laughed. "A paycheck? You think he'd pay me to do his books? You obviously don't know Hank. He told me I shouldn't expect walk-around money for doing my duty. My reward was the honor and privilege of contributing to a successful family business. Then, just the other day, it hit me. Embezzlement. Hank accused me of it to my former employer. It felt like poetic justice to me.

"I wrote the checks. I made the deposits. I prepared the P&L's. Hank never looked at the details behind the figures. He only cared about the bottom line. I realized that I didn't really have to commit a crime. All I needed to do was put myself on the payroll. I could get the twenty thou I needed in record time without raising any suspicion. If he had the books audited after I left, the CPA would find nothing illegal."

I wondered about her logic. Would a judge regard it all the same way she did? "Did you put your plan into motion?"

"No. Haven't had time or a payroll period yet. Besides, I had to help Pops. He'd been so good to me. I couldn't abandon him without first helping resolve his problem with Hank."

"Did your father-in-law offer you money?"

Mary Alice pulled her chin back to her throat and opened her eyes wide. "To do what? Kill my husband? Kill his son?"

Funny that she jumped with alacrity to that lethal conclusion. Perhaps it was more revelatory than she knew.

Chapter Seven

"Were there any other problems?"

Mary Alice swiped a stray hair out of her face. "I know you can't tell me yet if it was murder, but I also know, as a spouse of one of the victims, I'd be a suspect. I thought you'd think that gave me a strong motive. Honestly, I'm surprised you haven't arrested me already. I didn't think you'd need to ask any more questions."

"We need more than a motive to arrest someone."

"Still, I suppose that places me high on your list of suspects?"

"As you said, you are a spouse, and all spouses are suspects. You're no exception."

I understood why her husband's death did not distress her and felt badly for what he had done. I knew, however, what she told me about her relationship with Hank did place her high on the list of possible perpetrators. Nonetheless, a conflicting theory was also likely: that she concocted the whole story of mistreatment to make him look bad to justify her actions. I hardened my voice to disguise any empathy I felt.

"Let's go over the events of the day leading up to your husband's departure from your home yesterday through to this morning, with a little more detail, please," I said.

Mary Alice sighed and shook her head. "Two mornings ago, my day began with Hank's foot pushing me out of bed. I fetched him a cup of coffee and made breakfast, feeling like a blindfolded fool in a maze. When he left the house, he plucked my key ring off the hook by the door, jiggling the keys to make sure I knew that I was stuck at home without wheels again."

"He did that often?"

"Whenever he felt the need to remind me of my helplessness."

"Continue, please."

Mary Alice ran through the household chores she'd tackled and completed that morning.

"Did you work on your computer?"

"Oh, sure. I updated the financial records for the business there—you can check. You'll see they are all up to date, as of this morning."

"Anything else online?"

"I probably checked email and Facebook because that's pretty much a habit. I don't think I sent any messages or posted any comments, though."

"Could you jot down the passwords to those apps for me?" I asked.

Her eyes narrowed, and she tilted her head as if my request was tromping all over her privacy protections. "Sure," she said and grabbed a pen and a slip of paper from the table beside her.

"Thanks. Did you do any searches on the internet this week?"

Mary Alice's eyes widened, and she looked out the window. "I imagine I did, but I don't remember what," she said, picking up a small blue stone from the end table and rubbing it between her thumb and index finger.

"You don't remember? It wasn't that long ago."

She kept staring out to the front yard. "Oh, you know how it is. An idle thought flits through your head, raises a question, and you look for any answer. Not particularly significant or memorable."

"Did you click on any links on Facebook?"

Mary Alice shrugged. "Maybe."

"What's that in your hand?" I asked.

She startled as if surprised that she was holding anything. She held it up. "This? It's angelite. You want to see it?"

She passed it over, and I turned it in my hand, feeling the moisture of her perspiration. The heart-shaped stone was a lovely medium blue with a rust-colored vein twisting through its center.

"I've never seen anything quite like this. Where did you find it?"

"I picked it up when I went to a gem show with a friend way back when I was still in high school. It's very comforting when I'm stressed."

"You're stressed now? Why is that, Mary Alice? Are you hiding something? Are you protecting someone?"

"No, ma'am," she said, straightening her spine and raising her voice. "I am stressed. I'm not used to having family members possibly murdered, am I? For God's sake, aren't you human?" She buried her face in her hands and sobbed.

When she settled down and looked back up, I continued, "I am sorry. I know this is difficult. But it is vital to our investigation. Let's resume your chronology. You're at home alone. What did you do the rest of the day before your husband arrived?"

Mary Alice rubbed on the stone, stopped, clutched it in her palm, and set it on the table as if it burned her fingers.

"I fixed Hank's favorite dinner: real fried chicken—not the oven-baked kind that I usually fix—but good, old-fashioned, greasy, crispy chicken. Hank loved it. And I made the slow-cooking, southern-style green beans with bacon he adored. And I used unpeeled redskin potatoes to fix the mashed potatoes like his Momma made.

"Hank had to get up and leave the house very early—or as he put it, 'before the butt crack of dawn'—so we both went to bed before our usual time. We woke when the landline rang. I looked at the clock by my bed automatically. It was 9:50. Hank left the room to answer the call, but he was close enough I could hear him talking. He said, 'What is it, Pops? What? Pops?' And he might have said 'Pops' a couple more times.

"Hank was still buck naked from bed when he came back into the bedroom. He jerked on his jeans without taking the time to pull on a pair of boxers first. I asked if something was wrong with Pops. He said he didn't know. The only word he understood Pops to say was 'Help!' I jumped out of bed and grabbed a tee-shirt, ready to go to the farm with Hank, but he insisted that I stay home in case Pops called again. I asked if I should call 9-1-1, and he said he would if he got to the farm and there was a real problem and not just an old man's panic.

"I sat up in bed with my phone in my lap, waiting for it to ring. It was almost midnight when I called Hank's cell, but got no answer. I called the farm, but no one picked up there either. I managed to stay awake another hour and tried both lines again. I slumped sideways and fell back to sleep. I jerked awake when the sun shone through the blinds. Hank's side of the bed was still empty.

"I drank my coffee and started the beef stew in the crock pot for dinner. I fussed around the house, mad at Hank for not calling and worried about what had happened to him. I called his number and the farm landline yet again. When I got no answer at either one, I called the sheriff's office and asked for a wellness check."

"When was that?" I asked.

"You don't know? I thought someone would have given you the exact time. It was about 8:30 or 9:00, I guess."

"Then, what did you do?"

"I did a little business paperwork, put out the mail, and washed my hair, fretting the whole time. A couple of hours passed, but I still hadn't heard back from the sheriff's office. I called the farm landline again. When a strange voice answered, I hung up and then regretted it. If the person who answered was one of the deputies, I could've asked what was going on. I thought about calling back, but decided to wait. I'm not too good with patience, but I do try to exercise it now and then," she said with a little laugh.

"Why did you hang up? Who did you think answered?" I asked.

"I really didn't think at all. It was just a reflexive reaction."

Interesting. A sign of guilt? Maybe. What isn't she telling me, I thought. "What did you do then?"

"I ate a sandwich and decided to clean the house. I was vacuuming in the bedroom when you arrived."

That explained her delay in answering the door, but still, I couldn't get past the feeling she was hiding something from me. My thoughts were interrupted by my cell. It was a call from Rose Culpepper out at the farm.

"Spencer," she said, "you need to get back out here right away. We found something odd in the basement."

"Like what?"

"Like someone was living behind the furnace. We've taken photos, but I told Chip not to disturb the scene until you can eyeball it."

"Good. Thanks. I'll be there as soon as I can." To Mary Alice, I said, "Excuse me a moment. I need to check in with the searchers. I'll be right back."

I walked down the hall to a bedroom transformed into a home office. Entering the doorway, I faced a wall with an open cabinet filled with trophies. The wall above it was lined with photos of little boys in football uniforms. In the front row, they knelt with one knee up, their helmets resting on top of that knee. In the back two rows, they stood with their headgear tucked under their left arms. In every photo, Hank beamed beside the teams.

Most of the wall to my right was filled by a tilted drafting board, a set of blueprints spread on top. Opposite that was a closet without a door. Across the back wall of the space were broad shelves filled with flat sketches on large sheets of drafting paper. On the two sides, cubbyholes were filled with rolled-up blueprints. On the fourth wall, a sectional computer desk stretched the whole length. One segment had a bookcase filled with binders; in the middle one, a keyboard sat on a lower, retractable shelf with a large monitor at the height of the other two sections; and the third had three regular drawers with a deep file drawer on the bottom.

Randy Pippen had a small stack of office boxes beside the doorway. The top one had its lid off, and he was dropping a handful of documents into it as I entered the room. "I think I've gotten all the business materials in here," he said, tapping on the side of the stack. "I put the desktop in the container over against the wall to take to the cyber guys. I added all the memory sticks I found, as well as all the CDs and DVDs that didn't contain music, movies, or TV shows. Anything else I should secure?"

"You looked through everything in here?" I asked.

"Sure did. Nothing looked to be of value to the investigation. I'll get back to the kitchen next. Chad is finishing up the bedroom and will take apart the bathroom after that."

"I have to go back to the crime scene in a few minutes. Work in the kitchen while I'm gone and try to keep Mrs. Monroe at the table in there. Don't let her leave the house. I'll be back as quickly as I can. Don't forget the basement or the upstairs."

"Yes, ma'am. We'll cover every square inch."

I walked back to Mary Alice with Randy following me down the hall. I took my seat at the table across from her, and Randy started opening cabinets, removing all the edible contents, and packing each item in a box.

"Mary Alice, I saw the trophies and team photos on the wall. Was that Hank in all of them?" I asked.

"Yes, he loved his boys. He coached in Pee Wee Football every year without fail. His company sponsored the team, bought the uniforms for the players. And every time the mothers had a bake sale to buy new equipment, he'd bring home armloads of cupcakes and cookies."

Using a gloved finger, Randy tapped on the top of the slow cooker on the counter and asked, "What's this?"

Mary Alice swayed in her chair. "My dinner," she said with a distinct quaver in her voice.

I stared at her, hoping to see some other indication of the state of her mind.

Randy lifted the lid and sniffed. "Beef stew?"

Mary Alice nodded her head three times in rapid succession. "You gotta keep the lid on or the temperature will drop." Her breathing sounded uneven, and her eyes darted all over the place. I wondered what that was all about.

"It sure smells good," Randy said as he dropped the cover on top of the crock and looked at me for directions. "Should I take this in?"

Mary Alice gasped.

I acted as if I didn't hear her. "Oh, for heaven sakes, no. Poor woman needs to have something to eat. She's had a rough day."

Randy gave me a peculiar look, then shrugged and continued with the cabinets. I tossed a smile at Mary Alice and went back to the bathroom. I asked Chad to call out and tell Randy that he was needed back here.

When Randy got to the bathroom, I said, "Get a sample out of that crockpot. But do it when she's not there. I'm going to tell her to stay in that spot, but she'll need to go to the bathroom eventually. You can take the sample then. Until then, try not to even look in the direction of that thing."

"Gotcha," Randy said and returned to the kitchen.

I told a wild-eyed Mary Alice to remain in her chair and reminded her if she needed a glass of water or a trip to the bathroom to speak to one of the forensic team. Then, I left her place to see what surprise waited for me in the basement of the crime scene house.

Chapter Eight

Arriving at the other Monroe home, I again slipped on booties and gloves and went down into the basement. I heard voices behind a wall on my right and followed them to the source. Conversation broke off as I entered the dimly lit space.

A furnace took up the major portion of the partially walled-off area. Spider webs owned the ceiling line and the corners. The air smelled musty and stale with an undertone of sweaty shoes.

"Charley," Rose Culpepper said, "we've taken stills and video of the area already. Feel free to move anything around."

Rose and Chip backed up to let me pass through and see behind the oil-eating behemoth. I acknowledged them with a nod and peered into the dark. As my eyes adjusted, more became visible. An unlit candle burned halfway down sat on a saucer surrounded by a hardened, lopsided circle of melted wax. A cot with a throw pillow and a blanket on top of it nestled against the wall. A metal box sat under the cot.

I pulled out the box and flipped the lid. A half a dozen packs of snack crackers sat on one side, and a bottle of what appeared to be water lay prone on the other. At the foot of the cot, an old apple crate contained a plastic bag with a cellophane wrapper inside of it.

My rising suspicions of Mary Alice Monroe were now spattered with doubt. I didn't think it was possible that Mary Alice had bunked here, but who had? And why? Was it the lair of someone who'd committed a triple homicide?

"Take everything," I said. "Shouldn't be a problem finding fingerprints or

DNA somewhere in this set-up." I stood and squeezed through the entry behind the furnace. It was a tight fit to pass through without bumping the cot or anything around it. I managed, but only by a tissue-thin margin. "Let me know if you find any documents pointing toward an identity."

"One more thing, Charley. The basement door was shut but unlocked."

"Is it possible it's been that way for some time?"

"I doubt it," Rose said. "The key is still in the padlock, and it's shiny and bright. Couldn't have been exposed to the elements for long."

"Show me."

Rose and I went up the steps that stretched up to an angled wooden door. Rose pushed up, and we climbed out. The padlock was indeed quite new. The sun glinted on it as it hung from the rust-encrusted hasp. Not wanting to surprise a hidden snake with my bare hands, I grabbed a hoe leaning against the outside wall and poked at the margin of overgrown grass circling the basement entrance. The tool hit an object that thunked like metal. I knelt, pawed through the vegetation with my gloved hands, and found another lock. The body of it was as corroded as the closure on the door. Scratch marks marred the surface around the keyhole. The shackle was open but twisted out of alignment, indicating that a lock-picking attempt had been replaced by brute force.

Rose reached over my shoulder with an evidence bag. I slid the relic inside it, and she sealed and marked it, asking, "Wonder when it was removed and who replaced it?"

"Big question, Rose. Somehow, I doubt it was the homeowner."

I walked around the house and entered on the main floor to check on the processing of evidence on that level before leaving. Someone wanted to enter the house secretly, and that indicated a devious intent. Mary Alice? Hank? Or someone whose name had never crossed my mind?

*　*　*

I returned to Mary Alice's house with a new batch of questions. I found Randy still at work in the kitchen. He nodded at me, and I took that as a signal that he'd obtained a sample from the crockpot. Chad had moved to the bathroom search. I sat down at the kitchen table across from Mary Alice. The furrows on her brow were threatening to become permanent fixtures.

"Who lived in your in-laws' house, ma'am?"

"Charles Monroe, my father-in-law, and Florence Monroe, my mother-in-law. Her friends called her Flossie."

"No one else?"

"No. Not that I was aware."

"Did your husband have any siblings?"

"One—a brother," Mary Alice said, her brow's wrinkles becoming more pronounced.

"His name?"

"Chuck. Charles Monroe, Jr."

"When did you last see him?"

"It's been nearly ten years since I've seen him. I don't remember exactly where or when."

Her hands were busy, alternating between clasping the knuckles of her right hand with the fingers of her left, then grasping the left with the right.

"Is it possible he could be living at the farmhouse?"

"Oh, no. He couldn't. Pops disowned him years ago. That's why I hadn't seen him for so long."

"Why was he disowned?" As I asked, I wondered if that was at the bottom of this tragedy.

"I don't know. I asked Hank, and he said it was family business and not to ask about it again."

"Did that upset or anger you?"

"Damn right," she said. "What kind of husband keeps family secrets from his wife?"

"Not the best ones," I said. "Is it possible that the dead body lying across the bed is really Chuck and not Hank?"

Mary Alice pulled back her chin and looked at me as if I just turned inside out in front of her eyes. "My first inclination is to say 'no,' but then Chuck certainly would have a motive and probably be more likely to commit suicide.

Much bigger motive than Hank did."

"Why do you mention suicide?"

"It seems logical to me that murder-suicide is a possibility. There must have been a deep, dark story behind his parents disowning him. I would think that anyone who would commit a murder-suicide would be riddled with shame or guilt. Am I right?"

"I can't argue with that. But what do you mean about Hank's motive?"

"I can't imagine Hank would kill his parents while he was attempting to gain control of their assets."

"Your husband was that greedy?"

"I hadn't thought so until Pops' visit the other day, but that opened my eyes. He could have seen them as expendable, still—"

"Could your husband be aware of your father-in-law's plans?"

"I sure didn't tell him."

"What if your father-in-law told him that night, and Hank flew into a rage?"

Mary Alice's mouth formed an elongated circle. She stammered before saying, "I hadn't thought of that. I wouldn't think Pops would have been that foolish."

"Could your father-in-law have been so angry that he just blurted it out?"

"I guess so. But why that pitiful phone call so late at night?"

"There are a lot of questions I don't have answers for right now, Mary Alice, but we're doing our best to figure it all out. Back to Chuck. Are you certain Chuck is not in the area?"

Mary Alice shook her head. "No. In fact, Hank asked me if I had seen him since someone told him that Chuck was back in town."

"Who told him?"

"I think he said Harley saw him at Pat's Saloon."

"Do you know Harley's last name?"

She looked up to the ceiling, then shook her head as she said, "If I ever did, I don't remember."

"Excuse me for a moment, please," I said to Mary Alice and stepped outside to call Rose Culpepper. "Any results on the GSR test?"

"Yes. I had a deputy run it to the lab. It was negative on the body we presume to be Hank Monroe. And we used the latest technique that can pick up particles fifteen times smaller than the width of a human hair. Without a doubt, there is nothing there."

I ended the call and went back inside. "Would you come down to the station with me to make a statement and confirm the identity of the body?"

"The body?" Mary Alice bit her lip. "You want me to look at it? Is it necessary? If it's not Hank, where is he?"

"I can't answer that," I admitted. "First, though, we need to be certain one way or the other."

"Don't we need to wait until these guys are done in here?" she asked.

"No. That's not necessary."

Randy said, "We should be finished in a half-hour or less."

"What about my stew?" Mary Alice objected.

"I should be able to get you back home in time for dinner, so you won't need to worry about it," I said.

"But when they leave, the house will be empty and wide open for anyone to come in here," Mary Alice complained, her furrows deepening again.

"Give me your house key, and I'll lock up when I leave," Randy said. "I'll bring the key to you at the station."

I patted the back of Mary Alice's hand. "See, everything is fine. Let's go."

Mary Alice stood, her eyes bouncing from wall to wall. I took hold of her arm. Something about leaving her home bothered her. Had we missed something? Or was she just concerned with what we might do with her stew once she was gone?

The Monroe family seemed riddled with dysfunction. Was it one of them or was it someone else entirely? Or a combination of the two?

Chapter Nine

A deputy placed Mary Alice in interrogation room two and informed me that Travis Ferguson and his lawyer were waiting in the first room.

"The little punk turned himself in," the deputy told me. "His lawyer said he had important information about other situations that would be of value to law enforcement."

I rolled my eyes, grabbed the file folder on the case, flipped through it, and opened the door to the small, boring space. I introduced myself, and lawyer Cynthia Tremont returned the favor. Her suit was a conservative navy blue, albeit with a noticeably short skirt. Travis leaned on the back two legs of his chair with a sneer on his face. I sat across from them at the ratty, paint-chipped table.

I looked straight at Travis. "Mr. Ferguson, all four chair legs on the floor, please. We can't have you abusing government property now, can we?"

Travis shrugged his shoulders but didn't change his position or his expression. I rose from my seat and turned toward the door.

"Wait just a moment, please," said Cynthia. She turned to her client, grabbed the back of the chair, and gave it a hard jerk, bringing the upraised legs back to the floor. "Cut the crap, Travis. Sit properly or, so help me, I'll walk out of here."

I waited for Travis' protruding bottom lip to return to its regular pose before I got started. "Quite the illegal enterprise you had going in your grandmother's basement, Mr. Ferguson. How long have you been in business?"

Cynthia tapped a manicured fingertip on the tabletop. "Let's postpone the questioning until we have cleared the air on possible leniency for my client in exchange for information he has that has the potential to be of great significance."

"I'm all ears."

"He can provide the names of the three teenagers who vandalized the property off Crest Street."

"And…"

"He is willing to testify in court on behalf of the state."

"Although I appreciate that very much and vandalism is a good trade for bike theft, it doesn't quite measure up to drug dealing." I leaned back in my chair and crossed my legs. "Not to mention that we also could level charges of assaulting a police officer and evading arrest."

"Mr. Ferguson is willing to provide more important information which would put him at serious risk of bodily harm."

"And what would that be?"

"The name of his supplier."

"And the address of his crib, too," Travis added.

"Why would you be willing to do that, Mr. Ferguson?"

"Sergeant, please address your questions to me. My client has a conscience, and he has thought about his role in the opioid epidemic and deeply regrets it."

I couldn't help it. I laughed out loud.

Cynthia's nostrils flared twice their normal size. "Sergeant Spencer, if you will not take these negotiations seriously, my client and I are leaving right now."

I leaned forward and folded my hands on the table. "If you attempt to do that, Ms. Tremont, I will immediately arrest your client and charge him with every count I can conjure up."

Travis leaned forward and looked at me. "What she said was bullshit."

Cynthia placed a hand on his forearm. "Travis, that's enough."

Travis pushed her hand away, rose, and backed up to the wall out of her reach. "I do have a conscience, but not like she said. I ain't no saint. My supplier didn't live up to our agreement. He promised pharmaceuticals—like you get in a drug store. But he tried to sell me this street shit that's poison. I looked at those little blue pills, and I could tell they were crap. They had a "30" on one side, but it was crooked and misshapen, not like the precision you find on store-bought goods. What if I gave one of them to my grandmother for her pain? It could kill her. That's not right. I told him so. I told him I wouldn't pay for that inferior garbage, and when he wouldn't take the package back, I threw it in the trash."

"Travis, please sit down, and don't say another word," his attorney urged.

"Did he threaten you, Travis?" I asked.

"What do you think?"

"So, you need him off the street?"

"And off my ass."

"Thank you for your honesty, Mr. Ferguson. Ms. Tremont, if you and your client would wait for a few minutes, I'll consult with the Commonwealth Attorney's Office."

Even though everyone was cracking down harder than ever on opioid dealers, it was still possible to get a good deal if you rolled over on the guy above you in the food chain. A lot of the time, it depended on the CA's mood. I sure hope he was in a good frame of mind. I didn't much like the thought of Travis getting away without prison time, but I sure wouldn't mind bringing in someone worse than him.

Mindful that I still had Mary Alice waiting for me, I didn't take the time to go over to the prosecutor's office. I picked up the phone and hoped for the best. I was surprised that he didn't require much convincing.

"Tell the lawyer, we'll need time to draw up the agreement," he said. "We'll hold her client on bicycle theft for now and get down to business Monday afternoon. I'm open after lunch—set up a time that works for you and the defense attorney. Gotta run. 'Bye!"

It took less than a half-hour to get Travis Ferguson locked up, even with Cynthia Tremont attempting to roadblock the whole thing. Finally, I stopped talking to her and asked Travis, "Hey, are you okay with this? Do you mind spending a couple of nights in the jail while we work out the best deal possible for you?"

"Nah. I can be pretty sure I won't run into my supplier while I'm inside, right?"

"If you tell me his name, I can guarantee it."

"Don't you dare," Cynthia scolded.

Travis looked her in the eye and took pains to enunciate each word. "His name on the street is Mo' Money. His name in high school was Marvin Givens."

I raced downstairs to put out a BOLO and to ensure that Givens would be taken directly to another facility. I didn't know how long Travis would be in intake, and I didn't want Givens to be there at the same time.

* * *

As I stepped into the other interrogation room, Mary Alice slid a couple pages of a handwritten document across the tabletop. "All finished," she said.

"Excellent," I responded, surprised she didn't need any prodding to use the paper and pens in the room to write her statement. "Let's go downstairs to the morgue."

Her pace by my side was not slowed by dread as most spouses would be. I walked a little faster, and she kept pace with me without any difficulty. I wondered what she was thinking. Was she unperturbed, or was she good at hiding it?

We stood in front of the drape-covered glass window as I pressed a button to let them know we were ready. The curtain drew back to reveal the sheet-covered body with its hideous bullet wound. Mary Alice's face bore a solemn expression but one that lacked emotion. Definitely not the aspect of someone who'd lost the love of her life. Then again, considering the bruises I saw on her arms, who could blame her for being grateful that the daily nightmare was over.

"Is that your husband, Henry Monroe?"

She nodded her head with slow and sure movements. "Yes, it is. Can I leave now?"

"Certainly, I'll run you home."

Normally, I would have gotten a deputy to perform that errand, but I hoped to get something more from Mary Alice on the ride.

I checked with Randy to make sure he wasn't already on his way over here and explained his response to Mary Alice. "If they finish up before we get there, they won't lock the door. They'll leave the house key on the kitchen counter and wait for us to show up."

"Thanks," she said, and I noticed moisture in the corners of her eyes. The second she pulled the car door shut, she burst into sobs and buried her face in her hands. She was still crying when I pulled up in her driveway. I couldn't decide if her tears were genuine or if she was a good actress.

Chapter Ten

I t was Saturday, the first forty-eight hours after the Monroes' death were coming to a close, and I still wasn't certain of what to think of Mary Alice Monroe. I couldn't tell if she was full of grief or full of guilt or both. I didn't know if she tried to kill all three of them, if she was only responsible for her husband's death, or if she was blameless for all three lives.

I went to the autopsy suite with a head full of questions and no answers in sight. Perhaps the medical examiner or the lab techs could give me some resolution.

I walked through the door, and the medical examiner waved me away. "I'll meet you in my office in two minutes. Go have a seat."

I followed directions and waited. He slammed the door shut as he entered. "Your victim is not right-handed, is he?" he asked.

"No."

"I don't think you have a suicide."

"Why not?"

"First, no GSR on either hand. Plus, the angle is awkward for a self-inflicted wound. Not impossible, but unlikely. And if it were self-administered, he would have had to use his right hand, which makes no sense since he is left-handed. But as I said, not impossible that it happened. Just doesn't look right to me."

"I didn't think it was suicide. What about the female victim?"

"My, oh, my, that poor woman's brain looked like swiss cheese, but brain damage wasn't what killed her. She was poisoned with something, but I haven't gotten any toxicology reports yet. She showed all the signs of opioid overdose, but that could be off base. We'll have to wait 'til we have the spectrograph run. That still isn't definitive. She could have had a drug problem."

"The male found with her?"

"He looks like an opioid death, too. Otherwise, he was in good shape for a guy in his seventies. But again, I need the toxicology. If both are opioid deaths, it indicates they were drug users, or it was a suicide pact, or it was poisoning. I don't know anything for sure right now."

Another possibility—a highly improbable one—popped into my thoughts. "I know it's unlikely because of the position of the bodies, but could the older male have shot the younger one and then overdosed his wife and himself?"

"I hadn't considered that. I suppose the older guy might have taken an intentional overdose, climbed into bed, and then shot his son before the drugs had taken his life. I'll keep that in mind, but it seems far-fetched. Any reason behind that suggestion?"

"Just my wild imagination darting everywhere. Let me know if you find anything from your lab."

"You got it," he said.

I went upstairs to the forensics lab, where Rose had a partial answer for me on another front. "I checked that stew sample," Rose said. "I found toxic glycosides in it."

"Could you explain what that means?"

"I need more refined testing, but right now we have two possibilities. Either we have an overdose of heart medications or a plant-based poison. Since they found no prescriptions for digitalis or similar drugs in the house, I'm leaning toward something from outside."

"But it's winter. Nothing is growing now."

"Correct. However, the roots of some plants contain glycosides. Oleander, for example, but that's unlikely since it doesn't grow around here. There's foxglove and milkweed, though the latter propagates by reseeding, and I don't think it would be easy to find the seeds in the dirt. Probably could order those from Amazon, though. Periwinkle and lily of the valley both survive our winters here. Most people who grow them would know where to find them if there is a patch in their yards."

"And the roots could kill?" I asked.

"Yes. And the poisonous components would survive being cooked in a stew."

"Could glycoside poisoning appear to be death by opioid overdose?"

"Unlikely, but I'd never say never."

Perplexing. Mary Alice's stew was at her house. Her in-laws were poisoned at their farmhouse. I had a hard time thinking she was responsible for that crime. The only person I could imagine killing the elder Monroes was Hank, and he was shot dead at the scene. I needed to bounce everything off Lieutenant Holcombe. Maybe he'd have an idea.

I went to the office and sought him out. "Hey, Holcombe, got a minute?"

"What's up?"

I explained my confusion over Mary Alice. Holcombe leaned against the wall and folded his arms across his chest before he spoke. "So, let's say, Hank took some of the stew over to his parents' house. Fed it to them. And that suicide is off the table for Hank."

"According to the ME, most likely."

"Mary Alice went to the farmhouse and when she saw what he had done, shot him in the head and fled."

"Okay, but I would think she would have at least called for an ambulance either at the house, from her cell, or a pay phone somewhere, in case the older couple were still alive."

"She could have panicked and deliberately or unintentionally left her cell at home. And pay phones are an endangered species these days," Holcombe suggested.

"True. But still, it doesn't fit with what Mary Alice is telling us that she started the stew in the crockpot the morning after Hank went to his parents' house. She could have lied about that, I suppose. I need to dig deeper. I need ballistics reports, toxicology on the senior Monroes."

"Do you need me to put on some extra pressure in Forensics?"

"Thanks, but I don't think so. Triple homicides—or three unexplained deaths in one house—are rare enough that they know to focus and fast-track it. I also need to find Chuck Monroe. I need an emotional map of the Monroe family dynamics."

"Let me know if there's anything I can do."

* * *

Returning to my desk, I found the reports from ballistics and started reading. They made no sense. The revolver found at the scene bore the fingerprints of Henry Clay Monroe, and it was registered in his name; however, it was not the weapon that fired the shot that killed him. How could that be possible? And what did it mean? None of the weapons found at the victim's house were a match for the murder weapon either. I must not be reading the reports right or misinterpreting them. I read all the documents again.

I went up to the ballistics lab to see Joe Wilder. I waited until he came out of the testing chamber, trying to reach a different conclusion from what I read.

"Hey, Sergeant," he said when he emerged. "You ready to return the guns? All but one is registered to the victim. The shotgun is not listed anywhere, but it's an antique and not functional, so that's irrelevant."

"Actually, Joe, I'd like to make sure I understand your findings."

"They're pretty simple. In short, you haven't found the weapon that fired the projectile that penetrated the victim's skull."

"That certainly rules out a suicide, then."

"Unless your dead guy shot himself in the head, disposed of the weapon away from the crime scene, and resumed his position on the bed without dripping blood on his path along the way."

"You've always been a smart ass, Joe."

"Beats the alternative. Bring me another weapon, Sergeant, as soon as you find one."

On the way back to my desk, Deputy Jack Preston intercepted me. "I called Charles Monroe's attorney at home, and he agreed to meet me at his office and turn over a copy of the will. He said that it was a recently modified version, so I asked for the previous one, too. Here you go."

"Thanks, Jack. Did you look them over?"

"While I was waiting for you, I skimmed through."

"What stood out?" I asked.

"The changes were dramatic. Originally, Henry Monroe inherited everything. In the latest rendition, there is a trust fund for the care of Florence Monroe, and the remainder of the estate goes to Mary Alice Monroe. And the lawyer said he told his client it wasn't necessary to add a prohibition to block his sons from inheriting anything, but the old guy insisted on it. Spelled it out at the end—nothing for Hank or Chuck."

"Holy crap. So, it's either Chuck getting belated revenge, Hank thinking the changes had not been made yet, or Mary Alice getting greedy. Then, of course, there is the possibility that it is someone else entirely. I, however, am inclined to follow the money."

"Odds are in your favor, I say."

"Thanks again, Jack." I sat down to read it all through. Mary Alice never mentioned the will to me. Either she didn't know, or that was at least a part of what she was hiding from me. I told Jack to take another officer with him and bring Mary Alice in for questioning. And bring in that slow cooker with her. He had no trouble locating the widow, but the crockpot was nowhere to be found.

Chapter Eleven

Seated across the table from Mary Alice, I remained uncertain on whether I should start with the glycosides and the now-missing slow cooker or the will. To give me time to think that through, I asked her once again to run through the twenty-four-hour period before the bodies were discovered.

"I already told you," she sighed. "And I wrote it all down."

"I assume you want me to get to the bottom of this, don't you?"

"Well, yes, but…"

"Then humor me."

She slumped, resting her arms on the table. She reiterated her story in a monotone. No variations stood out.

"Did you or Hank own any guns other than the ones I collected at your house?" I asked.

"No. Oh, wait. There were two others. A revolver that Hank kept in his work vehicle in the glove compartment and a small pistol he usually carried in his pocket or waistband."

"Any other weapons?"

"I don't think so."

"Are you sure?" I pressed.

"I am not aware of any, and Hank liked to show off new weapons when he bought them. I can't be 100% certain, though."

"You don't own any?"

"Absolutely not. My dad didn't hunt, so I've never been used to having guns in the house before Hank. Living around here, I've gotten used to rifles and shotguns—lots of people have those—but I'm still uncomfortable with handguns."

"Why didn't you tell me about your father-in-law's will?"

"What about it?"

"Who is the beneficiary?"

"I don't really know since I've never seen it, but I'd assume it was Hank."

"What about his brother?"

"I was told Chuck had been disinherited years ago, so I doubt if he's included in the will."

"So, I imagine with Hank dead, it would all come to you?"

"I don't know. When Pops came to the house the other day, he did say he would set up a trust fund for me so I wouldn't have to worry about my future. But I doubt he'd gotten around to doing that."

Did she intentionally avoid my question?

"But if Hank was his sole beneficiary, wouldn't his inheritance now pass on to you and make you financially secure?"

"It's more complicated than that."

"What do you mean?"

"Well, he knew about—he knew Hank and I had problems, and he wanted me to do him a favor."

"Is that why he came to your home the other day?"

"Yeah."

"You'd better explain it all to me, and don't leave out any of the details."

Mary Alice inhaled deeply. "Okay. I was fixing lunch—just for me. Hank was at work. The doorbell rang, and my father-in-law was out on the stoop. The sight of him made me smile." A dreamy look passed over her face as she remembered. "He was so darn cute with his black and red plaid cap with ear-flaps hanging down, framing his wrinkly face. He was wearing a green flannel shirt and denim overalls as if he were a character in a hayseed play." Tears seeped from the corners of her eyes. "Damn, I'm gonna miss that man." She grabbed a tissue from a box at the end of the table and blew her nose.

"Okay, your father-in-law showed up unexpectedly. What happened next?"

"I got him a cup of coffee and asked if he wanted chocolate chip cookies or peach pie with it. As soon as he was sure I baked the pie, he asked for a slice. He loved my peach pie," she said with a chuckle. "Once I served him, I asked why he'd come to see me.

"'It's about Flossie,' he said. That's my mother-in-law. And then he said, 'I had to get a power of attorney. She used to pay all the bills, balance the checkbook, and all that. Now, though, if I put a blank check in front of her, she wouldn't know what to do with it.' I just about died when he hung his head down and shook it from side to side. My heart broke when he added, 'Dementia is an ugly thing. It's been so sad watching a bit of her die every day.'

"When I saw the tears welling up in his eyes, I rose and wrapped my arms around him. He rested his head on my shoulder, wrapped an arm around my back, and held on fast. I never felt so helpless in my whole life. He pulled himself together and said, 'I have a woman coming in three times a week to help her shower and comb her hair. As long as she knew who I was and where she was, I was doing okay.' He then told me that now Flossie doesn't recognize him and keeps asking to go home.

"When Pops told my husband that he put Momma on the waiting list for Oak Forest, Hank erupted and said it was too expensive and that Pops needed to put her in the cheapest place he could find. Hank said she was too out of it to appreciate the finer things. Pops said, 'I'll never forget what my son said. It just broke my heart. He told me his mother was just a shell of organic matter, and I shouldn't be wasting his inheritance like that.'

"Then he said that Hank showed up the next day with a power of attorney document, insisting that Pops sign it. When he refused, Hank threatened to take him to court. So, I asked, 'What can I do?' Pops said that he knew I had an unhappy marriage and suggested that I end it and move out to his place to help with Flossie and to get the farm ready for sale. After that, he told me, I'd be able to use the trust fund and start a new life.

"But I knew Hank better than Pops. Hank would not tolerate that situation. I believed he'd carry out his threat to kill me. I worried that my in-laws would get seriously hurt in the process. But the pathetic plea in Pops' eyes persuaded me to say that I'd think about it. Honestly, though, it seemed hopeless."

Mary Alice slumped her shoulders and rested her face in her palms. I studied her intently. Much of what she said and did seemed genuine. Yet something seemed off—odd to the point of unbelievable. Is she setting up the case for the justifiable homicide of her husband? Or did she kill them all to inherit?

"What about the new, revised will?" I asked.

Mary Alice looked up at me, her brow furrowed. "What new, revised will?"

"Are you telling me you were unaware of it?"

"Pops told me he was redoing his will and setting up a trust for Momma Monroe and one for me. That's all I know. I wasn't aware that he actually did anything."

I decided to keep her off-balance and asked, "Are you going to tell me what pills or plant you used in that beef stew, or are we going to have to dig up your whole yard to find it?"

Mary Alice swayed in the chair, her hands gripped the tabletop, her face turned as white as the bells on a lily of the valley. She hung her head again, and her breath grew ragged.

"Mary Alice?"

She looked up at me. Her eyes looked as wild as those of a deer fleeing from a predator. She gasped and cried, her nose running like a storm-laden stream, her lips opening and closing without a word escaping.

"Where is the slow cooker, Mary Alice?"

She moaned and slumped. I went to her side and put a hand on her shoulder. Her body fell towards me. I grabbed her to keep her from sliding off the chair. I lowered her to the floor. I checked. She was still breathing. I called to request an ambulance. In minutes, my prime suspect was on her way to the emergency room.

Chapter Twelve

Yet, there was a silver lining. With that interview cut short, I had time to go home, change my clothes, and slap on lipstick before dinner with my Dad and sister. Entering the restaurant was like stepping into a beehive—buzzing with noise and the quick movements of the wait staff. Fortunately, Dad was already there and had secured a table in a back corner where it would be easier to hear each other talk.

When I reached the table, Dad stood and wrapped me in a hug. "I've told our waitress that it's Ruby's birthday, and they'll bring her a surprise and sing to her."

I sighed and smiled. Ruby was going through a distinct stay-in-the-background phase—she did not want to be noticed by anyone, ever. She would not be pleased. I knew, however, it would bring Dad a lot of pleasure. He wanted both of his daughters to be noticed by everyone, always.

"What's new in your life?" he asked.

"I finally got the lead on a murder investigation—a triple homicide."

"This is good news?"

"Yes, Dad. Very good news."

"Then, I'm happy for you even though I feel a little ghoulish saying it." He patted the back of the hand I had rested on the table. "She's here! Look!"

Ruby most certainly had arrived. As soon as she spotted us, she lowered her head, ignored the hostess, and barreled back to our corner. "We both said, "Happy birthday, Ruby!"

She put a finger to her lips. "Shhh! But thank you."

Ruby and Dad studied the menu. I folded my hands atop of mine. I knew what I wanted—salt and pepper catfish—this place made the best ever. Dad ordered the rib-eye steak and Ruby the grilled salmon salad. Traditionally, we didn't hand out gifts until dessert, meaning that now was the time for Dad's big news. Ruby and I looked in his direction.

He saw us both staring at him and squirmed. "Well, well, I guess it's time for the big reveal." He shifted his weight in his chair from one side to the other. He moved his eyes back and forth. "I am getting married."

Ruby bounced in her chair and said, "It's about time."

"Is it someone we know?" I asked.

Ruby playfully slapped my arm. "Of course, it is, silly. Will Lucinda want us to be bridesmaids, Dad?"

"Lucinda?" he said. "What does Lucinda have to do with it?"

"The bride always makes that decision, Dad," Ruby said in a teasing tone of voice.

"You think I'm marrying Lucinda?"

"Of course, Dad, who else?"

"Ruby, Lucinda and I are not romantically involved."

"What do you mean? You two are like an old married couple already. She's part of the family. She's been there for us through everything," Ruby protested.

"Yes, Ruby, she has been a rock. She saved your sister's life, got justice for the murder of your mother, and helped us get our bearings afterwards. We owe her a huge debt of gratitude accumulated over the years. We can never pay her back in full, but Ruby, she's a friend—an exceptionally good friend—nothing more."

"When are you going to let her know you're dumping her?" Ruby said through clenched teeth.

"Charley, help me out here," Dad pleaded.

"Ruby, Lucinda is not interested in marrying Dad. She made that clear more than fifteen years ago. She cares for us—all of us. And, yes, she's part of the family, but that's not going to change, is it, Dad?"

"Oh, no. Absolutely not. I've told Emily all about her. I've told her how important Lucinda is to both of you—and to me. She understands and is looking forward to meeting her."

Ruby's lowered brow forecast a major storm ahead, but I, for one, did not want it making landfall at our table at this time. Nothing to do but change the subject away from Lucinda. "Where did you meet Emily, Dad?"

"In Syria."

"Oh," Ruby sneered, "another doctor in the house?"

"Actually, she's a Physician's Assistant."

Ruby folded her arms across her chest and leaned back into her chair. "A P.A.? Of course, that way you can boss her around like the rest of us."

Dad looked shocked at her pronouncement and totally at a loss for words.

"Ruby, that's not fair, and you know it," I said.

"Oh, really? He's a doctor—next thing to God. And he goes out on assignments with Doctors without Borders, so that makes him a saint. He thinks he's above us all."

Now, I was speechless. I had no idea that Ruby harbored these negative feelings towards our father.

Ruby turned to me with a sneer on her face. "And you're almost as bad as he is."

"What?" I asked.

"Charlotte Spencer, the great protector. Saved her baby sister. Now saves everyone in the county from criminals and blackguards. Oh, please, give me a break."

Dad and I stared at each other.

"Lucinda is the only one who doesn't treat me like I am damaged," Ruby added.

I wanted to hug her and pat her on the back. I wanted to rock her like I did when she was a little girl. I forced myself to stay in my chair.

"Ruby, that is because I am damaged, Dad is damaged, and, yes, you are damaged. All three of us. Mom was murdered, horribly in our own home. But you? You were the youngest. You were the one who found the body. All I ever wanted to do was to protect you from ever being hurt again."

I spared a glance for Dad, who looked as broken as he did when he learned Mom died. The sound of sobbing pulled my attention from him to my sister.

Oh dear, Ruby had shifted from don't-notice-me to high drama in record time. Her face was in her hands, and her shoulders heaved. I wrapped my arm around her shoulders and brought her to her feet.

"Dad, you'll be okay for a few minutes?"

He nodded with all the energy of roadkill. I led Ruby back to the restroom. Once we got inside, Ruby continued to cry as she gasped, "I'm sorry, I'm sorry, I'm sorry."

Wrapped in my arms, the heaving slowed and stopped. She backed away from me.

"I won't lie, Charley. I've had those thoughts in my darkest moments. I just feel so worthless next to you and Dad. I feel guilty, too. I should have saved Mom. I was the only one there. But no, I hid until the bad man was gone."

I placed a hand on both her upper arms. "Ruby, lift your head and look at me." She took a moment to comply. "Mom would be proud of you if she were here. You're in college. Your grades are terrific. You are beautiful. You are smart. Dad and I love you so much. We are grateful that you hid. If you hadn't, we may have lost you, too. How much more would the two of us been damaged if our sweet little three-year-old Ruby were brutally killed that day, too?"

"You mean that?" Ruby had an odd gleam in her eye that made me doubt her sincerity, but I decided to accept it at face value—peace at any cost.

"Absolutely!" I swallowed my doubt. "Wash the tears off your face, and let's get out there and celebrate your escape from your teens, okay?"

Ruby smiled, turned to the sink, splashed, dried her face, and slid her arm in mine. We marched back to the table, grinning. Dad, frozen at the table, looked ready to puke, saw the smiles on our faces, and the tension melted from his shoulders. A sad smile stole across his face. I gave him a thumbs up. Before we could sit and pull our chairs to the table, our dinner was served.

We dug in, exchanging fragile looks that gained in strength with the passage of time. We all chose cheesecake and laughed all through dessert, exchanging silly family memories. Still, I was worried about Ruby. She had not recovered as fully from the murder of our mother as I thought she had.

Chapter Thirteen

I awoke with an unpleasant sensation. In my sleep, my arm had gone up over my head, and now it felt like someone was scrubbing my underarm with sandpaper. In no time, I realized that it was Flash licking my armpit. Gross.

"Oh no, kitty cat, you will not make a habit out of this."

I pushed him off the bed, threw my feet on the floor, and went into the kitchen, where I scooped out food for the pesky little creature. Belatedly, I realized that I'd probably enabled his disgusting behavior because I gave him exactly what he wanted.

I sighed, grabbed a yogurt, and sat down in front of the TV to catch a little news. Before the eternal commercial break was over, my cell rang.

"Spencer."

"We've located Marvin Givens, and the state guys are putting together an extraction team to get him out. Thought you might want to be part of it," Jack said.

Really, I just wanted to go back to bed, but I had to be there to question this guy. "Text me the address."

* * *

I pulled up where other police vehicles had gathered, in front of a string of brick row houses. Some had polished marble stoops, others were so darkened with age that I couldn't tell what the original surface of the steps or the landing was. The location for Givens was around the corner and down a block. An interagency drug task force coordinated the takedown—I was merely along for the ride.

Two lieutenants I didn't know called the shots, placing officers in front of and behind the residence in question. They placed others across the street behind bushes and other structures in front of a long run of connected houses. The breach team quick-marched down to the house and mounted the stairs. They pounded on the door and screamed for someone to open up. When that failed, the battering ram slammed into the wood once, making it bow and splinter. Then twice more, causing it to collapse inward.

That team stepped to the side to allow the next group, who was charged with the job of clearing the house and taking anyone present into custody, to enter. When they finished that task, we found a diverse bunch inside: one white boy, one dark-skinned Haitian male, a Puerto Rican girl, and one black guy. All of them claimed they were not Marvin Givens.

A lieutenant with the state police busted through the crowd, flipped the backwards hat off the head of the tallest one in the bunch, and pinched his ear, pulling him away from the others.

"Givens, why you lying to these folks? You think we're stupid. You think no one here would recognize you? Shit, Givens, in some places, you're a celebrity." He turned to me and said, "You gave us this tip, right?"

"Yes, sir."

"I'll send him back to your station, if you'd like."

I nodded.

The investigators present paired up, and each duo took an occupant of the house to a room for questioning. Obstruction of justice charges felt pretty slim since, at this point, they were only guilty of not opening the door. I hoped the search team would locate illegal drugs or guns, or something to allow more charges and give us more leverage.

I accompanied Sergeant Jeremy Boone from a neighboring county into a bedroom with the unknown girl. Blankets balled up at the foot of the bed prevented us from sitting there. I led her to the side and told her to take a seat. She looked down at the filthy white sheets and grimaced. I couldn't blame her; it looked as if a recently surfaced coal miner slept on them.

She cooperated with Boone on the basics—name, Amaia Rivera; age, 22; address, right where we were sitting. I doubled checked her information on my cell using the station database, finding one previous arrest for marijuana possession that had resulted in a fine and a year of probation.

I asked, "What is your relationship with Marvin Givens?"

"What ju tink, bitch? Imma just gonna roll over on my friends?"

Boone slammed an open palm onto the surface of a dresser making both me and Amaia jump. "Respect, Miz Rivera. You want it from us, you give it to us."

Amaia just rolled her eyes and gazed up at the ceiling.

"Answer the Sergeant's question, Miz Rivera," he said.

Amaia made a what-fresh-hell-is-this face and swiveled her neck, turning her gaze in my direction. "I was livin' wit him. Ya need me to spell dat out?"

"That won't be necessary. Did Mr. Givens provide financial support for you?"

"No disrespect, ma'am, but is ya dat stoopid dat ya hafta aks?"

It was my turn to roll my eyes. I looked at Jeremy and jerked my head towards the door. He followed me to the hall.

"I feel like I am more of a distraction than an asset in there. You want to give it a go alone?" I asked.

"How 'bout if I ask, and you just sit there and glare. If that doesn't unsettle her, then I can go solo. Does that work for you?"

I nodded. "Works for me." We returned to the room.

"Well, then, Miz Rivera, what do you know about the other people in the house?" Boone asked.

"You think Imma gonna tell ya cause ya a black boy? Quit playin' cop games. I ain't sayin' nuttin. Arrest me and get me a lawyer, or leave me be."

Boone and I looked at each other and rendezvoused again in the hall. I shrugged. "She could be putting on an act because of me."

"Maybe. I kinda doubt it. But I'll go in by myself and see what happens."

Five minutes later, Boone returned. "I even told her we found opioids in the pockets of her jacket. She insisted the drugs did not belong to her. She wants a lawyer, or she wants to go. She's going back to your cop shop, so it's your call."

"If any illegal items are found in the house, from drugs to guns to counterfeit gift cards, we will charge her with possession of all of it since she lives here. We can always drop the charges later. After she's in custody and has a lawyer, we can see if she's willing then to impart some useful information."

I went back to the justice center to talk to Marvin Givens. By the time I arrived, Givens already had a lawyer—not a public defender but one of the foremost defense attorneys in the state, Kirk Fitzgerald. He cut an imposing figure in a courtroom or anywhere. At six-six, he towered over most people. His handsome face, dark hair, blue eyes, and ready smile would be certain to capture jurors' hearts. Word has it that there is a dartboard with his face on it hanging in a back room of the Commonwealth Attorney's Office.

Fitzgerald was easy on the eyes until my entrance turned his smile into a sneer—then he looked predatory and deadly. I had no doubts that if there was a deal to be made here, it certainly would not be a slam dunk. I introduced myself as I took a seat across from the two men.

"I understand that the only evidence you have on my client is the word of a compromised snitch and some illegal substances found in a house with multiple occupants. On top of that, your grounds for a search warrant are dubious, and I will move to throw out all evidence seized. Because of that, my client will not speak to you until I have a prosecutor here with the power to enforce any deal we might reach," Fitzgerald said. "Nothing you promise on your own is credible in my opinion."

"Are you telling me your client is ready to make a plea bargain?"

"I'm telling you, Sergeant, that it is among the many options available to this client—to most clients—and I don't want to bargain with someone as powerless as you."

"Since it's Sunday, there are no prosecutors upstairs unless they're working on a case with a Monday trial date. In other words, those who are here are not available to take on something new. It will have to wait till tomorrow."

"That's fine. My client has many friends in this facility."

I called for an officer to process him. I know it was spiteful, but I didn't bother to tell him his client was getting an immediate transfer to a neighboring lock-up. Before leaving, I went to my desk where a pile of papers waited for my review, but the most pressing matter was a phone message from the deputy who had accompanied Mary Alice to the hospital. I returned his call.

"Sergeant, I wasn't sure what to do because I didn't know if the Monroe woman was in custody when she had her medical emergency or not. She says she wasn't, but that doesn't amount to much in my book. Anyway, they are releasing her today, and I don't know if I should take her home or bring her back in."

"You stayed with her all night?"

"Yes, ma'am. Sheriff told me I needed to stay for her protection."

Interesting. I didn't think that her life was in any kind of danger. What did the sheriff know that I didn't? Did he think she was a flight risk? Or was he worried about Chuck? It didn't really matter, though, because I didn't have sufficient cause to arrest her.

"Take her home. Clear her house before you leave her there alone. I need to continue my conversation with her, but better to do it at her place."

I added the recent developments to my case notes and began the laborious process of clearing out the pile of paperwork on my desk. Some of it was departmental notices—why couldn't we all shift over to email for this stuff? What a waste of paper. Most of that category of communication didn't even apply to me, and those sheets made a quick journey into the waste basket.

After everything was sorted, I dug into the long print-out of Marvin Givens's arrests and releases. The only charge that merited lock-up went back to when he was fifteen. It was a simple possession of a controlled substance charge, most likely marijuana, considering the short time served at the juvenile facility. I guess all that his record proved was that he was a clever little perp. I put that document into the folder I'd started with multiple police reports from different members of the team that extracted him from the house. I printed out a copy and slid it all into my top drawer to take over to the C.A.'s office in the morning.

Monday was going to be a busy day. By then, I should have more answers from the forensics lab that, with a little luck, would make it all a bit easier—or complicate matters even more.

Chapter Fourteen

Monday morning, I went straight to the Commonwealth Attorney's Office when I arrived at the justice complex. First, I needed to check with the C.A.'s secretary to make sure that nothing had come up over the weekend to change the scheduled afternoon appointment I had with him, Travis Ferguson, and the defense attorney. With that confirmed, I moved into the cubicle jungle where the assistant C.A.'s had their desks.

Danielle Striker stood—the top of her head visible above the panels. I wondered if she knew that made her a target.

"Dani," I asked, "got space on your plate for one or two more cases?"

"Get real, Charley. None of us has any spare room, but y'all keep bringing 'em in and piling 'em up. What can I do for you?"

"I hope you can pick up one of these," I said as I explained my two post-arrest issues.

"Who is the lawyer for the Givens guy?"

"Kirk Fitzgerald," I said.

"What a sanctimonious prick! Yeah, I'd love to knock him down a peg. Send me the file. As for the Harding kid, what can he give you? You've got Travis Ferguson in custody already. And if Harding's willing to give you made-up addresses, then he's not ready to agree to testify against Ferguson. I'd let him rot for a while to see if he changes his attitude. If you get contacted by his lawyer, give her my name, but stall her by telling her you and I need to confer."

* * *

When I returned that afternoon, Commonwealth's Attorney Bradford Cummings stood by his secretary's desk. As soon as he saw me, he waved me into his office. "Okay," he said, "lay it out for me."

"Much to his attorney's displeasure, he already offered up his supplier, Marvin Givens, based on my promise of a plea bargain."

"A sign of good faith? We don't see much of that around here."

"True. But it also involved Mr. Ferguson's ethics."

"A thief and a drug distributor with ethics? You can't be serious."

"That's what he said. He was angry with his supplier because he had always insisted upon and received 'pharmaceuticals.' The last time he did business with him, the pills were street quality, and when his supplier wouldn't take them back, he threw them away. Now Mr. Givens is demanding payment from Mr. Ferguson, and he has threatened Mr. Ferguson to get it. Basically, Mr. Ferguson turned on him for bad customer service and a desire for personal safety."

"Oh, good Lord. Okay. Is he expecting nothing but probation and community service? I don't know if I can go that far—too many pills in his possession for that."

"I don't know what he expects or what his lawyer has said to him. I would like to get the names of the vandals at those townhouses, and I agree with you that he needs to serve some time behind bars."

A buzz erupted from Cummings' phone. "The lawyer's here," he said.

I got up and opened the door to invite them inside. "Sir, I'd like you to meet attorney Cynthia Tremont."

She stretched out a hand, shook Cummings', and said, "I believe we've met before—the Commonwealth versus Ruiz."

"Yes, indeed, Ms. Tremont, a pleasure to see you again. Have a seat. Your client should be up here any minute. Would you like a cup of coffee, a glass of water, anything?"

Every career prosecutor I knew took a dim view of their counterparts on the other side. Like the rest of the world, they tended to judge everyone's decisions based on their own personal lens. The good prosecutors knew they could make more money as criminal defense attorneys, but also knew they couldn't sleep well at night. They judged those who did as not having any more of a conscience than their most malfeasant clients and being as devoid of ethics. Never for a moment did many of them consider that on the other side, many of the lawyers were driven by different but equally strong and valid principles. But, boy, could they be polite and courteous to them at times like these.

We heard Travis Ferguson's arrival before we saw him. The clang of his shackles echoed in the halls. When he entered Cummings' office, Cynthia's jaw dropped. She spun her head to the Commonwealth's Attorney and said, "Brad, please. Is this really necessary?"

Cummings grunted and told the deputy, "Take off the shackles."

"Bradford!" Cynthia said.

The C.A. cringed at the familiarity, but his eyes widened as if an old memory popped into his mind. Just my imagination? Maybe? Still, I wondered about their previous encounter.

"Take the handcuffs, too."

"With all due respect, sir, do you think that's wise?" the deputy asked.

"Spencer, you got a problem with this?"

"No, sir, Mr. Cummings."

"Unfasten both, Deputy, but wait outside right by the door."

Unencumbered, Travis Ferguson took a seat next to me, across the desk from the Commonwealth Attorney. "Good morning, Mr. Ferguson," I said.

"Morning, Sergeant Spencer. Did you find Marvin Givens?"

"We certainly did. Thank you for the information."

"Please, let me do the speaking on your behalf, Travis," Cynthia said.

He rolled his eyes at me and then turned to his lawyer and nodded.

Cummings asked, "What are you looking for in a deal, counselor?"

"Two years of probation and fifty hours of community service."

"Dream on. You know, in the midst of a national opioid epidemic, your client is going to have to spend some time locked up."

Cynthia drew a deep breath and straightened her posture. "My client gave you a man who deals in poison. My client has displayed an ethical sense of obligation to the health and well-being of his customers by refusing to distribute anything below the standard of pharmaceutical quality. Surely, that demonstrates his character and justifies his redemption."

"What he did was illegal," Cummings bellowed. "If he'd killed someone, would you say the humane manner in which he took another human's life demonstrated his high ethical standards? I'm thinking ten to twenty years."

"Don't be obscene. I bet if you tried, you'd find dozens of deaths that could be linked straight back to Givens. I doubt you could find one linked exclusively to my client."

I had a feeling this discussion could go on forever. I listened to five more minutes of it before breaking into it. "I'd like to offer a compromise."

Travis breathed a loud sigh of relief. Cummings and Tremont glared at me in silence until the Commonwealth Attorney said, "Proceed, Sergeant."

"I propose that Mr. Ferguson's sentence be contingent on his testimony in court against Marvin Givens and against the townhouse vandals. Of course, he'll need to give us the names of the latter immediately."

"And then?" Tremont asked. "What kind of sentence do you envision?"

"Provided he meets all the conditions, I think that two years of incarceration, followed by two years of probation, twenty hours of community service, and a two-thousand-dollar fine would be fair."

Travis gave me a smile, but, of course, the two gladiators in the room scowled.

Cummings said, "You must be out of your mind." But as Tremont turned her head toward me, Cummings gave me a wink to let me know I was on solid ground.

"I don't think you are showing sufficient gratitude to my client for the cooperation he has given and the additional assistance he is agreeing to provide," Tremont said.

"You'll have to work this out with Mr. Cummings, ma'am. But if I do not get the three names of the vandals before I walk out of here, I will withdraw my support of leniency."

A soft triple knock and the door edged open as Dani Striker stuck her head through the opening. "Excuse me, sir, could I borrow Sergeant Spencer for a moment?"

"Spencer, I don't see any reason why you need to remain in this meeting," Cummings said.

"I really need the name of the vandals, sir," I objected.

"Not until we have a deal," Tremont said.

I sighed. "I'll take a minute to assist Ms. Striker then, sir."

Travis rose, looked me in the eye, and said, "Bobby Lee Hunter, Clarence Thompson, Donna Claridge."

Tremont bolted to her feet. "Travis, please! You are not helping me here."

"Thank you, Mr. Ferguson," I said. "Call my cell if you need me."

Back at Dani's desk, she said, "Sylvester Harding's lawyer called back. She said her client was willing to testify against Travis Ferguson."

"First of all, I don't trust that guy after he lied to me, but most importantly, Sylvester and his attorney are too late. That was Travis Ferguson and his lawyer in Cummings' office working out a deal."

"He's going to have to come up with something better than that, then. I'll let Trinity Bellows know."

"Any word from Kirk Fitzgerald and Marvin Givens?" I asked.

"We're meeting in the morning."

"Keep me updated, okay?"

"Yeah, if things get ugly, I'll ask you to come in to unsettle Fitzgerald."

I smiled. "Anything you need."

Chapter Fifteen

I paired up with Jack to find out as much as possible about the three vandals. Bobby Lee Hunter was nineteen and had no previous arrests. Clarence Thompson and Donna Claridge were minors, and neither of them had any record of trouble with the law I decided to pick up Hunter first, if I could, and then arrange for the other two and their parents to meet me down here.

Hunter's address was in a particularly squalid sector of downtown, a place filled with old Victorians suffering from one level of neglect or another. Peeling paint, fallen gutters, and weed-friendly, trash-strewn yards were common. Hunter had an apartment in one of those homes in better condition than most. The yard was surrounded by a short, wrought-iron fence. The exterior yellow paint couldn't have been more than a couple of years old, and the railings of the wrap-around porch appeared to be intact.

I couldn't find a doorbell, so I turned the knob and stepped into a once exquisite foyer. On the left, an elegant stairway of elaborate woodwork swept up to the second floor. To my right was a door with the letter "A" on it. Straight ahead was another one with the letter "B." Bobby Lee Hunter's entrance. Jack rapped on the door.

We heard footsteps bouncing across the floor before the door swung open and the pot smoke rolled out. The smile on the face in front of us sagged, and his eyes flew wide open. I looked at Jack and shook my head—we weren't going to worry about marijuana now. We could weaponize it later if we needed to do so.

"Mr. Hunter? Mr. Bobby Lee Hunter?" I asked.

The focus of his eyes bounced around the room, even over his shoulder. The look on his face told me he was contemplating flight. Obviously, Jack read the same signal because he grabbed one of the young man's wrists.

"Are you Bobby Lee Hunter?" Jack asked.

Bobby Lee's shoulders slumped, and he nodded his head.

"We need you to come in with us and answer a few questions, Mr. Hunter," I said.

Bobby Lee stuck out both hands in apparent surrender.

"I'll tell you what, Mr. Hunter," I said, "you are not yet under arrest. We don't have to cuff you if you'll come on out with us and get in the car."

"Sure," Bobby Lee said. "Can I check that my cat has food and water first? It's right in the kitchen."

We were by his side as he took care of his pet and walked to the vehicle with Jack's hand wrapped around the back of Bobby Lee's neck. After we pulled away from the curb, Bobby Lee spoke.

"I'll waive my rights to an attorney if you will let me speak to my uncle first, and he says it's okay—he's on the Richmond Police force. I think I know what you want to know."

Jack and I exchanged a glance. I said, "I think we can arrange that when we get back to the station."

* * *

We let Bobby Lee have privacy for his conversation. When he disconnected, we walked into the room.

"Did your uncle agree?" I asked. Bobby Lee nodded.

Jack handed him a waiver to sign and read him his rights before setting down a written copy and a pen beside him.

Bobby Lee picked up the pen without hesitation and executed his signature with a flourish. As he finished, he said, "My uncle told me to provide you with some interesting information I have in another, drug-related matter. There is a guidance counselor at my old middle school who bought marijuana from me for years until she started working at the same school. Recently, out of the blue, she called and asked me for fentanyl. I told her that she could kill herself with that shit—excuse me. I didn't mean to use that word. Anyway, I arranged a meeting with a dealer to purchase fentanyl-laden pills."

"Who is the dealer?" I asked.

"On the streets, he's Mo' Money, but I think his real first name is Marvin—I don't know his last name."

"And the guidance counselor?"

"Miss Jones. I think her first name is Natasha, but I'm not sure if I am remembering that right."

"Would you excuse us for a moment?" I asked and motioned Jack to follow me out to the hall.

I closed the door behind us. "Considering the drug dealer we arrested has the same first name and street name as this guy, that's too much of a coincidence to think we are talking about two different people, isn't it?"

"I'd say so."

"Go back in, chat with him, keep him relaxed, ask if he wants a soda, anything—I'm going to call the Commonwealth Attorney's Office and see if the prosecutor handling the Marvin Givens case wants to join us."

Jack nodded and stepped inside as I dialed. When Dani Striker answered, I ran down the information Bobby Lee provided, along with his current status of waiving his rights.

"I'll be down immediately," she said.

I went back into the room and explained the situation to Bobby Lee.

"My uncle didn't say anything about talking to a prosecutor," Bobby Lee said.

"Bobby Lee, you've trusted us so far. It is not a trick. In fact, we can work a deal to your advantage far more quickly with her present. It might even make it possible for you to get home tonight."

"Okay," he said, but his brow furrowed; his eyes rolled around like a crazed deer.

"I'll tell you what, Bobby Lee. How about if I call your uncle, explain the situation, and then let you talk to him again?"

"Yeah," he said with a vigorous nod of his head. "I'd feel a lot better."

A knock on the door announced Dani's arrival. I sent Jack out to hold her at bay for a few minutes. The phone rang at the other end of the line. I put it on speaker, and a voice barked, "Hunter."

"Hello, Lieutenant Hunter. This is Sergeant Spencer. Something has developed with your nephew Bobby Lee."

"Did I make a mistake telling him to waive his rights?"

"I don't think so, sir. Your nephew has unwittingly provided information connected to another case. The prosecutor handling that matter wants to be included in the conversation. I think that it would be in Bobby Lee's best interest."

"You know if you're bull-shitting me, you'll have trouble getting our cooperation on anything in the future."

"I certainly do, sir."

"Okay. Can I talk to the boy?"

"Yes, indeed. I am disconnecting the speaker from the line, and I am now going to cut the microphone. Give me a few seconds to get out of the room, and you'll be free to talk openly."

I nodded at Bobby Lee, handed him the receiver, and went to wait in the hall. I watched through the pane of glass in the door as Bobby Lee's head bobbed up and down and swung back and forth in response to the conversation. When he set down the handset, I walked in without the others.

"You can bring in the prosecutor," Bobby Lee said.

"Thank you, Bobby Lee." I opened the door and motioned Dani and Jack inside. I introduced Dani Striker and then asked, "I know the request I am about to make is tedious, Bobby Lee, but could you please retell everything you said to me to Ms. Striker?"

After a light sigh of frustration, Bobby Lee repeated everything he'd said to me up to that point. "When you left the room, Sergeant, me and the deputy here talked about sports—not anything else. You don't want me to repeat that part, do you?"

As Jack nodded in affirmation of Bobby Lee's statement, I said, "No. That won't be necessary." I passed a note to Jack: "See what you can dig up on the guidance counselor." Jack read it and stepped outside to begin searching for

Natasha Jones—or whatever her first name was.

Dani and I worked a deal with Bobby Lee: no jail time, two years of probation, compensation for his third of the damages, and agreement to testify in court against his co-offenders in the vandalism case, Marvin Givens, and Natasha Jones, if we could find her.

After one more consultation with his uncle, Bobby Lee agreed. The next family get-together was bound to be a doozy. Bobby Lee was released on his own recognizance with strict warnings about the consequences of not showing up when asked. With more reluctance, he also agreed to stop selling marijuana and cease acting as a go-between for buyers and sellers of other hard drugs.

Dani added, "And don't forget, Bobby Lee, getting and holding a legitimate job will have a big impact on the judge's attitude towards you."

When I walked back to my desk, Jack intercepted me. "I found Natasha Jones. Do you want to go see her now?"

"No, let's wait and allow Striker to light that match under Marvin Givens first. Then, we'll see if Miss Jones can feed the fire."

Chapter Sixteen

It was as if I had an activation switch in the seat cushion of my chair that caused my office phone to start ringing the moment I sat down.

"Spencer," I answered.

"Are you the one looking into the deaths at the Monroe farm?"

"Yes, sir."

"Good. I'm at the next farm up the road. I saw something that night that might not mean a thing, but I don't know. But I thought maybe you'd want to hear about it."

"Could I have your name, please?"

"Yeah, sure. Glass. Jeb Glass."

"What did you see, Mr. Glass?"

"There was this car parked at the end of my driveway—on the right-hand side of it. I thought maybe we had a visitor who was afraid to risk heading up my lane to the house. I'd plowed it and all, right after the snow stopped, and made it two blades wide. But city folks tend to be chicken about country roads and such."

"Yes, sir. What—?"

"Well, when I got to the house, there weren't nobody there but my wife. So, then I thought somebody got nervous of the roadway. It'd been cleared but still had bad spots. And those little sporty kinda cars ride pretty low to the ground. I figured somebody had come and picked the driver up. The next morning, the car was gone. But since I heard about the goings-on at the Monroe place, I started to worry about that car, so that's why I'm a'calling."

"Yes, sir. Do you remember the make or model of that car?"

"Oh, yeah. It was a cute little thing. A red Miata. Don't see many of those out thisaway."

"Did you notice the license plate number?"

"Can't say that I did, Ma'am. I'm pretty sure, though, it was a Virginia plate on accounta I would have remembered if it was from out of state."

"Have you seen that car since?"

"Can't say that I have. Hasn't been parked at my place since that night, but that's all I know for sure."

"Thank you, Mr. Glass. I can't tell you right now if it is useful. But who knows, it's very possible."

"You're welcome, ma'am. The missus and I would really like it iffen you'd give us a call when you know one way or another."

"I do my best to get back to you, Mr. Glass. Thanks again."

As I disconnected, I checked the time. I was twenty-five minutes away from my meeting with the parents of Donna Claridge and Clarence Thompson. I looked into the room we'd use to make certain there were seven chairs available, grabbed a cup of coffee, and walked up to the reception area.

One set of parents had arrived a bit early. They sat upright with their arms folded across their chests. I couldn't decide which set of eyes was more threatening—the dark brown wounded ones on Mrs. Claridge's frowning face or the medium blue piercing ones on her husband's scowling and reddened visage. They flanked a slouchy girl wearing jeans ripped at the knees, a big, pouty lip, and closed eyes. I stretched out a hand and said, "Hello, Mr. and Mrs. Claridge. Thank you for coming in to see me."

The parents' hands remained tucked tight on their chests, and the teenager shoved hers deeper into her pockets.

"What's this all about?" Mr. Claridge asked.

"There is another family involved. As soon as they arrive, we'll get started."

"But why are we here?" he pushed.

"Patience, Mr. Claridge. You could hang your overcoats on the rack over there. And if you like, I could get you coffee or water while you wait."

Mrs. Claridge smiled and opened her mouth, but before a word could escape, Mr. Claridge shouted, "Let's just get this over with!"

His wife pursed her lips in disapproval but did not speak another word. I turned to face the front desk. "Sergeant, let me know when the Thompsons arrive, please."

I started walking back up the hall when Mr. Claridge boomed, "Where do you think you are going? I am a taxpayer, and I pay your salary. I demand to know why we are here."

My steps did not falter. I badged the door ahead of me and slipped out of sight. I heard pounding behind me and then the boom of the desk sergeant's voice. I waited at my desk until I got the call informing me that the Thompsons had arrived.

I returned to take the group to the back. The newly arrived members sat at the far end of the row of chairs. Mr. Claridge saw me as soon as I came through the door, and his already red face darkened to a deep crimson. Mrs. Claridge looked like she wanted the earth to swallow her up. Pouty Donna stretched her legs out as far as they could go as if she hoped to trip me as I walked past her. I swerved and hugged the opposite wall. Mr. and Mrs. Thompson and their son Clarence rose to their feet with outstretched arms. I shook the hands of all three and introduced myself.

The six people followed me down the hall and into the interrogation room. As soon as everyone was seated, Mr. Thompson said, "Clarence informed us of his role in this crime, and we are ready to assume responsibility for the damages he caused."

I said, "Apparently, Donna has not shown the same courtesy to her parents. They have said they are clueless about why they're here. We'll start from the beginning." I detailed the vandalism at the construction site.

Mr. Thompson said, "According to Clarence, three teenagers were involved."

"That is correct, Mr. Thompson. The third individual was not a minor, and we have already gotten his confession."

"What proof do you have that my daughter was involved?" Mr. Claridge asked.

"We have the sworn statement of the third offender, and I suspect Clarence will confirm that statement."

"Even if she was there, that doesn't mean Donna was involved," Mr. Claridge argued.

"Clarence," I said, "whose idea was it to trash the condo?"

Clarence looked at Donna and said, "I'm sorry." Then he turned to me. "It was Donna's idea, ma'am."

"You're going to take the word of that little punk?" Mr. Claridge said.

Mr. Thompson rose to his feet. "My son is not a punk. You apologize right now."

"Gentlemen, settle down. Don't speak unless I address you directly, or I'll have a deputy remove you from the room and let the mothers settle this matter."

"I demand a lawyer," Mr. Claridge said, jumping to his feet.

"Sir, no one has been arrested or charged. You have no right to an attorney at this time. I am trying to prevent your daughter from having a criminal record. However, if you do not sit and remain quiet, that situation could change."

"I am sorry, Sergeant," Mr. Thompson said as he returned to his chair.

Mr. Claridge remained standing with fists clenched at his side. "Arnold!" his wife snapped. "Sit down and shut the hell up for once in your life."

He looked at her with his mouth agape and kept staring at her as he slid back into his seat.

"Clarence," I began again. "Why did you go along with Donna's suggestion?"

Clarence blushed and hung his head. "We both wanted to go out with her. I knew that if I didn't do what she said, the other guy would win."

"Do you both still want to date her?"

Clarence swung his head from side to side.

"Why not, Clarence?"

"After what she did, we thought she was crazy."

"What exactly did she do, Clarence?"

"Do I have to answer this out loud?"

"Son," Mr. Thompson said.

"But it's so gross."

"Just tell the truth, Clarence."

Clarence flinched and slouched deep in his chair. He cleared his throat before speaking. "She took a dump on the floor, swiped her finger in it, and wrote on the wall."

Again, Mr. Claridge was on his feet, "You lying little son of a bitch!" He lunged toward the boy, Mr. Thompson stepped in front of his son, and I yelled for a deputy.

I guess I should have seen that coming.

As he was led from the room by two massive body-building uniforms, Mr. Thompson said, "Would you like me to leave, too?"

"No, sir. Sit down. Donna, do you deny anything Clarence has said?"

Donna rolled her eyes. Her mother jabbed her with an elbow. "Answer her, now, Donna."

Donna let out a long, lengthy, loud sigh. "No. I did that. Can I go now?"

"Not yet, Donna. The other person involved has agreed to pay for one-third of the damages. Here is an estimate of that cost from the contractor," I said as I passed a copy to the three remaining parents. "Could you all do the same?"

"I have no problem with that," Mr. Thompson said. "Clarence has also agreed to go apologize to the contractor face-to-face."

"I'm sorry," Mrs. Claridge said. "I don't think this is fair."

I gasped, and the Thompsons' jaws dropped.

Mrs. Claridge continued, "I think we—or rather Donna—should pay half the damages. Obviously, our daughter is the most culpable in the bunch. We will take care of that immediately, and Donna will get a job to pay us back."

"Mo-o-o-m!" Donna moaned.

"Shut up, Donna," Mom snapped back. "This daddy's little girl crap stops right here, right now." She turned to me. "Sergeant, could you help me reimburse the other individual for his overpayment?"

"That won't be a problem."

Mrs. Claridge pulled out a checkbook and opened the calculator app on her phone. She wrote a check for half of the estimate and another with the name left blank for half minus a third and passed both across to me. "Mr.

and Mrs. Thompson, you have a fine son. You should be proud of him."

At that moment, a cell rang. Mrs. Claridge looked at her daughter and said, "Hand it over to me right now."

"I will not," she said and jumped to her feet. "And Daddy won't let you."

Mrs. Claridge rose to face her child, and my cell rang.

"Spencer," I answered and listened, disconnected, and said, "Mrs. Claridge, I regret to inform you that your husband will not be going home with you tonight. He assaulted one of our deputies. He's being processed into the jail right now."

Mrs. Claridge looked at me and nodded. With an outstretched hand, she turned back to her daughter and said, "Now."

Donna pursed her lips, narrowed her eyes, and reached into her pocket. She slammed that phone on the surface of the table, stomped across the room, and jerked on the handle. She smacked her face into the surface of the locked door. Dramatic exit thwarted; she growled her fury.

Meanwhile, the Thompsons had written a check and slid it over. I thanked the three parents again and let them all out of the room.

Chapter Seventeen

I swear. I couldn't believe how these damned blankets twisted around each other and my legs while I was sleeping. No wonder I felt more tired now than when I went to bed last night. I couldn't stop thinking about the strange connections between the vandalism case and the drug distribution case. I imagined the many unanswered questions popping into my head now had been tormenting me all night long. What if today I learned that my triple murder case was mixed up with them, too? I laughed and shoved off the blankets, heading into the kitchen to fix coffee.

The phone rang when I was halfway through my second cup. "Sergeant," the caller said, "this is Morris in digital forensics. I cloned the hard drive of Hank and Mary Alice Monroes' computer. I didn't find any questionable documents or photographs on there. I did, however, uncover suspicious activity in the internet history. If you'll drop by the lab, I'll give you the report and walk you through it."

"Give me half an hour, and I'll be there," I said. I scurried about feeding the cat and getting ready for work. I arrived at Morris's desk with five minutes to spare.

"What have you got for me?" I asked.

"The search engine reveals a number of interesting items. The first thing that caught my eye was on the Tuesday before the homicides out at the Monroe farm. Now, it wouldn't be notable out of context, but it sure looked interesting in retrospect. During the day, when Mary Alice Monroe should have been home alone, she searched small cities as if she were planning a move. She spent a lot of time looking through photographs, reading local stats and demographics, as well as sites of interest for each one.

"What cities?"

"Oh, let's see. Yeah, here it is. Beaufort, South Carolina; Portland, Maine; Portland, Oregon; Seattle, Washington; St. Augustine, Florida; and Savannah, Georgia."

"All over the map, but it does seem she had a preference for coasts—nothing in the middle of the country."

"I noticed that, too," he said. "Now, on Wednesday, it seemed as if she got more obvious with her searches. So blatant, in fact, it's hard to believe she didn't take any security precautions or wipe out her history when she was finished—if she was planning a murder. Mary Alice actually typed in 'best drugs to kill your husband.'"

"You're kidding?"

"Nope. She opened a link to an article titled, 'Ten Drugs that Can Kill You in Minutes.' It had some illegal stuff on there, like crystal meth and *krokodil,* but others were prescription drugs. From there, she searched 'fatal pharmaceuticals.' She followed links to information about opioids, anti-psychotics, and anti-depressants."

"All during the day when her husband Hank was most likely at work?"

"Yes. Of course, you'll have to confirm that he was on the job before you go into court. Anyway, then she switched to poisonous plants. She visited a page with photos of lethal mushrooms, but spent little time there and didn't click any of the links. Then Google sent her to Wikipedia, where she opened several other pages, finally narrowing her search to plants with glycosides."

"And that's what was found in the beef stew in her crockpot."

Morris nodded enthusiastically. "She read a lot of articles about oleander but spent most of her time on one specific page that discussed its use as a poison."

"Could you bring that page up for me?"

"No problem." His fingers bounced around the keyboard.

I scanned the document looking for anything to indicate the presence of a bad taste when ingested or its ability to maintain its lethal characteristic after hours in a crockpot. I saw nothing. If I were planning on using it as a poison, the necessity of driving south for hours to obtain a sample of the plant and the absence of information on taste and heat resistance would make me move on.

"Where did she go next?"

"Next stop: Monkshood, but that interest faded fast. Soon, she focused on lily of the valley."

"It's hard to believe those pretty little white flowers are poisonous."

"Not just the flowers. The roots, the leaves, the berries—every little bit of it is fatal if ingested. Botanical chemists have found forty different cardiac glycosides in that pretty little plant. Shoot, if you put a handful of them in a vase, the water becomes toxic, too. Her final stop on that day of poison education was on a story about a woman who poisoned her husband with a stew containing minced lily of the valley."

"Jeez! Did the article include a recipe? But her husband wasn't poisoned, and her inlaws didn't die from ingesting glycosides—it was fentanyl. It just doesn't make sense."

"I'm glad figuring that out is in your job description, not mine, Charley."

* * *

As I drove to Mary Alice's house, I called Rose Culpepper and asked if she could send someone over to the Monroe house to look for any disturbed soil in the yard. Of course, Rose presumed I was looking for a body until I explained the more pedestrian plant search. Her excitement level dropped at that realization, but she did agree to send someone out to check that afternoon.

I tried pushing around the puzzle pieces of my thoughts to form something resembling a big picture, but I could not get a coherent image. Nothing felt as if it fit the facts. This case jarred with the discordance of a really bad sci-fi film detailing a clash between alternate realities. I pulled into Mary Alice's driveway and sat in the car for a few minutes, hoping that she would see the car and feel intimidated before I walked through the door. When I saw a curtain twitch, I knew the time was right. Before I could knock, the door flew open.

"What now?" Mary Alice asked. A standard question for guilty perpetrators playing the victim card.

I forced a smile. "May I come in?"

"If I say 'no,' I'm certain you could get a warrant, so, yeah, come on in." Slumping her shoulders, she walked away from the door.

She sat down on the sofa with her hands clasped, arms resting on her knees, and her head hung low. I took the chair across from her. "Mary Alice, are you feeling well?"

"No. I doubt I'll ever feel well again."

"I need to ask you about a number of things. Do you feel up to it?"

"No, but I never will, so might as well get it over with."

"Let's start with the basics. Did you have anything to do with the death of your husband?"

"Well, I wished he was dead, and now my wish has come true. I can't deny that."

"Did you play an active role in his death?"

"No, I did not, but not for lack of trying."

"Would you explain what you mean by that?"

Mary Alice raised her head. Her eyes scanned my face. "Thinking about a crime isn't a crime, is it?"

"It can be, if you talk with others. When that happens, it's called conspiracy."

"I have an alibi for that night. I was here at home alone, sure, but that nosy old biddy across the street can tell you that my car remained in the driveway all night long."

"That still doesn't mean that you didn't form a conspiracy with someone or hire another person to shoot your husband."

"Prove it."

"For that matter, you could have driven out to the farm with your husband and then got rid of his truck."

"Except for the fact that my father-in-law called and asked for help."

"We only have your word on that, Mary Alice."

"Phone records should back me up."

"Your father-in-law called your landline from his landline. There is no record of local calls. You only get that when a cell is involved. The only people who can back up your claim are dead."

She glared at me and rose from the sofa. "I wish you would leave now."

"Just a couple more questions." Mary Alice slumped back down. "Where is your crockpot?"

A shudder passed through her body. "I had to get rid of it and the stew in it because it reminded me of Hank."

"I thought you hated the man."

"Yeah, well, grief is a funny thing."

"What did you put in that stew?"

"You want my list of ingredients? Okay. Stew beef. Potatoes. Carrots. Green Beans. Mushrooms. Onion. V-8 Juice. Red Wine. Beef broth. Salt. Pepper. Bay Leaf. A splash of Kitchen Bouquet. My grandmother's recipe."

"Did you alter that recipe in any way this time?"

"No, why would I?"

"We took a sample from your crockpot while you were in the bathroom. Our chemists analyzed the stew and found an additional ingredient."

"What parsley? I might have added that—I do sometimes."

"No. Mary Alice. I think you know exactly what I mean. They found glycosides in the stew."

"I don't know what that is. How could I add it to the stew?"

"It's poison, Mary Alice."

"Your sample must have been contaminated in the lab."

"Hardly possible when it is the first instance we've discovered that substance in any test since the new lab facility opened."

"What difference does it make? Hank wasn't poisoned."

"But his parents were, Mary Alice."

"I would not harm a hair on their heads," Mary Alice shouted as she stomped across the room and flung open the door. "Out, out, now!"

I rose and walked to the door. As I crossed the threshold, I said, "Mary Alice, we will be talking again. Soon. It will go better for you if you start telling me the truth."

"Go join Hank in hell!" she shouted as she slammed the door.

Chapter Eighteen

The door to the justice complex slammed shut behind me, but not before I heard a call of "Sergeant" slipping out through the cracks. I pulled it open, and dispatcher Deputy Waller struggled to catch his breath. "I'm glad I caught you, Sergeant. That Monroe woman. An intruder in her house."

"Now?"

"Yes, ma'am."

I hurried to my car and made the short drive to Mary Alice's home. Two marked cars beat me to the scene. I pressed the bell and knocked on the door for good measure. A deputy pulled open the door and invited me inside.

"What happened?" I asked him.

"Walsh and Montgomery are chasing the perp. I'm here watching Mrs. Monroe in case he doubles back."

"Thanks, Deputy. Where's Mrs. Monroe?"

"At the kitchen table."

I sat down across from her. "Are you okay, Mary Alice?"

She nodded her head.

"Not injured? Not shot?"

"Not shot. But I kind of injured myself." Mary Alice stretched out her right leg. A knot on top tied a bloody towel around her foot.

"Is it still bleeding?"

"I don't know."

"Does it hurt?"

"You better believe it. I stepped on glass from my shattered antique doorknob. I'm not sure whether I am more upset by my foot or the knob."

"Let me look."

I squatted down and unwrapped the tea towel. "Ouch, that must be painful, Mary Alice. It's still oozing blood." I didn't mention the piece of glass protruding from her heel. I should call an ambulance."

"Please don't. I can't bear the thought of going back to the hospital."

"Okay. I'll see what I can do, but you'll need to see a doctor soon. Do you have gauze bandages and adhesive tape?"

"In the bathroom medicine cabinet, unless your guys took them."

"Keep your foot up over the towel so the blood doesn't get on the floor. Don't put any weight on it. I'll get the supplies and be right back."

In the bathroom, I grabbed gauze pads, adhesive tape, tweezers, antibiotic cream, and a damp washcloth. I went to the floor beside her with one knee on the floor and the other raised. I rested her ankle on my thigh. I plucked out the glass and laid it on the towel.

"That was in my foot?"

"Yes. Relax, Mary Alice. I'll be done as quick as I can." I cleaned the wound, patted it dry, and applied the cream. I placed a gauze pad on the injury and ran adhesive tape across it and around her foot. I pulled up another chair and propped her foot on its cushion.

"There. All good for now. Any damage to your house?"

Mary Alice nodded her head and wiped away a tear.

"Can you tell me about everything that happened?"

She nodded again, closed her eyes, and told her story. "After you left, I had a cup of coffee and a scrambled egg on toast. Then I took a shower.

"I stood under the running water for longer than usual and then wrapped a towel around my body. The softness felt so comforting, like a cocoon shutting me off from all the ugliness of the last few days. Even the wooden floor of the hallway felt nice under my bare feet as I walked into the kitchen for a drink of water. At that moment, being home without Hank felt so good and so safe.

"Then, it all blew up in my face. A man was in my house. He said, 'You Hank's wife?' My throat shut tight. I couldn't speak. I could barely breathe.

I raced back down the hall into my bedroom and locked the door. I heard heavy footsteps coming towards me. I felt each one reverberating in the pit of my stomach. Fists pounding on the door." Mary Alice's breath grew labored.

I placed my hand on hers. "Collect your thoughts, breathe deep, and calm down. I'll wait until you are ready to continue."

A few minutes later, Mary Alice nodded and resumed. "I grabbed my cell off the nightstand and called 9-1-1 and reported an intruder. In the hallway, the man shouted, 'Where is Hank?' I told him 'Hank's not here.' I hoped that would make him go away. But he just said it again, 'Where is Hank?' I repeated, 'Hank's not here.' I added, 'I just called the sheriff's office. They are on their way. Get out of my house. Now.'

"I heard a gunshot and felt the wind of a bullet passing near my face. I ducked into the bedroom closet. I whimpered and whispered into the phone, 'Hurry! Hurry! Hurry!'

"More shots slammed through the door. I heard one that sounded like glass breaking. Then, a hard thud on the door followed by the sound of splintering wood. Again, he shouted, 'Where is Hank?' That time, I didn't answer. I stayed as still and silent as I could. After a moment of quiet, his voice changed, softened. 'Let me in, and I'll tell you about Hank's girlfriend.'

"At first, I was shocked. I didn't know Hank had a girlfriend. Almost as quickly, I realized that man could be lying to me to get me to open the door. My thoughts were fighting with each other, and I couldn't decide what to say or what to do. Then, I heard the approaching siren and didn't have to figure it out. A patrol car must have been close to the house when I called.

"Another shot fired through the bedroom door. And he said, 'God damn you, woman. I'll find that son of a bitch.'" I listened as his footsteps retreated down the hall and through the kitchen. The back door opened. His running feet stomped hard across the wooden back porch. I slipped out of the closet and shoved up the window when I saw a marked car screech to a stop out front. I screamed, 'He's got a gun.'

"The deputy immediately took cover behind his vehicle. 'He's out back,' I said to clarify the situation for him. I pulled on a pair of jeans and a sweatshirt. I had a really hard time opening the battered door. As I walked out of the room, I stepped on the shattered glass of the antique doorknob and raced to lock the back door. When I turned the latch, I noticed I'd left a bloody track of footprints into the kitchen. I went to get a rag to clean them up and then remembered that I shouldn't touch a thing until the cops got in here. I grabbed a tea towel in the kitchen and tied it around my foot.

"I peered out the window and saw the deputy disappear into the woods behind the house. I heard more sirens and limped to the living room window. Two more deputies ran straight for the woods.

"I heard a voice coming from my pocket and realized I'd forgotten about the 9-1-1 operator. I pulled my cell out and put it to my ear. The operator said, 'Ma'am, are you there? Are you there?' I told her I was, and then I heard you knock on the door and ring the doorbell. The woman on the line said, 'Please stay on the phone with me. Help is on the way.' I said, 'I know. They're here. They're here. I have to open the door.'

"She said, 'The deputies are there?' I said, 'Yes' as I jerked open the door. She said, 'Good. Okay. I'll let you go talk to them now.' And there you were."

I looked her over. She seemed rattled. No indication that she was acting now. I went down the hall. I examined the door and then looked for the final destination of the bullets. Using a grease pencil, I circled the points of impact on the wall beside the head of the bed. I walked back to the kitchen table.

"Was it a close call for you?" I asked.

"Except for that first shot, no. After that, I was hiding in the closet."

"Do you think he was shooting to kill?"

"I don't know. I don't know what he wanted. He just kept saying, 'Where is Hank?'"

"Do you know who he was?"

"I didn't recognize his voice. At first, I thought it might be my husband's brother Chuck. But he seemed to be a much bigger man. But I was scared. I just don't know for sure. It could have been Chuck but—"

"Mary Alice, why don't you gather up what you'll need for the night. We'll stop at an urgent care clinic and let them look at your foot. Then, I'll take you to the station to make a statement. After that, we'll get you wherever you want to go."

I warned her that she could have been shot tonight if she'd been standing in the wrong place at the wrong time, Mary Alice's face blanched an even paler shade than it had been when I walked in the door. When she was ready to go, I guided her out to the front passenger's seat of my car.

Before I pulled away from the curb, a pick-up truck with cages parked behind my car. Dogs were released to join the search. "They should find him in no time now," I told her.

"I'm just so numb, Sergeant, I don't know if I even care." Fear pinched her face around her eyes and nose.

"Mary Alice," I said, "where do you want to stay tonight. You shouldn't stay here in the house until your intruder is in custody."

"Oh, please, no. I just got back from the hospital."

"But we need to process the evidence in your bedroom, Mary Alice. You won't be able to sleep there."

"That's okay. I can sleep upstairs in the guest bedroom. I'll be okay. I'll feel safe with the evidence guys swarming around. I'll just need my night gown and my toothbrush, and I'll stay upstairs. I won't bother them at all. Please."

"I need to take you to see a doctor first, but I'd feel better if I didn't bring you back here tonight."

"Oh, Sergeant, please. Let me stay. I won't be any trouble."

Against my better judgment, I agreed to allow her to stay home. I hoped I wouldn't regret it.

Chapter Nineteen

My questioning about the crockpot probably had a lot to do with Mary Alice's altered attitude. Still, I was baffled—and that made me pause outside the restaurant. I took a deep breath and dreaded walking through that door. Although I was excited about meeting my dad's fiancée, I was apprehensive about my sister's response. I had urged Dad to give Ruby a bit more time to accept the reality he was getting married, but he was planning a wedding and wanted both of us to get to know Emily beforehand. I pleaded with Dad to make this first get-together over coffee. Seemed like a morning meeting had a lower chance of drama. I was outvoted.

Through the window, I could see the small table for four near the bar. At the moment, everyone was all smiles, but there was something in Ruby's grin that set my teeth on edge. With hope in my heart and caution in my head, I pushed inside. Dad stood and introduced me to his fiancée. She looked nothing like my mother—darker hair, shorter in stature, and definitely not as thin. But, when I looked into her eyes, Mom's warmth and kindness radiated in all directions. That mattered far more than all the rest.

I took my seat. Ruby patted the back of my hand. "Well, what do you think of your stepmother-to-be, Charley?"

Drawing my eyes to a slit and grimacing, I gave Ruby the big-sister look of warning to control herself. She was walking on the edge. All she did was flip her hair off her shoulders and stick out her tongue.

Looking at Emily, I smiled. "She appears to have all the basic characteristics needed—female and of an appropriate age."

"That's your only expectation? Really? You're usually so demanding." The ugly smirk on Ruby's lips made me fear what was coming next.

"You know, Ruby, some fathers have been known to pick a second wife the same age as their daughters."

"Our father has more sense than that."

"For which we should be grateful."

"I betcha anything that Dad would be willing to tell us if he thought either you or I were making an unsuitable match. I think we should do the same for him."

I turned directly to Ruby and said, "Apparently, you do not have a mature outlook on the parent-child dynamic."

Ruby graced me with a milk-curdling scowl and said, "Stop patronizing me. You may be a few years older, but that doesn't make you the font of all wisdom."

"We need to go to the restroom. Right now, Ruby." My sister jumped up from the table and stomped off. "Excuse us." I rose with a smile and followed her across the room.

Inside the closed door, she erupted. "How dare you treat me like a child!"

"I know I shouldn't do that, but when you act like—"

"Shut up. You know she's not the right woman for Dad, and I'll prove it to you."

"I don't know that at all. How in heaven's name can you prove it?"

"I will ask her blunt questions. If she's open and honest, maybe I'm wrong. But if she stalls or juggles the question, I'll know I'm right."

'What are you planning on asking her?"

"If their relationship has become intimate—you know, physical."

"You're going to ask if they're doing it?"

Yeah. I might even drop the F-bomb when I do."

"Good grief, Ruby. Has Dad ever asked you if you've been intimate with any of your dates?"

"No. So what? We have a right to know."

"No, we don't. Dad is entitled to his own private life."

"Not when we are going to have to live with the consequences of his private life. And it could last for years—ten, twenty, thirty miserable years."

Ruby jerked the door open and stormed out into the restaurant.

I hurried to catch up with her. I knew once Ruby's mind was made up; she was laser-focused on what she wanted to accomplish. I hoped I could at least soften the blow or, with a little luck, divert the conversation. Ruby resumed her seat, smiled as she focused on Emily, and said, "So, tell me, Emily, have you ever been married? Are you married?"

"Emily," I interrupted, "what I would like to know is where you have been stationed with Doctors Without Borders?"

Emily returned my smile. "Just about everywhere there is war or disaster or an unrelenting combination of poverty and poor medical facilities."

"What was your most fulfilling assignment—?" I began

"Tell us about yourself—any failed marriages?" Ruby asked

I tried to steer the conversation into less aggressive territory. "Ruby, stop being so cute," I warned. "Emily, when did you and Dad meet?"

Emily laughed. "It was a dreadful first encounter—over an operating table. We tried with all we had, but our patient died of his injuries."

"On your first date, did you have s—" Ruby started to ask, but I knew where that was going.

"Stop being silly, Ruby."

"Did you do it?"

I turned and glared at my sister. "Enough!" I hissed.

"Charley, I'm surprised at you," Dad said. "I've never seen you like this before. I know you're eager to get to know Emily, but you're not allowing Ruby to get a word in edgewise."

"Dad, you really don't want me to shut up. Trust me on that."

"Charley, I did not tell you to shut up. I am never that rude to you."

"I know, Dad. I am not upset with you."

"Well, then, let Ruby speak."

I braced for what came out of Ruby's mouth. I knew I'd spend days trying to figure out what I could have done to stop it.

Ruby looked at Emily, then over to Dad, and back to Emily again.

"Please don't, Ruby," I whispered.

She flashed me a grin and turned back to the expectant couple. "What I want to know is, have you tested *every* aspect of your relationship?"

Dad and Emily looked at each other, puzzled brows furrowed, blinked.

"What Ruby means—" I interrupted.

"You don't speak for me, sister. What I want to know is are you fucking on a regular basis?"

I slumped my shoulders and let out a huge sigh as my head hung down, nearly touching the table.

"Well?" Ruby asked.

Dad rose from his chair with an abrupt jerk, making the legs scrape across the tile floor, sounding like an explosion.

"Emily, we are leaving now. I thought my children were more civilized than this exhibition has shown."

Dad extended his elbow, and Emily looped her arm into his. Right before they went through the door, Emily turned and looked back at me with a weak smile.

"Well, once again, you ruined all my fun. I'm going," Ruby said. "You can pick up the tab."

It was the disaster I had expected it to be, but, Lord knows, I would have been happier if Ruby had proven me wrong. We were going to have to have a long talk before the wedding.

Chapter Twenty

Kitty on my lap, remote in one hand, Blue Moon in the other—I was ready to forget this day ever happened. Of course, my cell rang. I looked at the number and knew the day wasn't about to give up and let me relax.

"Sergeant Spencer?"

"Yes, sir."

"This is Deputy Kirby Waller in dispatch. Got some good news."

Good grief. When is that old dude going to retire? He always calls when I want to be left alone.

"They found that pick-up truck you were looking for. It was parked a couple spaces away from the front door of that twenty-four-hour Wal-Mart on the highway."

Yes, I was glad the vehicle was found, but, jeez, why now? I sucked it up, added a fake brush of perky to my voice. "Okay, I'll head out there now."

"No need for that, Sergeant. They're prepping it to haul it into the forensic bay in the garage."

"What about mud in the tires? Debris attached to the under-carriage?"

"They're using one of those new covers—the ones they call under-carriage condoms." The dispatcher laughed, coughed, and said, "Excuse my French, ma'am. Anyways, the whole truck will be covered in plastic before its loaded up for transport."

"Thank you, Deputy Waller. You sure I don't need to go out there?"

"Nah, the deputies didn't think I should bother calling you—said they'd catch up with you in the morning. I think they wanted to get out of the cold as quickly as possible. I figured, though, that you might be frettin' about it, so I decided to let you know."

"Thank you again. I really appreciate that you called." I guess I misjudged the old guy. He's still got more sense than a night-shift rookie.

* * *

In the morning, the techs in the forensics bay had peeled the top layer that covered the bed and cab of the pick-up before I arrived. All four doors hung wide open. The tires and undercarriage remained covered.

"Sergeant," Sam Patrick, the forensic tech in charge of the automotive forensics department, said as he stretched out his hand.

"Have you found anything significant?" I asked.

"I'd say so," the tech answered. Two distinct set of fingerprints on the driver's side exterior door handle and on the steering wheel. One set has been identified as the deceased, the other is still unknown. However, it did match with the samples that came from the basement of the farmhouse."

"Did they check to see if you had a match with the shooting victim's wife?"

"Sure did. No go. But we found some DNA and sent swabs up to the lab. Just waiting for results now."

"Did you find a wallet or a cell phone?"

"Neither one. Someone smashed open the locked box in the truck bed. Lots of quality tools in there but no way to tell at this point if anything is missing. However, we did have one more charge cord than we have chargeable power tools. Got somebody going through and matching them up. We might be able to figure out which one is either missing or got discarded without its cord, but we won't know if it is the only thing or if any manual tools are gone."

"Let me know when you finish your examination. I'll bring in one of his employees who might know what, if anything, was taken."

Sam's phone rang. He looked down at the incoming screen and said, "Hold on a second, Sergeant. The lab is on the phone."

When he disconnected, I said, "DNA results already?"

"I wish. It's interesting, but I don't think it would be admissible at trial. I had a GSR test run on the steering wheel and door handle. The door handle was negative. That doesn't mean any particles were never there, but they likely would have shaken loose from driving the vehicle around. The steering wheel, on the other hand, was positive. Not much residue but enough to suggest that you were probably right in assuming the shooter had stolen the victim's truck."

"Any possibility that Hank left the GSR there when he went hunting last fall?"

"An infinitesimal possibility. But who knows? Not enough research has been done on GSR transfer. When and if someone figures that out, a lot of convictions will be questioned."

I went back to digital forensics to talk to Morris. He confirmed my suspicion that the computer did have a roster of employees with addresses and phone numbers. I printed out a copy and decided to make cold calls at their homes since, in all likelihood, work would have stopped with Hank's death. As luck would have it, the first three men I visited had only worked with Hank for a short time and were vague about the items in the truck's tool chest. Number four was the jackpot, and I arranged to question him at his home.

Hank had hired Johnny Bouvier a decade ago. Like his employer, he was tall and lanky. His shiny black hair curled in an Elvis-like twist in front. His face, however, bore no resemblance to the star. His lips were thin, his nose narrow, and his eyes so brown I couldn't see where his pupil stopped and his iris began.

"At first, it was the two of us." Johnny smiled as he remembered. "Those were the scrappy days when we'd grab any contract that came along even if our bid was too low to make a profit. But I was always paid. Hank never stiffed me. Once when I knew he was struggling with bills at home, I offered to work for a week without pay. Hank wouldn't hear of it. Hank was a cold-ass, hard-driving son of a bitch, but he always treated me fair."

"Are you familiar with the contents of his truck, Mr. Bouvier? With the tools in the chest in back?"

"Oh, yeah. I engraved all the tools myself. I kept track of the inventory and let Hank know when we needed a replacement."

"Do you think you could tell if a piece of equipment was missing?"

"Probably could," he said.

"Would you mind coming with me to the forensic garage and check the contents of the chest?"

"You mean right now?"

"Yes."

"Sure, no problem. Give me time to replace these sweats with a pair of jeans and put on some shoes."

"Thank you, Mr. Bouvier."

I remained seated on the sofa, looking around the room, mentally gathering impressions of Johnny Bouvier. To my surprise, two shelves of his bookcase were filled with the classics, from *War and Peace* to *Wuthering Heights*—not what I expected from a guy working in construction. Then again, I was probably lugging around a few outdated stereotypes.

When Johnny walked back into the living room, I asked, "I noticed your collection of classics. Have you read them all?"

"Not yet. I'm working on it. The books were my mother's. I've read about twenty or so, but I hope to read them all before long."

"What was your favorite?"

"*Of Human Bondage* by Somerset Maugham. That book really stuck with me."

"I'm impressed."

"I guess you didn't expect to find that in a carpenter's library."

I blushed and grinned. "You got me there. Ready to go?"

"Yep. Just don't tell anybody at work about my reading habits."

In the car, I asked, "Did you and Hank get together after work hours?"

"Once in a while but not often. We didn't hang out together. I only met his wife because she occasionally brought forgotten or replaced depleted supplies to a job site. And I only went to his house once, but that was to drop by some paperwork."

"Was he a good boss?"

"Not always. He was a hothead. I quit and walked off the job a few times when I felt he was out of line. And once he fired me for interfering in his personal life."

"His personal life? Could you be more specific?"

"Well, his relationship with his wife. One day when she brought the last two gallons of paint to a house where we were finishing the punch list, her arm was in a sling. I asked her about it, and she turned beet red and stammered about an accident. I saw Hank glaring at her and heard him tell her, 'You should have taken that sling off before you got here. You're making me look bad.' I suspected he was responsible for her injury.

"I said something to him about treating his wife a little better, and he went off on me, fired me on the spot. The next day, he begged me to come back. That wasn't the last time I saw Mary Alice with an injury, but I never asked her about it again. And I never said another word to Hank. I didn't like it, but like Hank said, it was none of my business."

"Do you think she'd be capable of taking his life?"

"Mary Alice? Lord, no. That is one timid woman. I don't think she'd have the gumption to kill Hank unless he told her to do it. Even then, she'd probably back down at the last moment. He was shot, right? Can't see her taking a bead on anybody."

"Do you know anyone who was angry enough with him to shoot him dead?"

"Nah. You know, he pissed off his sub-contractors all the time. I've even heard a few of them say, 'I'm gonna kill that bastard one of these days.' But ya know, every time he'd offer them another contract, they'd be right there doing the job. Work is work," he said with a shrug.

"Do you know anything about Hank's family?"

"Not much. I know they own a big farm out in the county—been in the family for a few generations. I know he has a brother, but I think he was run out of town by the old man. I heard it was onna accounta he was gay, but I don't know if that's right or not. Seemed a harsh reaction even back then if you ask me. But maybe Hank's dad was as big of a hothead as Hank was."

"Can you think of anyone who would want Hank dead?"

"Well, I sure wouldn't blame Mary Alice if she did, but, like I said, I don't know that she'd be capable of something like that. Hank hasn't had any recent squabbles with subs or homeowners. The only person that I'd say was likely was his girlfriend."

"His girlfriend?"

"I shouldn't have said that. I'm not really sure he has one. I've overheard some conversations that sounded a lot like rendezvous planning. And Hank's made a few comments that led me to think that way. I don't know her name, though, or anything about her."

"To your knowledge, is this his first discretion outside of the marriage?"

Johnny laughed. "He's been accused of being a horny hound dog more than once. In fact, I know he messed around with the wife of a plumber a couple of years back. The guy came at him with a monkey wrench. You should have seen Hank run."

Chapter Twenty-One

At the forensic garage, Johnny went through the tool chest in Hank's truck. He explained that the extra power cord we'd found went to a drill he had tossed last week. He also noted that a screwdriver was missing from the set, but couldn't say if it was left at a job site or taken from the box.

I arranged for a deputy to take Johnny home and returned to my desk. I'd missed a call from Dani Striker two minutes earlier. I took the elevator to the tenth floor and took the skyway between the buildings. Truth be told, the real reason I decided to make a personal visit instead of returning her call was for the coffee—the stuff they made in the Commonwealth Attorney's office was far better than the swill we had in mine.

Dani knew me well. As soon as I poked my head around her cubicle, she said, "Go on. Go on. You know the way to breakroom. Grab a cup for me, too, okay?"

I returned and set our cups on her desk.

"Just a minute." Dani signed a document, slid it into an inter-departmental envelope, and placed it in her out box. I settled into the chair beside her desk as she finished up whatever she was doing on her laptop.

"There we go." She slapped down the lid to her computer. "Marvin Given's lawyer is ready to talk deal. If Marvin tells me the truth about the drug deal he did with Bobby Lee Hunter's teacher, I'll tone down my recommended sentence by a year or two—not much, but Fitzgerald knows we have his client cornered. They are in the mood to bargain for a shorter sentence. The drug task force search found so many drugs on the premises, his snotty attorney knows Marvin isn't walking out with a slap on his wrist.

"When we talked on the phone, Fitzgerald balked because he didn't think Marvin would rat out an acquaintance. I proposed he tell Marvin that he'd be backing up a friend's story, so Marvin wouldn't be the snitch. Apparently, it worked. I thought you'd like to be in the booth when I talk to the two of them. By the way, I will be referring to Mr. Givens as Marvin throughout the interview because he hates his first name, and I like to annoy drug dealers." Dani grinned. "You in?"

I nodded. "Let's roll."

* * *

I sat down in the booth in front of a monitor. Fitzgerald looked as haughty as ever in an expensive suit and silk tie. A smear of irritation or impatience marred the curve of his lips. Marvin looked like he hadn't a care in the world. He slouched in his orange coveralls and looked bored.

Dani entered the room, and Marvin rose to his feet.

"Sit down, Marvin. Sit down, now." Still standing, Dani looked down at him through slitted eyes.

"I jest want you to tell me why you put me in that shitty county lock-up."

"I'll tell you nothing until you sit down."

Fitzgerald tapped on Marvin's forearm. "Mr. Givens, please. I'll take care of this." He cleared his throat. "That is a question I wanted to ask you, Ms. Striker. The location of my client in the boondocks makes it difficult for me to handle his case."

"Boondocks? It's no more than ten miles outside the county limits. Besides, you know these decisions are made by jail staff, not me. I don't care where they keep them as long as they don't let them get away."

"What's the reason for his transfer out of this county?"

"I didn't ask."

In the booth, I sat in amazement at the tricky use of language—how to lie without lying. I'd never make a good attorney. Dani knew very well that I was responsible for his move because of the presence of Travis Ferguson in our lock-up. My face gives away far too much when I'm being dishonest or misleading. Maybe I'd get better at that with time—but did I really want to improve my ability to manipulate the truth?

Dani and Fitzgerald stared at each other until Fitzgerald blinked. "Fine. Let's proceed."

"Since this is a fact-finding interview, I need to hear directly from your client, not you. Is that clear?"

"I'll allow it for now."

"Marvin…" Dani began.

"Mo'. My friends call me Mo'."

For a moment, no one said anything. Then, Dani broke the silence. "Marvin, who told you about the woman from the school wanting drugs?"

"Did Bobby Lee tell you about that?" Marvin asked.

"Yes, he did."

"Okay, it was Bobby Lee Hunter. I took the order, and we set up a time and place for the meet with the woman."

"Where did you meet?"

"At the Kohl's over at the mall. She was driving a red Miata, so it was easy to spot her in the parking lot."

"Marvin, in your own words, please run through the sequence of events in the parking lot."

Marvin scowled and looked at his attorney, who prompted, "Just tell your story. Tell Ms. Striker what happened that afternoon."

"I pulled up in the parking space next to her car, but pointing in the opposite direction. We rolled down our windows and talked."

"What did you say to her?" Dani asked.

"We had a signal, like. I had to say certain words, and she had to answer a special way."

"And what was that, Marvin? Exactly." Dani leaned forward on her folded arms.

"I says: 'Hey, little lady, you lookin' for me?' And she says, 'I'm just looking for a girl from the Far East. Have you seen her?'"

"Okay. How did she seem to you?"

"She seemed like she never done this before. Her hands were shaky. She stuttered when she talk. For a moment, I thought she was gonna bolt. But she looked kinda familiar—like I seed her before."

"What happened then?"

I says to her: 'Sure have. Show me the Benjamins.' That's when her hands got real shaky. I didn't think she was gonna be able to open the glove compartment, but she did and handed me the cash.

"She was so jumpy, she made me twitchy. I says, 'You look awful familiar.' Then it hit me, and I says, 'Yep. I know you. Was it from school?'

"Her eyes be dancin' all over her face. 'School?' she says. 'I haven't been in school in forever.' And she said, 'Sure. I remember you,' or somethin' like that. I woulda been fine, but now she was makin' me real nervous. I axed her, 'You ain't a cop, are ya?

"She laughed, but it didn't sound normal. 'Do I look like a cop?' she ask me. I say, 'You might. Bobby Lee told me you're okay, but you're making me nervous.' She apologized and said she was nervous, too. She axed me to give her the stuff so we could both get out of there. Then, I axed her: 'You were a teacher at the high school, weren't ya?' She started shaking her head, and then she say, 'Yeah, right.'

"I reached over to her car with the package in my hand. I warned her to keep her mouth shut. She snatched it away from me and pulled out of her space pretty fast. I figured she'd be stopped for speeding before she got far."

"Do you know that woman's name?" Dani asked.

"Nah. Bobby Lee never mentioned it, and I don't remember from when I was in school."

Dani pulled out a sheet of paper and put it face down on the table. "Mr. Givens, would you recognize that woman if you saw her again?"

"Probably."

Dani flipped over the six-pack of photos, turned it around, and pushed it across the table. "Do any of these people look like her?"

Marvin scanned the page and broke out in a grin. "Yeah, yeah." He pointed to the middle photo on the bottom row. "That's her. That's the woman who wanted fentanyl."

"Are you sure? Look over them again."

"Yeah, that's the one. I ain't got a doubt."

"Thank you, Mr. Givens."

Fitzgerald cleared his throat. "Well, if that's it, Ms. Striker, let's talk plea bargain."

Dani shook her head. "I will prepare an offer and send it to you later today."

"Surely, we can discuss what you have in mind."

"Sorry, Mr. Fitzgerald. Because opioids are involved, I need to run it all by the C.A. and get his sign-off on it."

"That was not our understanding."

Dani shrugged and rose from her seat at the table. "Someone will escort your client back to lock-up shortly."

Dani and I didn't speak until we were back at her desk. "In case you missed anything, Marvin Givens admitted to selling the drugs to a high school teacher, not a middle school guidance counselor. But he did identify Natasha Jones from the six-pack we put together using driver's license photos. And he picked out the same one Bobby Lee threw under the bus. Too extraordinary to be a coincidence, I'd say."

I nodded in agreement. The thought of my murders having a connection to the bike theft-drug ring and vandalism at a townhouse community seemed far less humorous now than it did the other morning.

"Dani, what do you know about Natasha Jones?"

"Not much. Why?"

"Here's what I have: a drug distributor who stopped doing business with Marvin Givens because, instead of providing pharmaceutical-grade opioids as promised, he tried to foist off street opioids with a high fentanyl content. Right after that, a middle school counselor buys that street crap from Marvin. And the next day, I have a triple homicide, and two of the victims died of a fentanyl overdose. I need to know if Natasha Jones has any connection to the victims in the triple homicide."

Dani narrowed her eyes and tilted her head. "It sounds a little far-fetched."

"Agreed. But I've got to run it down for no other reason than she will bug me until I've eliminated her."

"Well, this is your lucky day," she said as she pulled a search warrant out of her inbox. "I also want to bring her in for questioning. You want to come along?"

"Absolutely. I'll grab a uniform to back us up."

"How about that dreamy deputy you have with you a lot?"

"Preston? Jack Preston?"

"Yeah, that's his name."

"Dreamy?"

"Don't tell me you haven't noticed."

"I haven't thought about it."

"That's tragic, Charley. Totally tragic."

Chapter Twenty-Two

Chaos erupted as the three of us approached the front door of the middle school. We stepped inside and flattened ourselves against the wall as a hoards of screaming, squealing, laughing examples of tomorrow's future streamed past us—or, in some cases, collided with us. When only stragglers were left, we dared to cross the hall and go to the office.

The receptionist turned bright red when she saw our badges, but soon the color drained away, leaving her as pale as a blank sheet of paper as she stammered, asking us how she could help.

"Where might we find Natasha Jones?" I asked.

"Th-th-the guidance cou-counselor?"

"Yes."

"Follow me." She walked deeper into the room to a door on the back wall. She knocked three times. "Miss Jones? Miss Jones?" she said.

She turned back to us. "She's not answering."

"Why don't you open the door?" I asked.

"Oh, that's against the rules. She could be having a confidential conversation with a student."

Dani stepped forward, put her hands on the woman's upper arms, and slid her to the side. She cracked the door a little and said, "Miss Jones? Miss Natasha Jones?" When she got no response, she pushed the door open. The room was empty.

"Where else could she be?" I asked.

"I-I-I don't know. I didn't see her leave. She didn't sign out."

I saw a window on the back wall. Beneath it stood a credenza, its top holding a couple piles of books that appeared to have been pushed to one side or the other of the sash. I pushed it up.

The receptionist gasped. "The windows are always supposed to be locked when the administrator is not in the room. I'm going to have to tell the principal about this."

The screen pushed up easily. I leaned out—a short drop straight down to grass, and next to that a sidewalk running the length of the building. I stepped up on the furniture and slipped my legs outside.

"That is against the rules," the receptionist said. "That is not allowed. Get in here right now, or I'll get the principal."

I looked back at her, not believing she threatened me with the principal—old habits die hard, I guess. I slid out the window, got to my feet, and followed the sidewalk to the end of the building, where it turned right, and there in front of me was the faculty parking lot. I jogged through the lot looking for a body in one of the cars, but found no one.

I returned to the window where Dani and Jack helped me get back inside. As my feet touched the floor, a tall, balding man as broad as the doorway bellowed, "We do have doors, you know."

"What is the make and model of Natasha Jones' vehicle?" I asked.

The man squinted his eyes. "And who are you?"

I whipped out my badge. "Sergeant Spencer. The woman on my right is Assistant Prosecutor Danielle Striker, and the man in uniform is Deputy Preston. I have a search warrant for Miss Jones' apartment, and I need to bring her in for questioning."

"And that excuses you from entering this building through a window?"

"Sir, let's focus on the urgent problem at hand. We have witnesses who have said that your guidance counselor purchased opioid drugs. We need to find her."

"What? Where? Surely, a pharmacy."

"No, sir. On the street."

"I find that highly unlikely, but, nonetheless, we will render assistance to help you resolve this matter." He turned to the receptionist and said, "Get on the public address system, and ask Miss Jones to report to the office immediately. Access the parking permit files and provide them with the information about her vehicle."

"Thank you. I assume you are the principal, but having a name for your title would be useful." I smiled, hoping it would help.

"I didn't—good grief—Sebastian Hopewell. And yes, I am the principal." He extended his hand. "What else do you need?"

"Can you verify her home address?" Dani asked.

"Give me a minute," he said and went into the main office. He returned and passed a piece of paper with the address written on it to Dani. "A young man has been showing up here for a few months. Natasha seemed bothered by his presence. I asked if she was being stalked. She laughed and said it was okay. He was harmless."

"Did she tell you his name?"

"She did. But I don't remember. I think it started with a D."

"If you remember, please let us know."

"Of course." The principal left again, and, in a few seconds, they heard his voice on the intercom. "Anyone who has seen Natasha Jones since the end of school day bell rang, please come to the office."

He stepped back in the room and said, "Here's her vehicle information."

"I don't recall a red Miata in the parking lot," I said. "Deputy Preston, here's the license plate number. Go see if you can find it. I'll call in a BOLO." I asked, and the principal granted permission, for Dani and me to search the guidance counselor's office with the caveat that we did not look at any student files. He left the receptionist to watch over us and keep us honest. She narrowed her eyelids and folded her arms across her chest. She regarded us with a baleful stare.

Dani went through the drawers on the right-hand side, and I took the left. In the second drawer, Dani pulled out a pamphlet and slid it across the desktop. "Look at this."

I glanced down and turned to the receptionist. "Pre-natal vitamins. Is Miss Jones pregnant?"

The woman's jaw went up and down a couple of times before she said,

"I don't know. Maybe. She could have it for a student. She counseled a pregnant one this week."

My cell rang, and the search team delivered the news that Natasha Jones was not in her apartment. I told them I'd join them there in a little while. Jack reported back that there were no Miatas in the parking lot, and he, Dani, and I began a search of the school. On my way out of the restroom, Principal Hopewell approached me and said, "A teacher came to the main office and said that she had seen Miss Jones get in her Miata and drive away—actually, she said she saw her 'Peel out of the parking lot as if Satan's minions were on her tail.'" He winced. "Drama teacher—they can be, well, dramatic. And one more thing, you should talk to the science teacher, Flora Moon. She and Natasha were close enough to do favors for one another. Unfortunately, she is out on a field trip to D.C., and the bus won't be back till rather late this evening."

"Thank you." I called off the search of the school, and the three of us headed out to the apartment building. The forensic crew had nearly finished their investigation, but found no drugs, only an old pot pipe buried beneath a stack of underwear in a dresser drawer. Rose Culpepper said, "We bagged up a mortar and pestle we found in the back of an upper cabinet in the kitchen. There are a lot of innocent reasons for having one—culinary and otherwise—but occasionally the reason is drugs. We'll test it and see if we can find anything."

Dani and I sat down in front of the desk in the corner of the bedroom to go through Jones' papers. I wasn't sure what we'd find there, but I couldn't assume anything. Rose entered the room.

"Do you care that I found a used drug store pregnancy test?" she asked.

"Yes. Positive or negative?"

"Positive. I found a bottle of prenatal vitamins in the medicine cabinet."

"Bag those, too. Not sure they'll be of any use, but it does give us more information about this woman."

"Found something else," Dani said. "It's just a note on a scrap of paper, but it has the name of the shopping center and beneath that, it reads, 'in front of Kohl's.' That's where Givens said that he met up with the teacher."

"Excellent. I haven't found anything of interest. I've got to get back to the station soon. I've got too many loose threads that need tending."

Rose joined us. "Charley, if I'm right, I've just found another thread for you to pull."

"What's that?"

"There's a framed photo in the top drawer of a nightstand that looks remarkably like the younger victim at the farm on Old Spotswood Road."

Chapter Twenty-Three

I looked down at the photograph. It was Hank Monroe all right. What was it doing in Natasha Jones's apartment, and why was it face down in a drawer—the drawer right beside her bed? Theories cascaded like fast-moving water over rapids. Hank's parents died from fentanyl overdoses. Marvin Givens said he'd sold fentanyl-laden opioids to a high school teacher, but Bobby Lee insisted she was a middle school guidance counselor. Too close for comfort. Natasha Jones disappeared right as Jack and I arrived at the school. In a rush to get to an after-school appointment? Not hardly likely since she exited the building through a window. Another doubtful coincidence—the kind that made my skin crawl.

Surely, a public-school employee would know the risks of using drugs, both to her health and to her career. On top of that, she might be pregnant. She couldn't be stupid enough to be using, could she? What other reason could she possibly have for buying those pills? If she'd done it to kill the Monroes, where was the evidence? What was her motive? Could she be the girlfriend that Johnny mentioned?

"Rose," I said, "there must be something we've overlooked. There must be more evidence tying her into the victims of the triple homicide. We have to keep looking."

Rose nodded. "On it." She dragged a chair over to the bedroom closet and started digging through the shelves. She pulled out a holster without a gun shoved back in a corner. She held it up in two gloved fingers. "Charley, could this be for the gun that killed Hank Monroe?"

"Could be. Bag it. Good job." I reached for my ringing cell. "Spencer."

"A patrol officer spotted the car with a woman matching the description of Natasha Jones entering the residence that is owned by Henry Clay Monroe and Mary Alice Monroe."

My heart beat a jagged tattoo. "Tell the deputy to keep watch on the house. Tell him not to enter until he has back-up. Don't let anyone leave the premises. I'll send another car to the location. I'm on my way."

I tersely explained the situation to Rose and ran to my car with Jack. As I raced down the road, I talked to myself incessantly. The innocent reason Natasha had gone to Mary Alice's—they knew one another, and Natasha was paying her respects. The two women were in this together. They were celebrating their success and plotting to divert suspicion onto someone else. Mary Alice's life was in danger. That last thought pressed my foot down on the gas pedal.

My radio crackled, and a dispatcher's voice spoke, "Shot fired at—" She gave Mary Alice's address. "Back-up not there yet. The deputy is going in."

The thought of losing a member of the department over my case swamped my stomach with acid. If I went any faster, I'd lose control of the car. I knew the scenery was flashing by at a high speed, but still it felt as if I were creeping along like a fat, pink earthworm on pavement.

I tried to think through the possibilities, but I could no longer put a positive spin on anything. A shot was fired. Someone was dead or injured or, at the least, terrified. None of the above were good outcomes.

The dispatcher interrupted my thoughts with an update: "Second shot fired. Back-up on scene."

An escalation. My heart raced. I pushed the car a little harder despite the risk. As I turned onto the street, the vehicle fishtailed. I went airborne over a hill and slammed back down, jarring my teeth and making all the miscellaneous crap in my vehicle rattle. I pushed over the curb, across the sidewalk, and into the white picket fence. As soon as the car stopped, Jack and I jumped out and raced for the house.

Chapter Twenty-Four

A cluster of deputies stood in the doorway at the front. Jack went inside to check on Mary Alice. I sprinted to the back of the house. As soon as I cleared the corner, a female ran from the rear of the home, heading for the woods. I raised my gun and fired. She turned back and paused. Then, she was off and running again. She had a good head start. I pushed hard to close the distance. My chest tightened; my breathing grew labored. As I entered the trees, I thought I was gaining on her. I heard an "oof" in the distance; that sounded to me as if she tripped. I hoped that was the case. I needed every advantage I could get.

I heard shouts behind me and glimpsed back over my shoulder. I saw men in uniform following me. Cheered, I spun around too hastily and tripped over a tree root. I didn't go down but had to brace on a tree. I could hear the woman I thought was Natasha Jones up ahead, but I could no longer see her.

I ducked under a low-hanging branch and past a clump of weeds, I saw pavement. I looked up and down the street without catching a glimpse of her. I darted across the road and into the trees on the other side. I paused, listening for any sound of movement. Desiccated leaves rattled to my right. I raced in that direction before realizing I was chasing a squirrel. I heard the deputies approaching, but up ahead, I heard nothing but the birds in the trees.

The men who were behind me were now beside me. "What now, Sarge?" one asked, panting.

I motioned them to spread out. We stretched to a line, each of us about twenty feet apart, and jogged side by side, looking for any sign of our prey. A half an hour—and lots of false alarms—later, we emerged into a neighborhood. We ran along fence lines, peered into yards, and looked for anything unusual. If we saw anyone outside, we asked if they'd seen a woman running through the subdivision. No one had. We didn't know where we'd lost track of her, but odds were, we were chasing our imaginations. Soon, we reached the fourteen-foot-high barrier running along a major highway. We had to admit she was gone and blowing in the wind.

Trudging back toward the pavement, I was pleased to see someone had called for transport. Two prisoner transfer vans were waiting at the edge of the trees. I felt peculiar boarding the back of the vehicle and sitting on the bad side of the cage used to secure prisoners, but nonetheless, I was glad not to have to walk all the way back through the woods again. The bench seats were hard, we felt every bump in the road, and it smelled like the inside of a jail. Still, I was grateful. I had more than a few scratches on my face and the back of my hands. We were dropped off at the sidewalk to Mary Alice's home.

Jack met me on the porch. "She's been asking for you and said she would talk only to you. She made a couple of phone calls. I think one was to a lawyer."

I groaned. The last thing I wanted was to deal with a legal eagle. Lately, it seemed as if more and more victims and witnesses were engaging attorneys. A lot of them simply wanted a barrier between themselves and the media. The unintentional consequence was that it slowed down our ability to get information. Often, time was of the essence. But, maybe, this situation was a falling out between co-conspirators.

* * *

"Hello, Mary Alice," I said.

"Sergeant Spencer. I'm so glad to see you."

"Can you tell me what happened here?"

"Yes, I can. And I want to tell you, but my lawyer told me to wait until she got here."

Seeing the huge bandage on her upper arm, I asked, "Were you injured?"

"Yes. The EMT said I might need stitches, but I said I'd rather go to my primary physician than the ER. He bandaged me up and told me to go see him soon. They have late hours tonight, so I made an appointment for 6:30. I should be able to get out of here by then, shouldn't I?"

I said, "Sure." I wasn't as confident as I sounded. A lot depended on what she had to say and whether the attorney made it difficult to get answers.

Jack stuck his head through the front door. "The lawyer's here. And the forensic guys showed up to check for digging in the yard."

I almost asked him why before remembering that I asked for technicians to check for a possible disturbed patch of lily of the valley.

"Sergeant?" Jack asked.

I shook my head. "Right, got it. Let the attorney in, Jack." I rose and greeted Cynthia Tremont. She was wearing a different suit, but the skirt was as short as ever and the spikey heels even a little taller than before. Of all the lawyers I'd dealt with, she was one of the better ones. She was hardly a pushover, but I could usually count on her to be reasonable. We shook hands, and Cynthia requested time alone with her client. I stepped out the front door.

Before long, I heard voices raised in disagreement. I pushed myself up to peer through the window and saw Mary Alice on her feet, waving her arms in the air. A call of "Sergeant" pulled me away from the window and into the backyard.

"You've got to see this!" an excited tech said. "This patch of snow is mixed with dirt. Somebody's been messing around here recently. Could just be a dog, but then again…"

I looked down at small clumps and smears of soil scattered through a white section about a foot long and eighteen inches wide. "Do we have photos of the spot?"

He nodded. "Yep. And don't worry, I'll be careful." He got down on his hands and knees and carefully pulled the melting snow off the surface and over to one side. He picked up the hand trowel and pointed at the clumped-up brown earth. "See," he said, "Somebody's been digging right here."

He removed a thin layer of dirt with a trowel, then pulled out a brush from his bag. He flicked it back and forth across the surface until something wormy-white poked into view. "I'll check it back in the lab, but it sure looks to me like that is the root of the lily of the valley."

"Take a photo in situ and then obtain samples," I said. I hoped Mary Alice wasn't noticing the activity out here. I'd rather she not be pre-warned of my latest surprise.

Chapter Twenty-Five

I entered the living room and sat down on the chair catty-corner from the two women on the sofa. "You wanted to speak to me, Mary Alice?"

Mary Alice opened her mouth, but Cynthia laid a hand on her forearm. "One moment, Mary Alice. Sergeant, I want you to understand that my client wishes to speak to you about matters against my advice. I am going along with her, but reserve the right for a time out to talk with her if I deem it necessary."

"I understand."

We sat in silence for a minute until Mary Alice broke it. "Remember the day you asked me about my slow cooker?"

"Yes, I do. We had to take you to the hospital."

"It wasn't in my house because I cleaned it thoroughly and tossed it into a dumpster a couple of miles from here. I disposed of it because it had been full of poison."

My head was spinning with questions. Is she about to confess to murder? Were we wrong in suspecting Natasha Jones? Or Charles Monroe, Jr.? Are they both blameless? If so, why were they running and hiding?

"I've been thinking about my husband dropping dead for a long, long time. But I only fantasized about the many ways he could be killed. I imagined him dying in a fatal car accident or because he was in the wrong place at the wrong time. No matter how bad he hurt me, I never thought of taking his life. When the snow was falling the other day, I had vivid daydreams of him losing control of his truck and plummeting down the mountain. I never considered the possibility of taking his life. No, that's not exactly true. I thought about it on many occasions, but I never thought about the specifics or really thought I would do anything to make it happen. But it was always there, like cancer eating at my brain, pushing me to stand up for myself. To end the abuse. To stop being a victim. That all changed when I learned what he was doing to his parents.

"I was appalled and afraid that Hank would never stop tormenting them until his mother was lodged in some place where the staff neglected or abused the elderly in their care. She was a really sweet woman once, and she deserved better. That's when I realized that an accident wasn't going to miraculously happen. The solution was taking Hank's life with my own two hands. It was the only way to end the suffering of all of us. I thought about shooting him, but I hate guns. Hank taught me how to use one, over my protests. Still, holding one in my hand made me a bit nauseous, and I wasn't a great shot. To be sure of success, I would have to be up close. The thought of all that blood made my stomach churn even worse. I didn't know enough about cars to cause an accident—didn't have any idea but to cut the brake lines, and I didn't know how to do that."

She sighed and blew stray hairs out of her face. "I even thought about hiring someone to kill Hank. But I didn't know where to look. And if I managed to find someone, how could I possibly trust a stranger to keep my secret? On TV, anyway, the shooter always gets caught and makes a deal that implicates the person who hired him. I scratched that solution off my list. If Hank hadn't been such an S.O.B. the other night, I might have let it all slide by."

"What night, Mary Alice? And what happened?"

"Tuesday? Wednesday? One of those nights. Anyway. I knew trouble was coming my way because he shoved the back door open so hard that it banged against the wall." Mary Alice continued describing the event that left her lying flat on the floor with a napkin over her face. She talked at a fast clip as if she believed the faster she went, the sooner the memory would be in the past. When Mary Alice finished, she bent forward with her face in her hands.

I hadn't had a great track record with men, but no one had ever treated me that way. I wondered how I would have reacted as I waited for Mary Alice to pull herself together. She looked up at me, her eyes glazed as if she were drunk, and her breath came as hard as if she'd run a marathon.

She still seemed to be mentally in another place, at another time, when she continued, "I remembered thinking that he just wasn't going to stop until he killed me. I knew I had to do something. Have you checked out my computer search history?"

"Yes," I said. "If it weren't for the death of your husband and your in-laws, I would have assumed you wrote crime fiction."

Mary Alice flashed a quick, sad smile. "Not exactly a good criminal mind. If I were, I would have destroyed the hard drive. Anyway, I settled for poison. I read about a bunch of them. I had a couple of pain pills in the medicine cabinet, but not enough to be fatal. I looked online for other things to give him. I considered visiting my cousin in South Carolina and getting some oleander leaves while I was down there. But then, I saw that I had something closer to hand—lily of the valley—a sweet name for a poison. I had a patch in my backyard.

"I didn't know if touching any root of the plant would be toxic or not. I wore gloves just to be safe. I scraped off the snow on top and started poking around in the dirt. I pulled out some little rocks before I hit the right spot. Even though the plants had died off for the winter, it was easy to find and pry up four lengths of fat, white root. When I chopped them up, they looked a lot like dirty minced garlic. I stored them overnight in a container that I shoved into the back of the refrigerator.

"I'd read on one website that people sometimes made the mistake of thinking they were wild garlic and put pieces in soup, and people died. So, the morning after my husband was out all night at his parents' house, I pulled out the crockpot and threw in all the usual ingredients for beef stew. Then, I added the lily of the valley root. I planned to serve that to him after he came home from work that night. But he never did. And then he was dead, so I tried to destroy all the evidence. I thought if you knew about the stew, you'd think I'd been the one who shot him.

"I didn't kill my husband, Sergeant, but I had every intention of doing so.

For me and for his parents. Sitting here today, I can't imagine how I decided that murder was the best option. I still don't understand how I was able to smother my conscience and decide to kill him. I know how and why I got there, but I don't understand how I thought it was the best thing to do."

"Perhaps the fact that he was having an affair helped?"

"I didn't know about Natasha Jones before she showed up at my door. They say the wife's the last one to know—I proved that maxim. I have been suspicious in the past, but not recently."

"If you didn't know her, why did you let her into your house?" I asked.

"I know it's stupid—but she looked nice. And she claimed to know me. Said when we were kids, I hit her over the head with a toy truck. And she brought my favorite pie. Man, you just don't expect something like that. Well, maybe *you* would, but I don't deal with people like that every day. Until she told me, I had no idea Hank was having an affair with anybody. For that matter, I still don't know it for a fact. She told me she was pregnant, but it's possible that she's just a nut who never had a relationship with Hank at all. I'd have to see the results of DNA testing on the baby to be certain that it was true."

"What happened when she came to your house?"

"I didn't recognize her—of course. I wouldn't, since I'd never met her. The pie and her friendliness made me think that my memory was off. I didn't want to hurt her feelings by telling her I didn't know who the hell she was. I mean, that's kind of rude, you know? I didn't have a reason to think she wasn't who she seemed until she pulled out the gun."

"I've lost you, Mary Alice—somewhere between the pie and the gun. Start from her arrival and tell me everything that happened," I said.

"Okay," Mary Alice said. Her memory unreeled like a spool of thread. "It was a tough day. I felt free for the first time in my life, but I couldn't enjoy it. I was disturbed by the knowledge that, despite my previous belief, I was not a good person. I had no principles. No boundaries. No morals.

"When the doorbell rang, I welcomed the distraction from slogging through the guilt swamp of my thoughts. I opened the door to a woman holding a box from the House of Pies. I struggled to recognize her, searching my memory for something familiar—eyes, nose, smile. Nothing except for a bewildering sense that the woman looked a lot like the image I saw in the mirror every morning. I wondered if there were a family connection. I asked if I could help her.

"She said, 'Oh, Mary Alice! You don't recognize me, do you? Well, it has been a long time. I wanted to come by and express my condolences, and, of course, one cannot come to a grieving household with empty hands. She straightened her arms, proffering the package. 'So, I picked up your favorite mixed berry pie on the way over. May I come in?' Now, that really threw me. I had to know her, or else she wouldn't know how much I loved that pie. I was confused, but still, I stepped back from the doorway and invited her inside.

"The woman sat down on the sofa and placed the pie on the coffee table. 'Oh, honey, you look so perplexed,' she said. 'I'll help you out. I'm Tasha. Natasha Jones. You remember now, right?'

"I sure didn't, but I didn't want to offend her. I had to figure it out. To delay further embarrassment, I said, 'How about I cut us both a slice and brew a fresh pot of coffee? Then we can catch up on old times.' I hoped I could figure out which old times by the time I served the coffee and pie.

"When I sat down opposite her, I hoped an open-ended question would spark my memory. 'Do you remember when we first met?'

"Tasha laughed. She said, 'As if I could forget it. Your mother came to visit mine and brought you along. We were told to go play in my room. My older brother wasn't at home, so I thought it was a great idea to go to his room instead. I told you it was my room. At first, you were amazed at all the trucks and cars I had. You started playing with a yellow metal dump truck. My Mom came upstairs and caught us in my brother's room. She scolded both of us. You picked up the truck and bashed it into my head because I lied to you.'

"I was appalled at that revelation. I had no idea I was such a violent child."

"Mary Alice, you know she could have made up that whole story," I interjected.

"But she had so much detail," Mary Alice protested.

"It actually could have happened to her, or she could have done it to someone else. If you have no memory of it, you might not have been there. What happened next?"

Mary Alice sighed. "She giggled and lifted a hand to her head and rubbed a spot on her scalp. She said, 'I can still feel where the stitches were. Anyway, I was crying, the blood was flowing—you know how those head lacerations are—and Mom took me to the emergency room.'

"I was feeling awful, but took a bite of the pie to keep from having to respond right away. The pie was sooo good—it made me feel as if I were melting inside. I asked her if we ever got together again.

"She said, 'Oh, yes. Many times. Many, many, many times. But then the summer before first grade, we all moved away when my dad's employer transferred to another state.'

"I still remembered nothing about her at all. I carried the empty plates in the kitchen and put them in the dishwasher. Returning to the living room, I asked her what she was doing these days.

"She said that she was in a rough patch because her fiancé died before they could get married, and to make it all worse, she was carrying his child. Then she said, 'He wanted to leave his wife for me and the baby, but she's a real bitch. Wrapped his parents around her little finger. He knew they'd disown him if he divorced her.' I expressed my empathy for her, and she said, 'Then you will understand why I have to do what I have to do.'

"I questioned what she meant by that, and she reached into her purse and pulled out her billfold. She opened it to a photograph of herself and a man, both smiling with their arms wrapped around one another.

"I thought I was seeing things. I squeezed my eyes tight and looked again. It was Hank and that woman sitting beside me. I looked at her, and she had this smug look on her face. I didn't want to believe what was in front of my eyes. As I started to accept what I was seeing, a surge of nausea raced up in my throat. I jumped up with my hand over my mouth and raced to the bathroom and emptied my stomach into the toilet. That woman ran water in the bathroom sink and handed me a cool washcloth, telling me to wipe my face, it would make me feel better. And it did, but when I pulled the cloth away, that crazy woman was pointing a gun at my head.

"Then, she chastised me. Told me that Hank said I was a drama queen, and I sure was proving it.

"I felt lightheaded and slapped both my hands on the counter to steady myself. I asked her what she thought she was doing. I thought about attacking her, or pretending to pass out, or just wishing she would disappear in a puff of smoke." Mary Alice bent over, panting hard. The memory was too fresh.

I leaned forward. "You're safe now, Mary Alice. Take a few deep breaths. When you're ready, you can tell me what happened after that."

Cynthia glared at me as if I, not Natasha Jones, were the source of her client's distress. It ticked me off, but I forced that feeling to stay out of the expression on my face.

Mary Alice straightened her posture, took a deep breath, and began anew. "She said that she needed to protect her child's financial future. That she had a note prepared, and I needed to sign it. I told her that I'd be glad to share my inheritance from Hank with her baby once we had a DNA test to confirm the genetic link to my husband.

"When I said that, she got angry at first—geez, it was like talking to Hank. Then, she laughed at me and said that I was kind of cute bargaining with her when she had a gun to my head. And she said, 'No, sweetheart, this note will ensure that my baby gets all of Hank's estate.'

"I agreed to sign it. I mean, she was holding a gun to my head, and I figured that the court would not take a document seriously once they knew the circumstances. She smiled at me and, once again, told me how cute I was. She added, 'Listen, sweetie, the world needs to know that you killed Hank. Let's go to the kitchen table and have a seat,' She motioned me to move with the pistol.

"I knew I hadn't killed Hank, but she seemed to believe I did. I tried to focus on breathing, trying to keep it even and steady, so I maybe I could think of a solution. She was so totally unhinged that I feared for my life with every step I took. I guess I was walking too slow for her because she kept jabbing me in the side of my neck with the muzzle of her gun.

"She jerked out a chair and ordered me to sit. She pulled another one next to me and took a seat without removing the gun barrel away from my head. She slapped a pen on the surface of the table and pulled a piece of paper out of her pocket, unfolding it and smoothing it flat on the table. She told me to sign it.

"All I could think about was stalling her for as long as I possibly could. If I had enough time, maybe I'd think of something to get out of this mess. Or maybe a neighbor would drop by. Or perhaps one of Hank's workers or subcontractors. I asked her if I could read it first."

"She chuckled as if she was certain I was trapped and said, 'You might as well. Read it out loud.' So, I did."

"What did it say, Mary Alice?" I asked.

"It's on the kitchen table."

I walked over and picked it up. "I, Mary Alice Monroe, can no longer live with my sin. I poisoned my in-laws with fentanyl. My husband arrived at their house and wanted to call an ambulance and the police. When I couldn't stop him, I shot him dead. I don't regret what I've done, but I know I must pay for my wrongdoing.

"I die without a will, but I request, in these final moments before my death, that all of Hank's assets be granted to Natasha Jones since she is the mother of Hank's unborn child."

Mary Alice continued. "When I read it, the reality of her intentions was clear. I couldn't deny it any longer. I asked, 'You're going to kill me?' And she said, 'No, you are going to commit suicide.' I objected. I told her that I didn't kill my in-laws. That I didn't kill Hank. That I never did anything to her. I said that I didn't know Hank was seeing anyone. I knew nothing.

"She said that it didn't matter because I knew now. And then she told me to wrap my hands around the grip and put my finger on the trigger. She said, 'You won't have to apply force. I'll wrap my hand around yours and squeeze. It will all be over before you know it.'

"That was when I started begging. 'Wait. Wait just a minute. I can give all of it to you. I don't care. You can have it all. Please. I feel free for the first time in my life, and I just want to live—I don't care about the money or house or anything.' While I spoke, I patted my pocket and realized my cell phone was in there. I slid my hand in and felt the surface with my fingertips. She was yelling at me to sign the damn note. And cursing me for not letting him go, to stop being a leech, that I should have let her baby have a daddy. She blamed me for Hank's death and insisted I had to admit to my responsibility.

"I was struggling to figure out the position of my phone by touch. I told her, 'He never asked for a divorce. I would have been glad to give him his freedom to be with you. I desperately wanted Hank out of my life. I didn't know about you.' I used my fingerprint to open the screen. Tasha's forehead wrinkled when she heard the opening sound. I kept my face blank, hoping she'd doubt that she heard anything. I moved my finger to the call button and then moved up to what I hoped was the 9 button and pressed it. The beep gave me away.

"Before I could get to the 1, Tasha grabbed my arm, jerked my hand out of my pocket with enough force to rip it down the side. The cell tumbled to the floor. 'What the hell are you doing?' she screamed. 'Sign it. Or I'll chop your fingers off one at a time before I kill you and forge your damn signature.'

"I jumped up and backed away with her hands raised in front of my face. I said, 'You can't do this, Tasha. You can't claim it's a suicide if you shoot me when I'm across the room.'

"She lunged at me, grabbing but missing. I bounced off walls and zigzagged down the hallway, ducking into the bathroom and locking the door. She pushed on it and kicked it and screamed. 'I will burn this house down around you, bitch. I will. I swear I will. Come out of the bathroom or die inside of it.'

"I remembered someone telling me a long time ago that crazy people need to be talked to in a calm, soft voice. I whispered through the crack between the door and the frame. 'Tasha, Tasha, you don't want to do that. If I'm killed through arson, how will your baby get anything? You need my help for your baby to inherit from Hank. And I'll help you. We can go to a lawyer and make it all legal. I think Hank's baby deserves to start his life with a nest egg. It's only right.'

"She said, 'You would do that?' I told her, 'Of course, I would. The baby is an innocent. The baby deserves something from his father.' I really meant it, too, but she didn't believe me. I leaned back against the wall, trying to think of what I should say next. Lucky me. That's when I heard the wood splinter and felt the bullet in my arm. I threw my hand over it and felt the blood seep through my fingers. It burned. Damn, did it burn. I didn't realize it was just a graze. I voiced my objection, and Tasha said, 'You got lucky. I meant to kill you. I was trying to shoot you right in your lying mouth.'

"I heard another shot ripping through the door and thought I was going to get hit again. But it exploded into the toilet bowl, shattering the porcelain. The water inside sprayed out everywhere. I slipped off my wet shoes and climbed into the alcove inside the bathtub. I pressed my back against the wall and tried to get as skinny as I could. I didn't think she could get the right angle to hit me in there. It was only possible if it ricocheted or if she got through the door into the bathroom. I pulled the shower curtain across to buy a little reaction time in case Tasha did get inside.

"Then the impossible happened—the front doorbell rang. I opened my mouth to scream, but before I could, Tasha threatened to kill whoever was outside and to make it look like I did it. I did not know who was there, but I did know I didn't want to be responsible for that person's death. I knew I had to get out there or else it would be too late.

"Outside, right below the bathroom window, the concrete stairs led down to the basement. If I fell straight down, the impact might kill me. But if I leapt across it, I'd land on the little porch. I wasn't sure if I could make it, but I knew I had to try. If I stayed where I was, I'd die for sure.

"I held my breath and leaned past the shower curtain. I flipped open the lock on the sash and retreated up against the far wall by the tub and listened. I was so scared. Making the scramble out of the window was risky. If Tasha pulled the trigger again, while I was doing it, I'd be right in her line of fire. Then I heard footsteps in the hall. Pounding on one of the outside doors. Glass rattling. A loud crash, almost as loud as the sound of the exploding toilet. A slammed door. The sounds were confusing. I stayed pinned to the wall, trying to understand all that I heard. I don't know whether it was a couple of seconds or many minutes, but I got to the point where I couldn't handle the anxiety of waiting any longer. I stepped one foot out of the tub and pushed up the sash. At that moment, I heard a loud male voice. He said, 'Sheriff's Office. Come out with your hands up.'

"I sobbed and hiccupped, but I just couldn't move. I was too afraid. I heard a knock on the bathroom door, and the man said, 'Lay down on the floor with your hands over your head.' I stretched out in the bathtub, my stomach on the porcelain, my legs bent up at the knees, my hands as far up towards the rim as I could reach. I heard another crash, more splintering wood. A hand touched my back, and I wet myself. The man asked, 'Mary Alice Monroe?' I nodded. 'Have you been shot?' I nodded again.

"He asked if I could stand if he helped me, and I managed to say yes, surprised at how raspy and gravelly my voice sounded. I flinched when his hand cupped the elbow of my injured arm as he helped me to my feet. Then, I heard another shot, and I doubled over and moaned. The man said, 'Ma'am, that was outside. You're okay. You're safe now. Can you lift your foot over the edge of the tub?' It was so hard, but I gave it my all. My whole body shook and felt immovable. Once I was out, the man wrapped an arm around my waist and led me to the kitchen table. He told me to sit down and rest until I felt steady on my feet. He said his name was Deputy Jack Preston.

"He wanted to ask me questions, and I tried to answer, but I just couldn't form any words. He said it was okay and looked at my gunshot wound. He told me that I was lucky that the bullet took a gouge out of my upper arm before passing through without hitting anything but skin, but it wasn't deep, and might not leave a scar. Then he said, 'Even if it does, it won't be bad. The neighborhood kids will all want to see it.'

"I smiled for the first time in a long time and pointed to the kitchen faucet. He pulled a glass out of the cabinet, filled it, and brought it over. My hands shook so much that he placed his over mine to keep the glass steady. I drank the whole thing down. He offered to get me another, but I shook my head. I got up from the chair to move into the living room, but my knees were shaking. He offered to help me and asked where I wanted to go. When I said, 'sofa,' he told me that wasn't a good idea because I might get blood on it. He said I should probably wait until the EMT bandaged my arm. I cried, and he eased me back into the kitchen chair.

"That's when I asked for you. He said you were outside, but he didn't know exactly where. I knew then I had to tell you everything, even though it meant I'd end up in prison."

Chapter Twenty-Six

"After that," Mary Alice said, "the EMT cleaned my arm, applied antibiotic cream, and wrapped it up. Then, I called my doctor's office and said I needed an appointment because of a bullet wound." Mary Alice grinned. "I had to stifle a giggle when she asked me to repeat myself. She kept insisting that I come in right away or go to the emergency room, but I finally convinced her that wasn't going to happen. That Tasha woman was right about one thing. If she is carrying Hank's baby, I do have a moral obligation to provide financial support for that baby."

"Did your husband have a will?" I asked.

"Yes, I believe that I am the only beneficiary."

"Yes, you are. What about your father-in-law's estate?"

"I don't know. Legally, I have no idea how they would work that out. Can they determine who died first? If it was Hank, then he wouldn't have inherited his father's estate. I guess it would go to Chuck. But I really am not sure."

"Have you read your father-in-law's will?"

"A long time ago. He gave a copy to Hank, and I read it. As I recall, everything went to Hank."

"When he was at your home last week, did your father-in-law tell you he planned to rewrite his will?"

Mary Alice tilted her head to one side. "No."

"Did you know he went to his lawyer's office when he left your home?"

"No."

"How do you think he changed it?"

"Hopefully, he decided to divide it all between Hank and Chuck."

"No. Think again."

"He did say that he was setting up a trust for his wife's care in case he passed first."

"He did do that, but that reverted to a new beneficiary upon his wife's death. Do you know who that is?"

"With Hank gone, his only living relative, to my knowledge, is Chuck. Is that his new beneficiary?"

"No."

"Then, I'm clueless."

I leaned in closer to her. "You expect me to believe that?"

Cynthia sat up straight and sucked in her breath. I was certain she knew where I was going, but Mary Alice did not seem to suspect.

"Maybe we ought to cut it all off here," the lawyer said.

Mary Alice looked back and forth at the two of us. "Why? What?"

I kept pushing. "Are you trying to tell me that you do not know that you are the sole beneficiary of your father-in-law's estate?"

"What? You're kidding."

"No. And I imagine you knew that. And I suspect you knew it's worth millions."

"I knew he was well off, but I didn't—"

"And the real story with you and Natasha Jones is that you were co-conspirators in these murders, and you two had a falling out—probably over the division of assets."

"What?"

Cynthia stood and stared at me. "Okay. We're done."

I sat back. "Really, Madame Counselor, you want to end it now with that big question still hanging in the air?"

"You have gone on attack, Sergeant, and I didn't think we were playing that game. I will take my client to a hotel for the next night or two until you apprehend that woman."

"Will you let me know where she is so we can monitor her and make sure she's safe?"

"No, I will not. I expect you to leave her alone. If you get an arrest warrant, let me know, and I'll bring her in to you. Grab your bag, Mary Alice. We're leaving."

"She has a doctor's appointment at 6:30. We were going to take her," I said.

Cynthia said, "I'll take care of that."

I watched them cross the room and go out the door. Mary Alice looked confused. Cynthia, on the other hand, was puffed up like a Mama bear, ready to attack to protect her cub. Interesting. I wondered if Cynthia knew something about Mary Alice that I didn't.

Chapter Twenty-Seven

The day had already been way too long, but I knew I couldn't postpone a visit to my sister. My dad and Emily had set a date for their wedding, and since Ruby wasn't responding to any of Dad's voice messages, I agreed to go tell her about it.

The way she answered the door to her apartment was not a good omen. "Oh, it's you," she walked away, leaving the door wide open, and entered her kitchen. "I suppose you'll want a cup of coffee."

"That would be nice, Ruby."

She started a fresh pot, seeming to be making as much noise doing it as possible. "Are you here to lecture me?" she asked.

"Ruby, how are Dad, or I supposed to communicate with you when your attitude toward us is so hostile?"

"Oh, and you're not hostile to me?" Ruby slammed the mugs on the counter.

"I want to get along, Ruby. It seems as if you don't."

"I want to get along. It's difficult when neither one of you have any respect for my opinion."

"Let's grab our mugs and sit down somewhere. The kitchen table? The sofa?"

"Right here is fine." Ruby plopped into a wooden ladder-back chair at the pine kitchen table.

I sat down across from her and wrapped both of my hands around the mug. "How do you define 'respecting your opinion?'"

"Listening to what I have to say. Thinking about it. Considering it."

"You don't think we do that?"

"No. When I first raised my objections to Emily, you both laughed at me."

"We did not. I objected to you thinking you could tell Dad what to do with his life. It is, after all, his life, not ours."

"But Dad… Dad didn't even stop for a moment to reconsider his choice. He just defended her, and you defended him."

"Ruby, Dad is in love. You expect him to ditch his happiness because you don't like his choice. He has to live with Emily. You don't."

"Well, it's clear. He chose her over me."

"No, he didn't. Choosing her over you would mean he adopted her and dropped both of us as beneficiaries in his will."

"You don't think he'll do just that? I mean, not adopting her but making sure she gets everything when he dies."

"Are you telling me that you disapprove of Emily out of greed?"

"No. You are not paying attention, again. I wouldn't be concerned about being disowned if he married Lucinda. But what do you think will happen if they have children? He'd have a new family then. It will be like we never existed."

"This is ridiculous. At their ages? You know, forget it. I came by to tell you about the wedding arrangements since you won't return his calls."

"Tell Dad to mail me an invitation."

"You'll come to the wedding?"

"No. But I might send a gift. That's probably all Emily cares about anyway."

"Ruby, listen to me. I am about to say something to you that comes completely from the love and caring in my heart. You are not coping well with past trauma. It is obvious now that you cannot do that on your own. You need to see a psychologist or a counsellor. You are carrying around a bucket full of bitterness, and your sense of self-worth is in the gutter. Please get some professional help."

Ruby jerked up from her chair. "You think I'm crazy? Is that it? If I don't toe the line, are you and Dad going to have me committed? Are you ready to lock me up and throw away the key? Get out. Just get out!"

"Ruby, please. I care about you. Dad cares about you. You are being self-destructive, and we hate that because we love you."

My sister dramatically threw her arm wide and pointed at the front door. "Out! Out! Don't ever darken my door again."

I knew she had a flair for the dramatic, but "don't darken my door" was a bit much. "Come on, Ruby. Be reasonable."

She grabbed my upper arm and pulled me out of the chair. "I said out, and I mean out." She dragged me toward the door, opened it, and shoved.

I planted my feet and faced her. "Ruby, you will regret this. Not today or tomorrow. Maybe not for years. I'll leave now and won't come back without an invitation. But know this, I am always there for you. Call me. Drop by. Anything."

"Get out!" she screamed.

Chapter Twenty-Eight

In the morning, I felt hungover—muscles throbbing, stomach churning, and head pounding. Yesterday was truly crappy. A disappointing chase, Mary Alice's startling confession, and my sister throwing me out of her apartment.

I did have a glass of wine last night when I came home, but only one. That wasn't the reason for my discomfort and ennui. It was a hangover, but an emotional one. I didn't think I'd ever get fully awake. I was tempted to call in sick, take a Xanax, and sleep the morning away, but I knew I'd feel guilty if I did. I was on my second cup of coffee when the phone rang.

"Sergeant," a deputy said, "I understand you're looking for Charles Monroe, Jr."

"You found him? Where?"

"A homeowner went out to his garage this morning and spotted a man sleeping inside his car. He held him at gunpoint 'til the deputies arrived."

"Is he there now?"

"He's over at the jail. He was being processed after his arrest on the breaking and entering charges, and they found a wallet and cell phone on him that belonged to a dead man."

"Henry—Hank—Monroe?"

"Yep. Do you want him brought down the tunnel over to your office?"

"Yes, please. Put him in an interrogation room. Let them know I'm on my way. Thanks." I dressed, then fed and watered Flash, and exceeded the speed limit all the way. I couldn't wait to talk to Chuck. Whether he killed his family or not, he had to have answers to some lingering questions.

* * *

I looked through the window of the door and saw a disheveled man in a waist restraint connected to a pair of handcuffs and shackles by a thick chain. He looked like he'd been needing a bath for days. The pocket on his flannel shirt was torn down one side, and the elbows were worn to the point that you could see the skin through the fabric. His jeans were blackened with dirt, and the sole on one of his shoes flapped to the floor when he lifted his foot. Still, he bore a striking resemblance to the victim in the morgue. I imagined it might be difficult to tell them apart if they were both cleaned up and alive.

"Charles Monroe?" I said as I walked into the room.

"Yes, Chuck, please," he said in a monotone.

I turned to the deputy leaning against the wall. "Could you remove the belt, please?"

"I'll have to re-attach a pair of cuffs."

"Understood." I turned to Chuck and watched the deputy remove the apparatus and re-cuff Chuck. "Do you know why you're here?"

"Trespassing 'cause I took shelter for the night in the wrong garage. He had a crucifix hanging from his rearview mirror. You'd think he would have shown a little Christian kindness and let me leave of my own accord."

"Be that as it may, Mr. Monroe, you are charged with breaking and entering."

"You can't do that. I didn't break in. I was looking for shelter from the wind. I tried doors on a few other garages before I got to that house, and the one there was hanging wide open—I guess it hadn't been shut tight, and the wind blew it in."

"You're also suspected of breaking into the home of Mary Alice Monroe." Chuck shook his head. "Didn't do that."

"Let me advise you of your rights before we talk about what you did or didn't do. I pulled out the card and read it to him verbatim.

"Fine. Where's my lawyer?"

Not for the first time, I resented the Miranda Rights decision. "Fine, Mr.

Monroe. You will be charged with breaking and entering when you return to the jail. You can call the lawyer of your choice there."

"Do I look like I can afford an attorney? You just said you'd get me one if I didn't have any money."

"After you finish processing, a magistrate will decide on the bail for your release and set an advisement date. That's when a judge will appoint an attorney for you."

"Sounds like that's going to take a while."

"I really don't know, Mr. Monroe."

"Well, see, the thing of it is, I have information about the murder of my parents and brother, which I was thinking will be valuable to the solving of the case. I would think with a killer loose out there, you'd want me to tell you what I know."

"How do you know it?"

"I was a witness."

I waved my hands like windshield wipers in front of my face. "Stop! Don't say another word. You want a lawyer, and I can't talk to you since you did not waive your rights but instead asked for an attorney."

"What is this, some sort of Catch-22? Damned if I do, damned if I don't. I don't trust you, Miss Policeman. I need a lawyer to protect me from you, even though I want to help get justice for my parents. Can't you short-circuit this process?"

At first, all I could do was stare at him. I wanted to talk to him. I longed to circumvent the rules. But I knew it was likely to smack me in the face. I needed thinking time. "Would you like a cup of coffee, water, a soda?"

"A Dr. Pepper would be good."

I crossed the room to the door. "I'll be back as soon as I can." I believed there might be a kernel of truth in what he said, but knew it was bound to be wrapped in at least one strand of lies. I clunked coins into the vending machine as I tried to untangle the mess in my head.

Lieutenant Holcombe came into the break room and said, "Whoa, you look like your brain is about to explode. What's going on?"

I explained my dilemma. "I sure can't figure out a way to find out what he has to say without waiting. And as he said, there's a killer on the loose."

"I certainly pushed you into a quagmire with this case. If it actually had been a murder-suicide, you wouldn't have to be worrying about a thing. Go talk to someone in the D.A.'s office. They might have a solution," he said, "but then again, they might yell at you for asking."

"That won't be a first."

"And you can handle it."

I rolled my eyes. Famous last words.

Holcombe clapped me on the back, and I returned to the interrogation room.

Chuck was slumped over in his seat, staring at the tabletop. He raised his head. "Well, did you figure out how to get around the bureaucracy?"

"Not yet," I said as I placed the Dr. Pepper in front of him. "I'm still looking."

I left him with his drink and the deputy and took the elevated walkway over to the building across the street, hoping to find Dani Striker or anyone I'd worked with in the past. I was not in the mood to spend the time initiating a new relationship when all I wanted to do was weasel around the rules.

As I walked toward Dani's cubicle, I saw her head rise above the panel. She was taller than I was, but not by much, until she put on spiked heels, then she towered over me. "You stop by for coffee?" she asked.

"I sure wouldn't mind a cup, but I do have something else on my mind."

"Of course, you do. Coffee first."

"Do you have to go to court today?"

"Do you really have to ask? I never wear these heels to work except for those days."

"I don't want to hold you up."

"No worries. Court isn't until this afternoon."

When we settled back at Dani's desk, she asked, "What's up?"

I ran down the situation with Chuck Monroe. "I think I'm stuck with waiting until his advisement date, when the judge will assign an attorney. Do you see any way around it?"

"You got a ten-dollar bill?"

CHAPTER TWENTY-EIGHT

"Yeah, why?" I asked.

"Take those furrows off your brow. I have a defense attorney friend who occasionally helps me out. All he asks is a ten-dollar retainer. I'll give him the cash so you won't get your ethics knickers in a twist. You in?"

"You betcha," I said, slapping down my ten.

"I'll get Kent Howard to meet you over at your place."

I had regrets about forking over the money before I got back to my office.

Chapter Twenty-Nine

I sat at my desk, wondering if serious consequences would ensue for accepting Dani's offer of assistance. What she helped me to do might screw up my case or my career. Or maybe there would be no price to pay because Dani's lawyer friend was a no-show? And I'd be back where I started with nothing more than a guilty conscience for my trouble. The more I thought about it, the darker my prospects looked.

Finally, I got a break from my musings of doom when a phone call summoned me to the front desk. Waiting for me was a man too good-looking to be a lawyer. Glossy black hair, prairie flower blue eyes, and shoulders wide enough for a linebacker. "Sergeant Spencer?" he asked.

I swallowed hard and extended my hand. "Yes, and you're Kent Howard?" He nodded in response.

"I'll show you back to your client."

When we reached the door to the interrogation room, he said, "First things first. To be perfectly clear: I accepted a retainer on behalf of Charles Monroe from a friend of mine. I am under no obligation to continue representing him after today. If I am dissatisfied with him, I'll drop him after setting up an advisement date. If I want to take his case, I will accept him as a pro bono client. However, what happens from here on out is between me and my client."

"Of course," I said, fervently hoping that I travelled on a two-way street of silent complicity that left me sheltered from negative outcomes to my career. I opened the door and motioned for the deputy to come out and wait in the hallway. I saw the attorney shake Chuck's hand and went back to my office, still internally debating my decision and struggling to keep my anxiety at bay. I had a couple of Xanax in my drawer. I touched the prescription bottle but jerked my hand away. I needed to be alert for the interview with Chuck and left the pills undisturbed.

Forty-five minutes later, I was back in the interrogation room. Kent smiled a welcome suitable for a reunion with a long-lost friend. Chuck sat back in his chair with a smug look on his face as if he just pulled a fast one. The combination raised my anxiety level a little higher. Maybe that was the point. I sat down across from the two of them.

Kent's face darkened with the seriousness of incoming storm clouds. "You need to understand that my client wants to tell you what he witnessed because he wants justice for his parents. I have advised him against it."

He paused, and I felt as if I'd just fallen into a trap of my own making.

"I assured my client that I could easily get the breaking and entering charge thrown out of court. Additionally, I advised that because of the bitter cold last night, I could probably convince the court to be lenient and spare my client any jail time on the trespassing charge. However, he disagreed with my advice because he wanted to answer your questions. I told him to do so honestly, or not answer them at all. I have no problem with you asking questions to detail your clarity, but if the interrogation becomes accusatory, I will terminate this session immediately. Do you understand?"

Honestly, I wanted to say, "Screw you," and walk out. Instead, I said, "Certainly. Mr. Monroe, please tell me what you witnessed."

"First, I knew that something was wrong when a woman started yelling at my parents."

"Yelling at your parents? Whoa, let's go back a bit. When did this happen?"

"The night they died."

"You were there?"

"Yes. In the basement."

"Was your brother Hank there?"

"Not at first."

"You were in the basement?"

"Yes."

"Were you camping out behind the furnace?"

"Yes."

"For how long?"

"Almost two weeks."

"Why?"

"I was worried about Momma." Furrows formed on his brow, and the crow's feet tightened at his eyes as tears flowed down his face. "I wanted to know what was wrong with her. I wanted to see her again. I wanted to talk to my father. I wanted them to know that I didn't do what Hank said."

"Why didn't you just knock on the front door and tell them?"

"They disowned me and told me never to come back."

"Why, Mr. Monroe? What did you do to cause them to be that angry?"

"Watch it, Sergeant," Kent said. "You're walking close to the edge."

"I *live* close to the edge, Mr. Howard." I turned and stared at the lawyer before softening my expression and looking at Chuck. "Okay, Mr. Monroe, let's go back to basics. Let's start with your estrangement from the family. Do you remember when that happened or why it happened?"

Chuck sighed long and hard and shook his head. "I wish I could forget. It was a little more than nine years ago. I finally got up the nerve to tell my parents I was gay. They took it hard. I thought that they would get over it, though. When I came down to breakfast the next morning, everything had gone to hell in a handbasket. Momma wasn't cooking as she usually did. She was sitting at the table sobbing. A crumpled tissue in one hand and her head resting on the palm of the other. Hank was leaning against the kitchen counter, his arms crossed over his chest and a nasty grin on his face. Pops' arms were akimbo. His face was red. He sneered at me and said, 'Pack up all the things you want and get out of my house. Don't ever show up here again. You won't get shelter. You won't get a penny from me when I'm dead. What you did to your brother is unforgiveable. He's your baby brother—how could you?'

"I asked, 'How could I do what?' as Momma's sobs grew louder. Pop yelled, 'You know what you did. You sicken me. Get out, or I'll call the police. I'll have you arrested.' Then he turned his back on me. I looked at Momma and said, 'Momma, I did nothing to harm Hank, no matter what he told you. Help me.'

"Instead of coming to my aid, she dropped her head on the table and rested her forehead on her folded arms. Her shoulders heaved. Her wails filled the kitchen, but she wouldn't even glance in my direction.

"It wasn't until I called home a couple of months later and Hank answered the phone that I knew what it was. Hank admitted and laughed about what he told our parents. He said he told Momma and Pops that ever since he was seven years old, I'd forced him to give me blow jobs and then, in later years, I raped him. Hank thought it was funny that they believed him—funny that I'd been disinherited.

"I came back after all these years because I got my act together, and I wanted my parents to know the truth. I was waiting in the basement for the right time. I waited too long." He bent over, placing his forehead on the table, and sobbed like I've never heard a grown man cry before.

Everything Chuck had said made him a stronger suspect, and yet, here I was, feeling sorry for him and hoping he didn't do it. If he had told the truth, I wouldn't blame him if he did kill Hank. When he raised his head, though, his eyes were dry. That proved nothing but did raise my suspicion. After all, it stood to reason he'd be a good con man living on the streets like he did.

"Tell me, Mr. Monroe, when you were eavesdropping in the basement, did you hear anything troubling before that night?"

"A couple of times, my mother was yelling and pleading to go home. Pops kept reassuring her that she was home, but Momma didn't believe him. She was really very far gone. That just about broke my heart. And then, a few nights ago, I heard Hank and Pops arguing about something. I couldn't understand enough of it to be certain because they were in the kitchen and the dishwasher was running, but I think it was about Momma's care. It was obvious, though, that they were angry with each other, and I thought that might be a good thing for me. If Pops were mad at Hank, there was a better chance that he'd hear me out."

"What happened the night your parents died?"

"I knew someone came to the house. I didn't pay a lot of attention at first.

I heard a woman's voice and assumed it was Mary Alice. But when she yelled at my parents, I doubted it was my sister-in-law. It's been nearly ten years since I've seen her, but she'd never been a yeller before. For another, what she said should have been good news for both of my parents if it came from her."

"What exactly did she say?"

"'I'm carrying your grandchild. Your son wants me to get an abortion. You need to take my side in this.' At that moment, I packed up, thinking I'd have to make a quick exit."

I was stunned by this confirmation. Natasha's unsubstantiated remarks to Mary Alice and Johnny's wishy-washy suspicions were on target. Hank was having an affair. And that woman would be a prime suspect.

"Why did you prepare to run?"

"Pops said that if she didn't leave the house immediately, he was calling 9-1-1 to have her removed. I couldn't risk staying there with the possibility of police coming out to the farm. Even if she were gone before they arrived, they would have searched the whole house to make sure, and then they'd find me hiding behind the furnace. I nearly left then.

"But the woman said, 'I'm sorry I yelled. My hormones are making me overly emotional. Let's talk about this quietly over a cup of tea.' After that, things quieted down for a while. The only loud noise was the whistling of the tea kettle."

"And that changed?" I asked.

"Yes. I heard retching in the bathroom. But the woman said she was carrying their grandchild, and pregnant women do throw up sometimes, so I didn't think much of that. I heard what sounded like dragging noises in the hall above, but I couldn't figure out what that meant—maybe she was helping Pops move a heavy piece of furniture. But anyway, after that, Hank arrived—"

"How did you know it was your brother?"

"I recognized his voice. I heard him calling for Momma and Pops when he walked in the door. Then I heard him going down the hallway, and the yelling started again—back and forth between Hank and that woman. The furnace was running, so I couldn't tell what they were talking about.

"When I heard the gunshot, I ran up the stairs. I started to open the basement door when it suddenly slammed shut in my face. I pushed it back open and heard the back door close. I walked down the hall and looked into my parents' bedroom. They were both tucked into bed, and Hank was sprawled on top of Pops. I checked Hank for a pulse first—nothing. Then I leaned over Momma. Then I went to Pops. They were all dead.

"I ran back into the basement, grabbed my duffle bag, and left the house through the basement door. I kept running until I reached a neighbor's barn, I knew was warmed by a herd of dairy cows. I thought I could use bales of hay for a mattress, but no sooner I laid down than my sinuses rebelled. I knew I'd be sneezing all night long. I wished I'd stolen a little cash from my parents one night while they slept, but I hadn't. Even if I had some money to pay for room in a cheap fleabag, I had no way to get there. Never was good at planning ahead. That's it."

"It sounds to me like he should be released. The quality of his information certainly is of greater value than a lowly trespassing charge," Kent said.

I was growing to dislike that man. But I wasn't finished with Chuck. There was a gaping hole in his story. "Mr. Monroe, could you please explain how you ended up in possession of your brother's wallet and cell phone?"

"Oh, right, well, uh, I did go back to the farmhouse. I didn't think I'd sleep well in that barn. I didn't want to spend the night in that house—"

"Why not? It was warm, and there was a spare bedroom you could sleep in."

Chucks' eyes looked as if they would pop out of his head. "There were dead bodies in there." His jaw moved up and down as he stared at me. "I may have been living rough for the past few years, but sleeping with the dead was not something I ever experienced. I can't believe you had to ask."

"Then why did you go back?"

"I was thinking I could get a little cash out of the jar in the kitchen, but then I saw Hank's truck out front. At first, I was just going to sleep in it, but when I got inside, I saw Hank's wallet—there was a lot of money in there, big bills, too. And the keys were in the ignition. I drove away, went to a motel on the highway for the night."

"Why didn't you call the sheriff's office and report the crimes at the farmhouse?"

"I didn't have a phone."

"You had your brother's cell."

"I didn't know his password."

"What about the telephone in the motel room?"

"What could I say to the police? I didn't know if it was Mary Alice or some other woman having sex with my brother. And if I didn't know, I couldn't just point a finger."

"Okay, Mr. Monroe, I'm going to need a statement from you about all of that, but right now, let's focus on the night you broke into Mary Alice's home. Did you want to ask her if she killed your parents?"

"I did not break into her house. Sure, I wanted to know whether or not she was out at the farmhouse, and I wanted to know if she was pregnant; but I certainly wouldn't force my way into her house and scare the bejesus out of her."

A knock sounded on the door to the hall. I looked out the window. It was Jack waving around a document. "One minute, gentlemen."

Jack bounced on his toes. "Got the results. Know what killed Florence and Charles Monroe. An overdose of fentanyl."

"The medical examiner was right from the beginning. Check back with toxicology and make sure they tested the stew for any kind of opioids. They found glycosides, the last I checked. I want to make sure there was nothing else."

"Okay. But wait, there's more. The mortar and pestle recovered from the home of Natasha Jones tested positive for traces of fentanyl."

"Thanks, Jack."

I returned to my chair by the table. "Mr. Monroe, do you use any drugs?"

"Not any longer."

"You're sober?"

"Yep. Two years, three months, and five days."

"Still maintain contact with the dealers and friends in your drug days?"

"No. I don't trust myself to be around any of them."

"If someone asked you about where he could find some Oxy, China Girl, or Little C, who would you recommend?"

Chuck's voice raised an octave. "No one. I don't do drugs, and I don't help anyone to feed their habit. Not since I got clean."

I studied his face for any signs of deception, with the hope that my silence would make him reveal more. The stillness in the room did not appear to make him nervous. He seemed more than comfortable with the veil of quiet. I broke the peace.

"Mr. Monroe, when you broke into Mary Alice's home, were you planning on killing her so that you could reclaim your rightful inheritance?"

"I did not break into her home, and I had no intentions of harming Mary Alice."

"But if you talked to her and she said she was there that night, you would have killed her, right?" I pressed.

"No," he said loudly.

"What would you have done?"

Chuck paused for a moment, staring down at the tabletop once again. "I would have demanded that she turn herself in to law enforcement. I would have threatened her that I would tell you people if she didn't do it herself."

"Mr. Howard, I am holding your client on the breaking and entering charges at the garage and at Mary Alice's house for now. I need to confirm the details of Mr. Monroe's statement before I can release him. Chuck, if you remember something you think I should know, tell me."

Chapter Thirty

My computer filled with reports. I could hardly hang up the phone before another call erupted. Test results and tips. I had taken forever to narrow down my suspect list to two people. At the moment, it appeared as if only one of them was responsible, but I still could not be sure it wasn't a conspiracy, and if any other people were involved. I began to doubt I'd ever untangle the knots in this case.

The ballistic test results demonstrated that the bullet that killed Hank Monroe came from a different gun than the one Natasha Jones fired at Mary Alice. Fingerprints and DNA from Natasha Jones were found in the elder Monroe's farmhouse. But then, the same was true of Mary Alice. And in the basement, there was evidence of Chuck Monroe. Not only that, Chuck's fingerprints were on the steering wheel and multiple other locations in Hank's truck, but he'd admitted to stealing it, so that didn't prove anything. Was it a three-way conspiracy after all?

The forensics garage called to report that when they removed the bench seats in the back of the truck's extended cab, they found another gun hidden there. Again, I needed to be patient until I learned if it was the one that killed Hank and found out whose fingerprints were on it. I'd reached that state of confusion where thinking was more a curse than a blessing—my thoughts ran in circles and collapsed on themselves.

I tried to focus. I knew Mary Alice and Chuck were both in safe locations, but Natasha remained missing. That cast guilt more heavily on her than the other two, but was that fair or logical? The phone rang again. I picked it up expecting another squirrelly tip in response to the BOLO on Natasha

Jones. Each call seemed to be wackier than the last. Natasha was seen at Ellis Island, boarding a plane at BWI for France, and hiking the Appalachian Trail in the middle of winter. I sighed and answered the line.

"Spencer."

"Is this the detective working on the murders at the Monroe Farm?" a woman asked.

I rolled my eyes and said, "Yes, Ma'am. Who is this?"

"Flora. Flora Moon. I'm a science teacher."

"Yes?" I said, grateful that it wasn't another psychic—we'd had more than a few of those.

"I work with Natasha Jones. I'd like to speak with you."

Her name finally clicked—the teacher that the principal thought I should interview. "Do you have knowledge of Ms. Jones' whereabouts?"

"I don't know. I am concerned that I might—well, I have a theory, based on known facts. Could I come to your office?"

"Right now?"

"Yes."

"Okay. Check in at the front counter, and they'll send you up."

I called down to the Sergeant at the desk and told him I was expecting someone and requested that she be brought right up. I asked that he give me a buzz when she was on her way. When the call came, I walked out of my office and over to the elevator with my hopes on high. Then the doors slid open, a female deputy stood in front of her. I thanked her and turned to my visitor, a tall, slouchy woman who seemed to think that the only way to get a date was to diminish her height with a floppy posture. Her hair appeared as if it had been through a wind tunnel. In response, I glanced out the window to see how forcefully the breeze blew through the trees, but all was calm. The edge of her skirt hung as crooked on her frame as if some of the hem had unraveled.

"Flora Moon?" I asked.

She stuck out her hand. "Yes. Investigator Spencer?"

I shook her hand as I gave her a nod and led her back to my office. Once we were seated, I asked, "What do you think I need to know?"

"I don't know for sure. I don't have any facts or empirical evidence. I simply remember something she told me a while ago that might explain where she has gone."

"That information could be very helpful," I said.

"It's just I'm not sure. I can't believe Tasha would hurt anyone. I want to do the right thing, but I don't know what it is," Flora said, her voice pinching off every word.

"Tell me what you know, and I'll figure it all out, Ms. Moon."

She looked at me with a furrowed brow and tight lips as the rest of her face went through the contortions of indecisiveness.

"Maybe I shouldn't have come at all. Tasha is my friend, and I feel like I am betraying her."

"Ms. Moon, your friend is missing. From what I've heard, the fact that she is not in her house and has not shown up for work indicates that something is not right with her. Whether she did or did not commit a crime, we'll sort out later. Right now, we need to find her and make sure she is okay."

Watching Flora's eyes dart back and forth was like observing a squirrel in the middle of the road panicking over which way to go.

"Okay, you're right," she said. "Something is wrong. And an old boyfriend has been bothering her at work. Her disappearance could be connected to him."

"Do you know his name?"

"Dylan Flagg."

"F-L-A-G?"

"No two G's."

"Do you know where he lives? Where he works?"

"No. But I think he's been up to the cabin with her in the past. So even if she's there, she's not safe."

"What cabin?"

Flora braided her fingers together and twisted her hands. "Tasha's grandfather built a hunting cabin up in the mountains. Her father still uses it a couple of times each year. Tasha calls it her special place. It's where she recovers from defeats and heals over broken relationships. It's her refuge."

"Have you ever been there?"

"Just once. It was summer. School was out. Tasha's grandmother had died. Before she went up there, she gave me a map and asked me to come up and see her in a couple of days, and I did."

"Do you still have that map?" I asked.

Flora nodded and dug into her voluminous purse that looked big enough to hold a set of encyclopedias. She pulled out the map in record time and handed it to me.

"Did you go out there? What was it like?" I asked her.

"The road to the cabin is awful—like an old log trail. Deep ruts, big potholes—do you call them potholes when the road is all dirt? Anyway, I had to park at the bottom of the driveway because I didn't think my car would make it. As I walked, I worried that I might be following the wrong trail. When I reached a turn, I saw around the corner that Tasha had abandoned her car, too. And still the driveway continued uphill.

"The leaves of the trees blocked the view of the cabin until I was almost on top of it. Inside, there was a huge stone fireplace in the big living room/kitchen combo, and nothing more in the original log-built section. Off to one side, there was a short hallway with two bedrooms and a bath. Tasha told me that piece of the house was added on much later by her dad. I sure hope I'm doing the right thing," Flora said as she rolled her hands on each other.

"I think you are. I hope you will be certain of that soon," I said. "Is there anything else you think I should know?"

She furrowed her brow again and seemed to be deciding whether to reveal more information.

"Ms. Moon, if you know anything that could possibly be of use to this investigation and you do not reveal it to me now, you are risking an obstruction of justice or an aiding and abetting charge when the truth comes out."

Flora bit her lower lip. "She's a really good guidance counselor. She is always there for her students, helping them through tiny mishaps or big tragedies."

"That's nice to know. But—"

Flora blurted out as fast as possible. "Tasha has not been herself lately. Something is troubling her. I'm pretty sure she was having an affair with a married man. Maybe something about that relationship was bothering her lately."

"With whom was she having an affair? Do you know?"

"Not by name. When I asked why she wouldn't tell me his name, she just said, 'You know why people hide affairs.' I asked, 'Is it someone who works in the school?' She laughed and said, 'Are you kidding? Can't you think of a more universal reason for secrecy?' I said, 'He's married?' And she just smiled and walked away. She didn't seem bothered about that at all then—and maybe that's not what's troubling her now. But something is. And I suspect it's something important."

"Ms. Moon, do you know if Miss Jones used any street drugs?"

"No. Well, I don't think so. I know she tried pot in college. I mean, who didn't?" Flora furrowed her brow. "Then again, I suppose drug use might explain the recent change in her demeanor. Wouldn't have been very smart since she'd be putting her job at risk. But, you know, I just don't know—she's always been so secretive."

"Anything else you can tell me?"

She squinched up her nose. "Yeah, there's one other thing. She got flowers delivered to the school. She got angry and told Meg in the main office to take them home. Meg got curious after she left and looked in the trash can for the discarded note. It read: 'I will give you an alibi. Love, Dylan.' I hope that doesn't mean what it sounds like. Anyway, Principal Hughlett said he saw Dylan Flagg in the parking lot arguing with Tasha at the end of school the day before she disappeared. He said Dylan had parked his car blocking Tasha's in its space. He recommended that Tasha get a restraining order, but I don't think she did. Maybe Dylan carjacked her the day she disappeared. Maybe he killed those people.

"I think that's everything, but if she figures out that I told you about the cabin, please explain that I only did it because I was worried about her. She can get quite savage when she feels crossed."

Oh my, curiouser and curiouser. With friends like that…

I thanked Flora and led her back to the elevator. Doubt and worry filled her eyes as the elevator doors shut and whisked her away.

Chapter Thirty-One

J ack and I idled in the street for a moment, studying the residence we were interested in. A double garage had both doors down. To block anyone trying to exit one of the bays, I parked across the end of the driveway of the field stone ranch house where thirty-six-year-old Dylan Flagg lived with his mother. Winter-browned grass, bare-branched trees, and patches of dirty, melting snow gave the place a mournful look. I imagined, though, that the empty, mulched beds around the house and scattered in the front yard would burst into glorious color with the arrival of spring.

Jack stayed outside in case anyone decided to flee, and I went to the front entrance. After I rang the bell, a patrician-looking woman with an elevated chin that allowed her to literally look down her nose at me opened the front door. She raised her eyebrows when she said, "Yes?" with two distinct syllables.

I flipped out my badge. "Sergeant Spencer, ma'am. I'm here to talk to Dylan Flagg."

"He's not here at the moment."

"When do you expect him?"

"He's a grown man. He doesn't report to me."

"Could I come in and ask you a few questions?"

"Whatever for?"

"Dylan Flagg is your son, right?"

"That is correct."

"I would like to talk to you about him. It seems he has gotten entangled in a murder investigation."

"Dylan?" She exclaimed, pulling her chin to her neck and dropping her mouth open. "There must be a mistake. Dylan has good breeding and an exceptional education."

Yeah, like that ever stopped anyone. "Ma'am, I am not implying that your son committed murder. I am saying that he has been involved with someone who is a suspect."

"How distasteful. There must be a mistake. My Dylan is too respectable to spend time with those kinds of people. Yes, yes, do come inside where we can sort this out in private. We can't be discussing matters of this nature like washer women over a backyard fence."

Oh, brother. I sucked it all up and forced myself to be gracious. The sitting room, as she called it, was a space that appeared to be unused. Wooden tables with spindly legs in that familiar dark finish with reddish highlights indicating great age flanked two antique chairs and a medallion settee with elaborate, carved wood arms and legs. They looked as comfortable as a rumble seat.

I settled in and asked, "Do you or your son know Natasha Jones?"

"Of course," she said. "They're engaged to be married."

"Oh, really? How long have they been engaged?"

"More than two years, I believe."

"When did you last see Miss Jones?"

"It's been quite a while. Dylan said someone has been stalking her, and she has avoided coming here because she did not want to lead them to our home."

"I've been told about the stalking of Miss Jones, Mrs. Flagg. And word is that the stalker is your son."

"Oh dear. I can understand how someone would get that mistaken impression. In fact, I warned him about that. He said, though, that he needed to follow her around to keep track of her stalker and to come to her rescue if needed."

"Do you believe everything your son tells you?"

"Of course, I do. He's my son. He would not lie to me. Not my Dylan."

"When did you last see him, Mrs. Flagg?"

"Yesterday, at breakfast. He told me he and Natasha were going out of town for a bit."

She wouldn't look at me when she said that, and, on her cheeks, a light blush surged under the surface of her skin. She's lying. But why and about what?

"Where were they going?" I asked.

"I haven't the vaguest idea."

"You didn't ask?"

"I didn't want to pry."

"May I see your son's room?" I asked.

"Whatever for?"

"I'd like to see if I could find where he and Miss Jones could have gone. I am sure I can get a search warrant, but if we go that route, you will have to entertain me until it's delivered here to the house."

"I have an appointment in a little while. I will have to leave for that rather soon," she said.

I stared at her without comment.

She pursed her lips. "You are a bully, Sergeant. This way, please." She rose to her feet, pushed open a door in the hallway, and stepped back. "After you."

The wall opposite the bed was covered with photographs—some in color, others in black and white. Every one of them included Natasha Jones, alone or with others. Some were sharp and defined with bright colors. Others looked as if they were taken at a great distance or through window glass.

"As you can see, Dylan is very devoted to his fiancée."

Devoted? Obsessive is the word that came to my mind, but I kept that thought to myself.

"They are going to set a date for their marriage once they resolve the stalker problem."

"Have they reported that to the Sheriff's Office?"

"Oh, yes. Of course, nothing came of it. The stalker hadn't threatened her life, so they said that nothing could be done."

I made a mental note to check for a record of that report when I returned to my office. I poked around Dylan's desk looking for anything relevant.

"May I take his laptop with me and look for travel booking information on it?"

"No, I will have to insist on a search warrant. I can't have you walking all over my boy on a fishing expedition."

My head twisted towards the bedroom window. I thought I heard something. I crossed the room and pulled back the drapes. A shout of "Sergeant" rang out. A figure dashed between the house and the pool and out the gate beside the pool. I saw the top of Jack's head popping above the exterior fence down the side, moving to the corner, and across the back.

I bolted to the door with Mrs. Flagg grabbing at my arm. I shook her off, raced down the hall, out the front door, and into the backyard. The figure headed for the woods at the back of the lot, and Jack was behind him.

To my right, a man on a riding lawn mower jumped off and ran toward Jack, yelling, "Hey, hey! What are you doing? Stop, or I'll call the police!"

I intercepted him and flashed my badge. "We are the police. Back off."

Once I hit the glade of regal blue spruce trees, I spotted Jack, looking around in every direction.

"I lost him, Sergeant."

"Lost him? How?"

"I don't know. One minute he was right ahead of me, and then he was gone."

The forested area was narrow and long, carpeted with pine needles. We meandered through it for twenty minutes before we gave up. Back at the house, Mrs. Flagg stood as straight as a pillar beside the pool fence.

"Ma'am, I could charge you right now with aiding and abetting," I told her.

"I think I should call my lawyer."

"Fine. Go right ahead," I said as I slapped my card into her hand. "It's in your best interests to call me if he returns home."

"I didn't know he was here," she objected.

Right, lady, right. Jack and I went back to the car, and he called in a BOLO on the car and the person of Dylan Flagg. I never got close enough to be able to describe him with any accuracy, but I still had no doubt about his identity. Did I now have four possible suspects? Or did I have one growing conspiracy?

Chapter Thirty-Two

J ack and I met for breakfast at a little coffee place a block from the justice complex. I wanted Jack's company to help me find that little cabin in the mountains, but there were too many things that needed to be done back here. Jack argued with me about that, insisting that I needed him or someone to ride along.

With no guarantee that I'd find Natasha Jones, I didn't really want to use him or any other officer as back-up. I told Jack it was more important for him to continue the search for Dylan Flagg and try to find confirmation of the Chuck and Mary Alice versions of events. I hoped he didn't unearth another possible suspect in the process. I remembered that old saying: Be careful what you wish for, you just might get it.

If I failed in solving this case, I might have to pursue another career. I wasn't worried that I'd be fired. I just knew that if I didn't get this case right, I didn't have what it took. I would know I wasn't good enough. Others would be disappointed in me, but I'd be unforgiving of myself.

Once I left the highway and veered off onto a state road, the piles of snow left by the plow grew higher and higher. Soon, I was seeing smaller side streets that no one had dared to travel. The plowing grew more erratic as I turned onto the road leading to the mountains. In spots, only one lane was cleared.

I reached my final left before the turn-off to the cabin, but the road appeared impassable without four-wheel drive. I pulled into the parking lot of Ralph's Grocery. The corner convenience store looked like so many way-out in the country—paint peeling off the eaves, droopy awnings over the windows, a roof with as many patches as a multicolored quilt, and a stream of wood smoke emanating from a stove pipe.

Since the parking lot held only two pick-up trucks, the crowd gathered around the potbelly stove surprised me. A man behind the counter with a Z.Z. Top beard but none of the band's sartorial splendor, stood up and said, "How do, ma'am. What can I do ya for?"

After I deciphered the meaning of his statement, I did my best to fit in with the crowd, laying on my long-abandoned southern accent.

"Well, I'm lookin' for Natasha Jones. I heard her grandpa had a cabin out in these parts, and I was fixin' to chew the fat with her a bit."

"Sure, she's out at the cabin. Came through here a couple of days ago. There weren't no way she was a'gonna get her little sports car up that road, so she ax iffen I could let her park it in the shed till she was ready to drive home. I told her sure 'nough. Not a problem. I'm fixing to drive the car up to the cabin if she's still there when the snow melts."

A clean-shaven man with slicked back hair who was seated by the stove said, "Ma'am, you ain't gonna get that car of yours up that road either."

"He's right, ma'am," Z.Z. Topp beard said. "I do have space for you to park out in the shed next to Miss Tasha's car iffen you want to walk. Ain't no more than a mile up yonder, and the driveway's not too long, but it's all uphill."

I pulled out my cell and said, "Maybe I should call first."

"Do you have a signal on that thing?"

I looked down at the screen and shook my head.

"Didn't think so. I gotta a regular phone, but there ain't one out at the cabin so it won't do ya much good."

"Okay, then. I'll take you up on the offer of a parking space and walk up there."

As he put on his jacket to assist me outside, he said, "Make sure you pay attention to the passin' of time out there. I know it's hard when you wommin folk get to talking and such, but iffen you don't want to be caught walking back in the dark, make sure you check yer watch. The temperature drops like a rock at night, and this here mountain is crawlin' with bears and bobcats.

You wouldn't want to meet one in the dark."

With that cheery thought, I pulled into the parking spot and trudged off through the snow. The surface, which had melted during the previous day and frozen again the night before, now crunched as I walked through it, leaving deep indentations in my wake. Birds flew through the trees, and sparkles of sunlight pierced through the empty, overhanging branches of the trees.

Loud thumps heralded the dumping of burdens from the branches as the warmth of the day made the ice and snow slide to the ground. I found it hard to believe that a killer dwelled in the midst of all this pastoral peace, but if I was right, a person or one of the people who terminated the lives of three others was waiting at the end of my hike. Along the way, I saw traces of her footprints and more recent valleys carved down the middle of the road by tire tracks.

When I reached the driveway, I noticed that a vehicle had driven to some point beyond it. Most peculiar, though, were the footprints, fresher than those I followed and leading to the entrance but coming from the opposite direction that I travelled. Those gave me pause. Had someone joined Jones at the cabin? I followed those prints up the hill until the cabin was in sight. They only kept going a few feet further before leaving the drive and plunging into the woods. I considered the possible significance and decided in all likelihood a hunter tracking deer had passed this way in search of a target.

I hunkered down behind a clump of short juniper trees that concealed my presence while revealing a few glimpses of the cabin. I saw a shape move past one window and then the other. I waited. When the figure walked past again, I made another move closer and then closer still, crouching down by the edge of the porch. I focused on the cabin and the person inside, not thinking about any peril approaching in the snow.

That was a major mistake.

I heard the glass-breaking sound of cracking ice behind my back. I rose and turned to face the barrel of a handgun inches from my nose. A man shoved me sideways and jammed his weapon into my neck. Before I knew it, he slipped my service revolver out of my holster with one hand and, with the other, grabbed my right arm, twisting it painfully up on my back. The taste of chocolate chips lit up my tongue. I fought back tears at the realization of my mistake. I'd failed again.

He walked me up the steps, all the while poking me with the muzzle of his gun just because he could.

"It's not a good idea to barge in on a woman out in the woods alone," he said. "You could find yourself looking down the wrong end of a shotgun. Knock first."

It felt awkward using my left hand, but I did it.

Natasha called out, "Come on in, it's open."

My assailant turned the knob and pushed open the door open. "Tasha—" he began.

A loud thud rang out, and he dropped to the floor beside me. I looked up and saw Natasha Jones hanging over the door, wielding a large cast-iron skillet.

"Who the hell are you?" she demanded.

"Sergeant Spencer. Sheriff's Department."

"Well, thank heavens. Do you have handcuffs?

"Yes, but—"

"Get them around his wrists before he wakes up."

"Who is he?

"Dylan Flagg. He's dangerous. I think he murdered someone. He's been stalking me and harassing me, and he followed me up here. He used to be my boyfriend, and now he won't leave me alone."

"Are you standing on something?

Yes, a step ladder. We can talk once he's under control."

She stepped down and out from behind the door, setting the skillet on a small table.

The body on the floor groaned.

"Hurry, hurry. Cuff him, and I'll explain everything." She whipped out a rope, from God knows where, and wrapped it around his ankles, pulling them tight and tying the rope off.

I slipped on the cuffs and asked for a pencil. I stuck the end into the barrel of the gun and lifted it from where it had fallen. "You got a paper bag?"

She stepped into the kitchen area and pulled out a plastic grocery store sack. "Will this do?"

"It'll have to," I said. I slid the gun in and shoved it all in my jacket pocket. I then grabbed my service revolver from his back waistband. "Now tell me, Miss Jones, what's going on here?"

She squinted her eyes, picked up the skillet with one hand, and bounced the bottom of it on the other and asked, "How do you know my name?"

"I came to interview you at the school. But you left before I got there. I've been looking for you everywhere."

"How did you know about this cabin?"

If she didn't stop bouncing that skillet soon, I was going to have to take it from her. But how could I disarm and constrain her when my cuffs were already busy?

"Your friends were worried. You were missing. I had to find out if you were okay," I explained.

She set the skillet back down, and I relaxed a little.

"Well, I came out here to get away from him. I saw him creeping in the front yard. He was making all these pseudo-commando moves. He thinks he's this rugged outdoorsman, but he's just a city boy in a flannel shirt. I knew he was going to come into the cabin at some point. I set up the step ladder and put the skillet on the top step, so I'd be ready to bash him over the head when he did. He was really scaring me."

She looked at him with undisguised contempt. "I think he killed my fiancé."

Chapter Thirty-Three

Natasha explained that the man on the floor was Dylan Flagg, her ex-boyfriend, and she was in the process of recounting the history of their relationship when moans and groans from his prone body erupted into lots of squirming and a yell for help. Natasha picked up the skillet and bashed him again. She shoved a kitchen sponge into his mouth. She kicked his body to make him lie on his side. A trickle of blood ran from just above his ear, down across his cheek, and plopped onto the floor.

Her lack of hesitation in bludgeoning him was worrying. She could have been as quick to pull a trigger. Or if this ex-boyfriend found out about Hank, he could have fired the killing shot. I wanted him alive.

"Careful, Miss Jones. You could kill him with that thing."

"That would be no great loss, believe me." She stared down at the inanimate body on the floor. Her head pivoted; her brows furrowed. She waved the skillet in the air as she looked straight at me. "Why were you looking for me in the first place?"

"I wanted to talk to you about the deaths of Hank Monroe and his parents."

"Hank, who?"

"Really, Miss Jones. Do you think I'd go to all this trouble if I wasn't certain that you knew Hank Monroe?"

Natasha said nothing for two long minutes as she bounced the skillet on the palm of her hand. I remained silent, determined to wait her out. When she finally spoke, it was as if she'd forgotten that she denied knowing Hank.

"Are you saying Hank is dead? And his parents are dead?"

"Did you really need me to tell you?" I asked.

"How do you think I would find out about that out here in the middle of nowhere?"

"Because they died before you left town to come to the cabin, as you well know."

"Well, who killed them?"

I ran my gaze over her face, looking for any sign of deception. She turned her face away.

She said, "I think that piece of crap on the floor might be responsible. He was very jealous of my relationship with Hank." She shook her head. "Hank, dead. His parents, too."

"I thought you didn't know they were dead."

"Well, I'd heard, but it wasn't a reliable source.'

"Who told you?"

"That piece of crap on the floor—that's why I think he killed them."

"I suppose that's possible, but if he did, he must have had an accomplice."

"Don't look at me." She pointed at Dylan. "I've been trying to get rid of him. Did Hank's wife finally go over the deep end?"

"Perhaps."

"That one is mentally ill. Although my major was child psychology, I know it when I see abnormalities in adults, too."

"Have you ever interacted with her?"

"No. Never met the woman."

"She said you came to her house."

"She would. She's a liar."

"How do you know this?"

"Hank told me all about her. She hated his parents but was very sweet to them to keep them off balance. They adored her, and she wanted to keep it that way. That Mary Alice is a major manipulator and distorts truth out of habit, even when it's not in her best interest."

I felt she had wrested control of this situation, and I wanted to shake her confidence even though I was fearful of angering her.

"Is it true you're pregnant with Hank's child?"

"Who told you that?" she yelled.

I took a step back, getting out of the reach of the heavy, black iron pan. "Hank's brother Chuck."

Natasha blew out a gust of air and grinned. "Pfft! Now you know. Chuck wanted to get his share of the inheritance back, so he killed his whole family. You need to arrest him before he runs away again."

"You think so?" I asked.

"Either he killed all three by himself, or that bitch-wife of Hank's helped him. I imagine they've both claimed ignorance, but don't the guilty do that all the time?"

"That's true," I said, with a nod of my head. "Where were you on that night?"

"At home, of course."

"Really? The farmer up the road said that a car matching the description of yours was parked at the end of his driveway that night."

"A farmer? Like a farmer knows anything about sports cars."

"He said it was a Miata, and he said it was red. According to DMV records, you own a red Miata. How do you explain that?"

"Easy peasy. It wasn't my red Miata because I was at home."

"Another thing came up in our lab. Traces of fentanyl were found in a mortar and pestle on the top shelf of your closet. How did that get there?"

"Oh, that bastard! Hank asked to use it to grind up some pills. He said his mother was having difficulty swallowing, so he wanted her to be able to drink her medication. I questioned his logic at the time, but I always give in to Hank."

"Why don't you put that skillet away in the kitchen?"

"He might wake up again."

"He's cuffed and gagged, so who cares?"

"Okay. All right," she said as she walked past me, spinning around quicker than I could draw my gun. Excruciating pain turned into oblivion.

Chapter Thirty-Four

I sensed someone was rolling me around, manipulating my body, but I couldn't understand it or shake off the miasma that clouded my brain. As the fogginess dissipated, I felt cold planks of wood on my cheek. I tried to use my hands to push up, but couldn't make them move. Was I paralyzed? I kicked my legs, both moved together, and I felt a sensation of tightness around my ankles. I lifted my hands an inch, and the pain darted through my shoulders. I dropped them to the floor and heard the distinctive clink of metal. I was handcuffed.

I heard footsteps. I looked around. Natasha pointed my own service revolver at my face. Panic rose in my throat. I closed my eyes. My heart pounded like a battering ram, as if attempting to break free. I held my breath. For a moment, all was still.

I doubled over with pain as something forceful slammed into my gut. I didn't want to respond, but a loud yell erupted against my will. I heard laughter. Agony rang through my head. An image of the skillet flashed through my consciousness, then I was gone again.

* * *

My cheek was tender. Small particles pushed into my skin as if I were lying on a bed of gravel. The rest of my face burned from the cold. My shoulders and arms ached like I'd done a kajillion pull-ups. My gut felt bruised all the way back to my spine. I could not understand why I was unable to move or why breathing was so difficult. I kept my eyes shut, unwilling to open them and face the day.

The events of the night before rushed back into my thoughts like a tape played on fast forward. I suppressed my anxiety and thoughts of failure. I needed to assess my situation and weigh my options. I slowly raised my eyelids. I lay on the floor. If I moved my legs, I felt the scratchy abrasion of rope rubbing on my ankles. My boots were gone. My socks, too. My hands were bound behind my back. I raised them slightly, wincing at the pain and hearing the jingle of metal. Bound with my own handcuffs—how humiliating.

Every small movement brought a surge of distress to one part of my body or another. Regardless, I needed to sit up. I tried rolling to a sitting position. In my mind, moving my body from a rough L shape on my side to the same configuration in a seated position seemed like a simple, fluid motion. Unfortunately, my arms got in the way. I ended up flat on my face, my nose smashed, my mouth bashed on the floor.

My struggle awoke my compatriot in bondage. I heard him bucking at his constraints and gagging on the sponge shoved into his mouth. I used my feet to push my body into position to see him. I panted with exhaustion by the time he was in my line of sight. I pushed the top of my body up by arching my lower back.

"Dylan, settle down. You need to be still and think," I told him.

In response, he wiggled harder, and the muffled sounds from his mouth barked with anger and fear. I used my feet to inch closer to the wall. I wasn't sure how I could use the upright surface to get out of my predicament, but at least I was doing something.

I rolled up on my side at the bottom of the arched passageway to the addition. Pushing with my feet and grabbing with my fingers, I struggled to get my back up against the wall. I failed the first few times, quieted my breath, and tried again. Finally, I managed to get into a sitting position—a precarious one, but nonetheless, I was resting on my backside with a clear view of most of the room. A few feet away, I spotted the handcuff key on the floor.

I paused in my efforts to catch my breath. Once I stopped exerting myself, the cold surprised me again, seeping into my clothes, raising goosebumps up and down my arms. The fireplace held nothing but ashes, which made sense after the passage of time. Nonetheless, I couldn't understand why the baseboard heat wasn't warming the place. Was it that cold outside that the heaters couldn't keep up? I held my breath and listened. No wind. The drip of falling water. The sun was shining brightly—it wasn't rain falling from the sky but melt running down from the eaves and the trees. Then, I noticed that the little red light on the unit closest to the front door was not lit.

Thanks a lot, Natasha.

I'd always thought it was an urban myth that physically fit prisoners, given enough time, could pull their legs through the handcuffs and get their hands to the front. If I could do that, I could retrieve the key Natasha dropped and maybe, just maybe, unlock the cuffs.

I didn't really think it was possible, but I knew I had longer than average arms for my height, and I had to try. The sense of purpose kept my panic at bay. I forced my spine to straighten and, steeling myself against the pain, rolled my shoulders back and forth to warm up the muscles. I tucked my bound hands under my buttocks and pulled them down to the back of my thighs. It felt as if I were pulling my tendons from the bone. I paused, panting, reestablishing my balance, and calming my breath.

Leaning my back against the wall and pulling my legs into my chest, I inched the cuffs up the back of my thighs and finally to the bend of my knees. Squeezing my eyes shut and clenching my jaw tight to cope with the agony I caused my body, I lifted my lower legs slowly, taking time to steady myself with every increment of height. Sucking in my gut, I raised them higher and higher. My arms drew up to the back of my calves, then to my ankles.

Almost there. I tugged, but my cuffs were stuck. I could not get them past the back of my foot. I made my abdominal muscles tighten even more and squeezed my shins into my face despite the objections of my battered mouth and nose. I became aware again of the continued senseless thrashing and moaning of my bonded companion.

"Shut the hell up," I yelled at him.

For a moment, he was still. That precious moment gave me the peace to impose my will on my legs. I rolled my weight onto my left butt cheek and forced my right foot to slip down and through the handcuffs. Bound as I was, both feet moved as one, but it all stopped when the cuffs hit the back of my left foot. I shifted my weight to the right side, and both hands were in my lap.

I enjoyed a few seconds of triumph, and then the pain rushed full force into my limbs. My shoulders and elbows throbbed with every heartbeat. My legs cramped and ached, making me want to scream or cry or both.

Dylan's muffled babbling grew in intensity. I couldn't understand a word, but his writhing eyebrows communicated well enough to get the message across.

"You want me to remove the tape from your hands?" I asked.

He nodded once, twice, with slow deliberation, then, over and over with desperate vigor. I shrugged. His thrashing grew intense, and I wondered if it was possible for him to churn up enough friction to set himself on fire. I knew I needed to move, but I was so exhausted. My head ached, my arms and legs rebelled at the thought of exertion. Inertia, however, was not an option.

I had two choices: free Dylan's hands and depend on him to return the favor, or try to get over to the key and manipulate it into the keyhole of the restraints, hoping for success in unlocking the cuffs. I recoiled from anything that involved trusting Dylan. I put my restrained hands to the side of my left hip and pulled and wiggled my way to the key.

Again and again, I tried inserting that key, but my fingers were numb from the reduced circulation in the tips. I cried with frustration, and Dylan harmonized with his indistinct, out-of-tune objections. I scooted over to the outside wall, stretched my hands up to place the key on the table by the door so that I wouldn't lose it. I leaned forward to try to untie the rope around my ankles.

Chapter Thirty-Five

Not easy to untie ankle restraints with bound hands, but it was possible, and I did it. Feeling confident, I placed my palms on the little table and hoped the support might make a difference. Though my arms and shoulders protested, I pushed upward. My legs wobbled, and I plopped down onto the floor. I rolled to my knees, waited for the muscles to stop shaking, and succeeded in pushing myself to my feet again.

I leaned against the table, hoping to stay upright and unlock my restraints, but success eluded me. I had no choice—I needed to get down to that little store while still encumbered with my steel bracelets and get someone there to unlock them. I slid the key into my pocket and looked down at Dylan, who was once again raising a fuss.

"Dylan, Dylan, be still and shut up a minute." Still, he mumbled, grumbled, and squirmed. I squatted down in front of him. "Dylan, I'll take that sponge out of your mouth if you cut it out."

His eyes darted up to mine with a question in his eyes.

"Yes, I'm serious. Don't you bite me, or I'll shove it back in." I pulled it out, and frankly, it was disgusting—not as wet as I thought it would be, which spoke to his endless prattle and unquenched thirst. "Okay, I'm going to get you some water."

He spoke with a scratchy, raspy voice. "Take the tape off my damn hands."

"Sorry, Dylan. I don't trust you enough for that, particularly since I'm still cuffed."

He tried to voice his objection but was cut off by a fit of coughing.

"Hang on, Dylan. I'm filling a cup with water, and I'll see if I can find a straw."

Oh, my, he was in luck. A box of those bendy straws in the first drawer I opened. I stuck one into a mug of water from the kitchen tap and knelt in front of him. I bent the straw towards his mouth, and he sucked like a hungry piglet. I pulled it out of his mouth.

"More. More. C'mon. C'mon."

"Dylan, if you drink it too fast, you may choke or even throw up. Then, you could asphyxiate on your own vomit. I'm going to set this cup near your mouth so that you can raise your head and sip. If you squirm, you could knock it over. Sip it slowly, okay?"

Nodding his head, Dylan said, "Yes. Yes. I promise. Please. Are you just going to leave me here? I'll freeze to death."

"No, you won't. The baseboard heaters are off, but I'm going to turn them back on and go get help."

"Build a fire, too?"

"No. It would take too long. I've got to get help," I said.

I positioned his water and got the heat running. I fought the loose, uncooperative knob for a couple of minutes before I got it to open. I certainly have taken the free movement of my hands for granted. Outside on the shady porch, the cold slapped me in the face. I cursed my luck and hurried out of the shade around the house. The air was a bit warmer in the patches of sunshine splattered on the driveway. I trudged out to the dirt road, cautious not to step in a chuck hole and lose my balance.

I wasn't quite halfway to the store when I heard a vehicle approaching. I stepped out of the footprint path I was following and ducked down into the ditch on the side of the road.

The truck jerked to a stop, the passenger door flew open, and there was Jack running towards me and hollering, "Charley, Charley, is that you?"

"Yes. No other," I said with a grin as I stood up.

He threw open his arms to give me a hug, but was blocked from a close embrace by my cuffed hands. "Jeez, Charley! You escaped in handcuffs?"

"I'll tell you all about it later. Just get these damned things off me."

Jack obliged, and I rubbed the life back into my wrists as he talked. "We didn't think we'd find you here. We were coming up to haul Natasha Jones in for questioning. The guys at the store said you'd already left."

"I wonder why they thought that?"

"Your car was gone, and Jones' Miata was still in the shed."

"She stole my car?"

"Well, I guess so."

"You need to put out a BOLO."

"Already did."

"Modify it. Natasha Jones is armed and dangerous."

I winced as I hopped into the back seat of the extended cab truck. Up front, Jack got on the radio to change the alert. While he was at it, he requested a forensic team and back-up—in four-wheel drive or ready for a bit of a hike through snow. I leaned over the front seat and directed the driver up to the cabin.

Dylan was so glad to have his legs untied and the tape removed from his arms that he didn't give Jack and the other deputy any trouble at all. Jack helped him stretch out his joints. When Jack found a first aid kit, they rubbed salve on my wrists and ankles and then on Dylan's. All the while, the deputy brewed up a pot of coffee.

The only time Dylan objected was when Jack tried to put on the handcuffs. Dylan whined like a baby. "Don't cuff me. Puh-leez. I'll tell you everything I know. Pleeez."

"Jack, wrap gauze around his wrists and cuff him in front for now so he can have a cup of coffee with us before we go."

"We're going to have to move them to the back before we transport."

"I know," I said.

Beside me, Dylan whimpered. He blew on his cup and took a couple of sips. "Ahhhh," he said. "I can't tell you how great this is. But let me tell you what I know about Natasha Jones and what happened out at the farm the night those people died."

"Dylan, let's save all that until we get into town. We'll read you your rights and record every word you have to say."

"You mean I'm going to be charged?"

I closed my eyes, hardly believing he had to ask. When I opened them, his eager face was staring at mine.

"Dylan, you held a gun to my head. You forced me into this cabin. You may be involved in a triple murder—either in the commission or after the fact. Of course, you'll be charged."

"Will I go to prison?" Dylan asked, his eyes as full of tears as a little child.

"It depends on you, Dylan. Being cooperative may not keep you out of prison, but it can shorten your sentence."

"Okay. Okay. I was out at the farm—"

"Stop," I said, holding up the palm of my hand like a school crossing guard. "Save it. Finish your coffee. And relax. We are leaving soon. Just as soon as back-up gets here."

Chapter Thirty-Six

After we arrived at the justice center, Jack said, "I need a minute before you talk to Mr. Flagg.". "I had a visitor before we went out to look for you. Mary Alice Monroe came to the station. She told the front desk she needed to speak to you. The front desk told her that you weren't in the building. She sat down to wait.

"I guess it was about a half-hour later when they let me know she was still there and asked me what to do with her, and I came right down. I looked through the little peephole and saw her reading a Laura Lippman book."

"Whoa, Jack, wait a minute. You noticed the author's name on the book cover she was reading?"

"That writer is one of my favorites. I notice it all the time."

I shook my head in amazement. "Jack, you are full of surprises. Okay— sorry for the interruption."

"Anyway, I came into the public space and asked if I could help her. She insisted she needed to speak to you and asked if you were back yet.

"I told her you weren't and asked if she'd be willing to talk to me. She nodded, and I asked about her lawyer. She said, 'I'll sign a paper waiving my rights. I've been thinking a lot, and I found some evidence. If I don't tell you all about it, you might not find who killed Pops.' So, I took her back to my desk for a chat. I think you ought to listen to the tape. If I need to make an editorial comment, I'll hit pause."

"You think it will have some bearing on my questioning of Mr. Flagg?"

"It might."

"Okay, let's go."

I left Dylan Flagg to cool his heels in the interrogation room and followed Jack to his desk. He pressed "play" on the recorder. I listened as he read Mary Alice her rights, and she signed the waiver. Then, Jack asked the first question.

"Do you know anything about the whereabouts of Sergeant Spencer?"

"No. You mean you don't know where she is?"

"Not specifically. I was hoping that the evidence you found was related to that."

"I'm sorry. Do you think she's okay?"

"We hope so. Now what new evidence do you have?"

"Let me explain first. My lawyer took me to that hotel. I had a lot of time to think. I've been trying to sort everything out. I believe my attorney was too harsh on Sergeant Spencer. Ms. Tremont said that law enforcement always lies about wills and things like that to trick people. But then Ms. Tremont said something else that contradicted that. She said with the money I would inherit I could easily afford to stay at that expensive hotel. To me, that meant she thought the sergeant was telling the truth. That's when I realized that my lawyer wasn't totally honest with me. And it made me wonder if maybe Sergeant Spencer had been telling the truth all along.

"Then I remembered something that might be important. Hank's hiding place. I have known for a long time that Hank stashed things he didn't want me to see in a secret compartment in his dresser. At one time, I used to go there often to try to figure him out and know what he was doing. I hadn't done that in years because I stopped caring enough to bother. I started thinking that something might be in there that could answer a few questions about the murders."

"Your house was searched. We should have found that."

"Hank hid it very well in the dresser he built with his own hands. Even if you had found the hiding place, I don't think you could have opened it without my assistance unless you used an axe. I didn't examine his dresser before I left the house for the hotel, but I think I would have noticed if the stash hole had been bothered. And I sure wouldn't have missed it if you guys chopped it up.

"Also, if you had found it, I'm sure Sergeant Spencer would have asked me about the contents or what we used it for. The other thing that troubled me was that I told Sergeant Spencer that it might have been Chuck who broke into my house. But

sitting in that hotel room, I ran the scene over and over in my head and decided that conclusion was not logical. I would have opened the door for Chuck, and I think he would know that. He didn't need to break in. Because of that deduction, I decided to leave the hotel against my attorney's express instructions. Then, I did something that I think was illegal."

"Is that suspected crime necessary to your story?"

"Yes, it is."

"What did you do, Mrs. Monroe?"

"I had to check it out. I called Uber and went to my house. I broke the 'X' of yellow police tape across the front door and went inside."

"Oh, jeez. This new evidence, you found it in that hiding place?"

"Yes, but don't blame the searchers. It was well concealed. Between the top and second drawers on his dresser, there is a skinny document drawer. It's nearly invisible. You need to remove the other drawers and press two release spots simultaneously to open it. Inside, I found this letter."

Jack pressed pause. "I didn't read it out loud. I can read it to you now. Otherwise, the rest of the tape won't make a lot of sense. Jack picked up a folded piece of paper, smoothed it out, and read:

"Dear Hank,

This is your brother Chuck. A friend of mine was driving through your town, and he offered to leave this letter in your pick-up truck. I am writing to let you know that I am coming back to talk to Momma and Pops. I am telling you so that you can do the right thing and tell our parents the truth. Admit that you lied when you said that I sexually abused you. If you do that, I will gladly sign over my share of the estate to you. I simply want to make peace with my parents before it is too late.

See you soon, Chuck.

"At this point," Jack said, "Mary Alice started to speak, but I held up a finger to get her to stop so I could read it again." Jack pressed fast forward, then started the tape rolling.

I listened as the recording continued rolling for a minute without any conversation. The first person to speak was Jack.

"Okay, Mary Alice. What does this letter tell you?"

"That Hank lied to his parents about Chuck sexually abusing him. Momma and Pops believed Hank, and that was the cause of the estrangement. Also, it tells me that Chuck would not have killed his parents because he wanted to reconnect with them. I don't think Hank would have either. Hank was a nasty piece of work, but I don't think he would commit murder."

"Who do you think did?"

"Most likely that Tasha woman. She tried to take my life, and that tells me she was capable of murder. And, it is possible that the man who broke into my house helped her. But I don't know anything about him, so I probably shouldn't have said that."

"Don't worry. We won't arrest anyone based on your guesses. It takes more than that. I've been typing your statement as we were talking, and am printing out a copy. Someone will bring it in right away. Look it over and make sure it's accurate. If it is, sign it. If not, let me know what changes I need to make. I must make a phone call, but I'll be right back."

Jack pressed pause on the tape recorder and turned to me. "I forgot to turn off the machine, and it kept recording after I left the room.

I listened to the quiet sounds. Mary Alice's sighs. The pen scratching across paper. The pen dropping on the table. A scraping noise that sounded like the chair legs rubbing against the concrete floor.

Jack stopped the tape again. "While Mary Alice was in there alone, I got the search warrant and the order to roll out to Natasha Jones' cabin. At that point, I briefed Deputy Rodgers. You'll hear her come into the room and talk to Mary Alice."

I heard an opening door on the tape. A young female voice—that I assumed belonged to Rodgers—spoke first.

"All finished? Were you able to sign it?"

"Yes."

"Good. Deputy Preston asked me to apologize to you. He had to rush out on important business. If there is nothing else, I'll show you to the door."

"Was it something I said?" Mary Alice asked.

"Excuse me?"

"I mean, did I say something that made him run off like that?"

CHAPTER THIRTY-SIX

"Oh, no. There're always emergencies around here."

"Did they find Sergeant Spencer?"

"Oh, I know nothing about that."

"Sergeant Spencer will see my statement, right?"

"I'm sure she will."

"Tell her to call me if she has any questions."

Chapter Thirty-Seven

I paused outside the door to the interrogation room, gathering my thoughts. If Dylan Flagg truly wanted to tell the truth to save himself, the interview could be very straightforward. However, there was a possibility that he was involved or directly responsible for one or more of the deaths at the Monroe farm. I hoped for the former but mentally prepared for the latter.

I took a deep breath and pushed my way inside. I'd have to describe Dylan as handsome even in his battered state. However, despite what he'd been through, he appeared as arrogant as someone who inherited from his mother, by accident of birth, a sense of superiority that meant the rules didn't apply to him. He proved my impression with his first remarks.

"Hey, about time. I thought you'd forgotten all about me in here. Did you break for dinner? I haven't eaten a decent meal in…well, I don't remember when."

"I thought a deputy brought you a sandwich and a drink," I said, noting the crumbled paper and aluminum can on the far end of the table.

"You call that a decent meal? A snack. That's all it was. A snack."

"If it makes you feel any better, no, I didn't have dinner. I made do with a pack of crackers.'

"Pfft! You're a woman. You're used to starving yourself."

I wanted to light into him for that remark, but I let it pass.

"First order of business, Mr. Flagg, is the reading of your rights. Please pay attention. Here is a written copy for you to follow along."

I slid the paper across the table. I read to him from my copy, careful to enunciate each word. I ignored his hand motions indicating I should speed it up.

"I don't want an attorney because I didn't do anything wrong. I'm here as a good citizen with a desire to help law enforcement," he said.

"Yes, sir. Are you saying you want to waive your rights to legal counsel?"

"Yes, I am. Let's get this thing going."

"All in due time, Mr. Flagg. Here is a waiver affirming that you are giving up the right to an attorney at this time." I placed the form and a pen in front of him, and he started signing without hesitation. "One moment, Mr. Flagg. Please read the statement before you sign it."

"Why? Are you lying to me about what's in here?"

"No, sir. But…"

"Pffft!" He slid the document, with his signature, over to my side of the table. "Let's get on with it."

"Where were you on the evening of Thursday, January twenty-third?"

"I was out at the Monroe place. At the time, I didn't know who owned the farm. I learned that later."

"Why were you there?"

"I was following my fiancé, Natasha Jones."

Fiancé? I doubted that. For now, though, I'd let that lie pass. "Did she ask you to follow her?"

"No. No. Nothing like that. Tasha thought she could take care of herself, but I knew better. I followed her everywhere to keep her safe."

"Did she know you were following her?"

"No. As I said, she thought she could take care of herself."

Admission to stalking. I put that on the back burner and let it simmer.

"What did you do when you reached the Monroe farm?"

"I saw her park, and I kept driving up the street until I found a place up the road to pull off. I jumped out and walked back to her car. She was gone by the time I got there, but I followed her footsteps to the front yard of the farmhouse up the road. I saw her path go up on the front porch. I went to a window and pulled myself up on the windowsill. I saw her talking to an old couple. I eased down as quick as I could and listened."

I visualized the house with its farmhouse porch and the long distance from the ground to the panes of glass.

"You pulled yourself up on those windowsills with your hands?"

"Guns, baby, guns," he said, extending and flexing his arms, grinning like a demented clown. Spreading his elbows, he added. "Poke these babies in the corners, and it's a piece of cake."

I couldn't help it. I rolled my eyes. I did, however, resist the temptation to ask him how much experience he had peering into people's windows.

"What did you hear?"

"Not much. Everything was muffled, and none of the words were distinct. But it was obvious they were arguing when the man started yelling. Then Tasha raised her voice. After that, everything quieted down. Tasha's voice sounded more distant at that point, so I crept around looking in other windows, trying to find her until I got back to the original room. She was carrying a tray loaded with a teapot, teacups, and stuff into there. I dropped down to the ground again." Dylan cleared his throat and clutched at his neck. "Hey, could I get another drink? I'm really parched. I'm too thirsty to keep talking much longer."

I wanted to bop him in the nose, but instead went to the door, spotted a deputy, and asked for his help. Returning to my seat, I said, "The drink is on the way."

He clutched his throat, employing a faked rasp, and said, "Wait. Gotta have a sip."

I sat and studied him. He smiled and winked. I wanted to throttle him. The deputy came in, placed the soda on the table. Dylan grabbed it, flipped the top, and guzzled as if his life depended on it.

"Okay, Mr. Flagg. Can we continue now?"

He waved his hand sideways, grabbed the can, and took a sip. "Okay. Much better. Well, I was getting a bit bored and rather cold. I was thinking about going back to my car and warming up." He paused.

I felt as if I were his puppet, but asked another question anyway. "Did you go there, or did you stay where you were for some reason?"

"Weird sounds started coming from the house. Tasha was using that voice

I always teased her about—the one I call her social worker's voice. I pulled up again to look and saw her back with one arm stretched out and wrapped around the old man, leading him to the hallway. I darted around the house again and could hear someone barfing in the bathroom, but couldn't see who because it had frosted glass. I waited and heard movement again. I went back to the side of the house and pulled up on a different window. I watched as she eased the old man into his bed. I dropped down when she finished and tried to hear what was happening inside. It sounded like dragging. I eased up again and saw Tasha with her hands under the armpits of the old woman, pulling her to the side of the bed opposite the old guy. She tucked her under the covers."

"Were they alive?"

"I don't know. The old man was when she pulled him into the bed, but the old woman didn't seem to be. I couldn't really tell. For a minute or two, I heard nothing in there and took another glance. The old guy had the telephone receiver in his hand. Then he dropped it to the floor. I didn't know if he called anyone, but I thought I ought to warn Tasha.

"I spotted her through the kitchen window. I waved and waved at her, trying to get her attention, but she was too busy doing something on the counter by the sink and never looked up. I headed around to the front of the house to knock on the door."

"Why didn't you go to the back door? It was closer to the kitchen."

"I didn't want to scare her," he said, giving me that look that told me he thought I was stupid.

"Okay. Go on."

"Anyway, before you interrupted, I was saying that I headed to the front of the house. Just then, I saw headlights turn up the driveway, and when they got close, I saw that Hank Monroe's truck. I hid behind the spruce at the corner of the house and peered around at the front door. It was Hank Monroe all right. He burst right in, shouting for his parents."

"Wait a minute, Mr. Flagg. How did you know that it was Hank's truck?"

"Do you really have to ask?" He looked at me as if he again thought I was too dumb for words. "I told you. I kept a close watch on Tasha, right?"

I nodded.

"So, of course, when I saw that same truck parked at Tasha's house, I followed it when it left. He parked at his place, and I asked a neighbor for his name."

"You asked a neighbor? What? You just knocked on a stranger's door and asked?"

"Well, yeah."

"Really?"

Dylan smiled. "The first two doors I approached, the people acted like I was up to no good. The third one was a white-haired old lady who looked like the neighborhood gossip type. She told me that Hank and Mary Alice Monroe lived there. Ain't no big thing."

He looked so smug, I wanted to smack the grin off his face, but didn't indulge in my impulse.

"You do this a lot?" I asked.

"Enough times. Whenever I need that kind of information."

"Okay. What happened next at the farmhouse?"

"Where was I? Oh, yeah, Hank arrived. I hurried around to the bedroom window and heard Hank and Tasha yelling at each other. I heard Tasha scream, 'I did it for you—I did it for us.' Then Hank said, 'You stupid bitch.' Tasha hollered, 'Fuck you!' and footsteps went down the hallway, and I heard the back door slam. Next thing I know, Tasha was racing across the field. I started to follow her but stopped when I heard a gunshot."

"A gunshot? After Natasha left the house?"

"Yes. She was…wait a minute. I'm not sure."

I watched his facial expressions as he rolled his eyes upwards with concentration lining his face. Was he recreating the events of the evening in his mind, or was he fabricating a better story on the fly?

"Honestly, I don't know. The gunfire was shocking—like it unplugged my brain for a moment. The next thing I knew, Tasha was halfway across the field before or after the shot, I don't know. She stopped and looked back once and started running again. I was going to follow her, but I heard the other door slam shut and saw Hank run out the back of the house to the field."

"Are you sure it was Hank?"

"At the time, I was. I mean, who else could it be?" he said, with a shrug.

"Did you see his face?"

His brow furrowed. "No. But it looked like him. His height. His stride. At the time, I was certain it was him."

I was nearly breathless. I struggled not to show how much the story impacted me.

"What did you do then?"

"I waited to see if the man came back. I was thinking about following him, but figured if he had a gun, it wouldn't be a good idea. I stayed concealed behind the spruce. I heard Tasha's car start up and heard it back out, spin the rear tires a bit, and then head back down the road fast—too fast, I thought. I had one thing left to do. Race back to my car and follow Tasha. I had to make sure she didn't run off the road or get shot, and that she got home safely."

"Did she?"

"Oh yeah, I had to drive faster than I wanted, but I was able to catch up to her before she got out to the highway."

"Did you go to Hank Monroe's house?"

"Not that night."

"But you did go there."

"Yeah, I needed to talk to him. I needed to make sure he wouldn't rat out Tasha."

"You broke in, right?"

"Yeah, sometimes you just do crazy things to protect the one you love. You're a woman. You can understand that, can't you?"

"You terrified Hank's wife."

"Yeah, kind of sorry about that. I didn't know Hank was dead 'til the next day."

"What do you think happened that night out at the farm?"

"At the time, I figured the old folks got sick and died—or almost died—and Hank finished one of them off."

"Have you changed your opinion on that?"

"After thinking about it and listening to the news, I realized that Tasha, the woman I thought I loved, probably poisoned those old folks. Still can't believe she shot Hank, though."

"Who was she, Mr. Flagg?"

"What? What do you mean?"

"Well, you said you were engaged to her—your mom said it was for the last two years. You must know her very well."

"She was not a very open person."

"And yet she agreed to marry you?"

"She didn't talk about herself a lot. But she liked to read thrillers. She liked walking in the woods. She loved her coffee." Dylan paused and wiped his hands over his face. "But—but, even though we were engaged, she kept a lot of secrets. I didn't know how many, and I didn't know how dark they were. She played me, Sergeant. It's embarrassing, but she took me for a fool."

"Mr. Flagg, you've never really been engaged to Natasha Jones, have you?"

"She said yes. She really did. We were at a mutual friend's wedding, and I asked her at the reception. She said yes. She did."

"Had you both been drinking?"

"Well, I was a bit snockered, but she seemed sober. I asked her, and she agreed."

"Okay, Mr. Flagg. Have you talked to Miss Jones since you and I met out at the cabin?"

"Not really, but—"

A sharp knock on the door interrupted his answer. Jack stuck his head in the room. "A minute, Sergeant."

"Really? Now?"

Jack nodded his head. "Urgent."

I shut the door behind me, and Jack said, "Tennessee State Police on the line. They want to talk to you about the BOLO you issued. They said they needed to talk to you immediately."

Chapter Thirty-Eight

I pressed the blinking light on my desk phone. "Spencer."

"Hello, Ma'am. This is Hooper with the Tennessee Highway Patrol."

"Did you locate Natasha Jones?"

"Yes, ma'am, we sure did. We have her in lock-up at the Shelby County Jail. She was driving the car in question but insisted that she did not steal it. Said you loaned it to her."

"She would. Have you charged her?"

"Not yet, but we are holding her on suspicion of car theft. I imagine you'll want to talk to her."

"Absolutely, I'll be there as soon as I can. How was she apprehended?"

"I stopped at McDonald's. When I was waiting for my order, I saw a woman duck down the hallway to the restrooms in a hurry. At first, I thought that her bladder got the best of her like it can when you're on the road. When she came back up the hall, she'd pulled a hood up over her head and kept her face turned to the side away from me.

"I grabbed my order, stepped outside, and watched her speed-walk across the lot. I saw the vehicle she entered and thought it looked a lot like the one in the BOLO we'd received that afternoon. She wouldn't look up, just stared down at her food, so all I could see was a profile, but it fit the description.

"I pulled out of my space and went down the road a bit before pulling over. I checked on the bulletin to confirm it was the correct vehicle, saw the notification that she was possibly armed and dangerous, and called for back-up.

"We caught up with her in a few miles down Route 40. We were getting close when she spotted us, switched lanes, and sped down a ramp. She pulled into a strip mall and slipped into the alley behind the stores. We split up and came at her from both ends. She realized she was trapped, got out, jumped on a loading dock, and went into the back entrance. We followed her into a storeroom and found her hiding behind the furnace.

"I put her in my vehicle and drove her to the Shelby County Jail. For a little while, she was silent, then she wouldn't shut up. Prattling on, asking questions. 'Why are you arresting me? Do you know who I am?' She insisted she was a middle school guidance counselor and a law-abiding, tax-paying citizen. After that, she asked for an attorney.

"I told her she could make a phone call after she arrived at the jail. She demanded her cell from her purse to make that call immediately. I didn't respond. After a pause, she asked about the charges against her. I told her I wasn't certain, but car theft was pretty obvious. At that, she went off on a story about an armed intruder holding a gun to a detective's head and her narrow escape."

"The detective with a gun to her head is true—I know because I am that detective. But she knocked both of us out and tied us up," I said.

"She was too busy painting herself as a victim to make that point," Hooper said, laughing. "What a piece of work. Anyway, at that point, I asked her to be quiet until she'd been read her rights. She insisted she only ran from us because she was frightened and not thinking clearly. Then she played the helpless card—oh, I'm just a woman kind of thing. When I took her inside, she turned real nasty. Nailed me in the shin with a hard kick. Spit in a deputy's face. Shackles went on her ankles, and we locked her up in an intake cell. She was a handful. Hard to believe she works in a school system."

"She does. And that should be enough to give parents nightmares for months. Thanks a lot for nabbing her. I wonder what stories she'll dish out for me."

I disconnected from the call and looked for Jack. When I found him, I asked that he re-interview Dylan on tape so we can compare it with the story he gave me. I wanted to know if there were any inconsistencies.

Once he got started with Dylan, I went to see the Sheriff. His office door was shut tight, and laughter seeped through the cracks. I explained to his administrative assistant that my problem was urgent. She checked with him and ushered me inside. A deputy sat with an ankle crossed on his knee in a wooden chair across from the sheriff. Another one lazed against the wall. All three men turned their gaze to me as I entered.

"Sergeant Spencer, you got a problem?" Sheriff Dwayne Hatcher asked.

"Yes, sir. I need to go to Memphis."

"What for? Another sighting of Elvis?"

The two deputies guffawed and exchanged glances with the sheriff. By instinct, I knew if I were a man, my statement would have been treated with more gravity. I squelched my anger and replied in an even voice.

"Sir, the woman who stole my vehicle has been picked up by the Tennessee Highway Patrol outside of Memphis."

"They've charged her?"

"They are holding her on suspicion of car theft, sir."

"So, what's the rush?"

"I anticipate that we will need to file further charges against her."

"Like what?"

I knew he had to know what had happened up at the cabin and couldn't understand why he was being so difficult. Showing off for his buddies? Who knew?

"Possibly two or three counts of murder and two counts of abduction."

"You have evidence?"

"Physical evidence and witness testimony, sir."

"Someone saw the killings?"

"Not exactly, sir, but compelling and persuasive testimony, nonetheless. I need to talk to that woman, and Tennessee is holding her at the Shelby County Jail awaiting my arrival."

"This the Monroe case?"

"Yes, sir," I said. You know it is, you old fart, I thought, why are you dicking me around?

The deputy against the wall stood up straight. "You should have taken the advice of the sheriff and called it a murder-suicide from the get-go, and you wouldn't have such a mess to deal with," he said.

The sheriff said, "Shut up, Carson," out the side of his mouth as I gritted my teeth to keep my opinion from slipping out. "Spencer, you'd best get going, then. Sign out a department car and make sure it has a full tank. Take a deputy with you, and you can drive your own car back home. Make sure you don't take someone who you'll need back here to coordinate on this end."

"Could I take Miss Striker from the Commonwealth Attorney's Office? She's female, and that would save the department money on overnight lodging since we can share a room."

"Fine. If you can get clearance from the Commonwealth Attorney. No shortcuts. Do it right. Get it in writing. Including a split on expenses."

"Yes, sir."

"Get going."

"Yeah, girl, get going," I heard behind my back, followed by another comment from the Sheriff, "Shut up, Carson. If I need your help, I'll ask for it."

I grinned as I went up the hall to see Jack and brief him on the developments. I took the skywalk over to the C.A.'s office. Danielle agreed with alacrity. She was eager to take a "road trip"—her words, not mine—but objected to getting permission.

"I can write a note."

"No. Gotta have the big guy's approval in writing. Sheriff's orders," I said.

"Okay. C'mon."

Danielle barked at the Commonwealth Attorney's secretary, "Police emergency. Pressing business," and placed her hand on the doorknob to her boss's office. The secretary buzzed the door lock.

Danielle stated the situation in a professional manner, making multiple references to securing extradition cooperation with Tennessee. Permission granted and the C.A.'s handwritten note in my hand, we hit the road.

The ten-hour drive with added time for bathroom breaks, gas, and food, would get us to Memphis by midnight. After a decent amount of sleep, we would be ready to go to the Shelby County Jail first thing in the morning.

Every time Danielle took the wheel, I called Jack for updates.

He had a lot to report, something new each time. Dylan Flagg was charged and locked up until my return. Jack compared my interview tape with the story Dylan told him. "No significant changes, only the addition of being victimized by you. I won't repeat what he called you."

I could imagine.

On another call, Jack told me that an old friend had bailed out Chuck Monroe and taken him home for a night or two. Lawyers for Travis Ferguson and Sylvester Harding had called in to talk to me, and Martha Ferguson dropped by to raise a fuss about her grandson. Mary Alice Monroe had called to make sure I was okay. Wasn't sure what to think about that last one, but Jack swore her concern for my welfare seemed genuine.

The last time I called, fate had turned. "I don't have good news this time. I finally got the ballistics report from the lab on the gun found in Hank's truck," Jack said.

I waited for a bit, and when he didn't continue, I said, "Spit it out, Jack."

"That was the weapon that killed Hank Monroe."

Another long pause. "And?" I asked.

"The prints were wiped off the gun, but he missed one. It matches the third finger of Chuck Monroe's right hand."

"Bring in Chuck."

"He left his friend's house. He wasn't where he said he was going. We're trying."

"Try harder."

* * *

Danielle and I were both beat when we checked into the hotel. We dropped our bags just inside the door and collapsed across one of the beds sideways. After a few minutes of rest, Danielle offered the shower to me, and I told her to go first. When she came out wrapped in a towel, holding a glass of water, she asked, "You want an Ambien to help you sleep?"

"You have a prescription?"

"No. I've been raiding the evidence lock-up. Really, Charley, did you have to ask? Of course, I have a prescription."

The sarcasm stung, but I was too tired to care. "I don't, Danielle. Thanks, but no thanks. The possibility of getting caught in a random drug test is too much of a risk to take."

"Oh, please. I'll tell them that I dropped it in your soda because I felt sorry for you or because I thought it was mine. No problem."

I sighed. "I'm taking a shower now. Sleep well."

Danielle sure had no problem with dodging the rules. I had to watch my step around her, or I'd pay the price one day.

Chapter Thirty-Nine

Despite our exhaustion from the previous day's ordeal, Danielle and I were both awake before six that morning. Danielle, however, blinked a lot, and her gaze was less than steady as she sucked down coffee to counteract her Ambien hangover. Anxious about the upcoming interview, I was not eager to eat but knew I needed to fuel up before the day ahead. I ate my scrambled eggs and toast without tasting a bite. Danielle, on the other hand, devoured her stack of pancakes and bacon with gusto.

* * *

I turned in my weapon at the front desk of the jail, and a deputy escorted us down a long hall. I peered through the window at my suspect. Natasha looked imperious with her perfect posture and jutting chin. Looking into her face was like gazing into February, all frost, ice, and storms. She sat next to a long-haired man wearing a disheveled suit jacket and a tie half-undone at the neck.

The deputy said, "Don't be fooled by his appearance. Martin Vanderbilt—or Marty as he likes to be called—is a prominent and successful defense attorney here in Memphis who makes prosecutors cry in their beer."

"We'll see about that," Danielle said. "I'm a red wine gal. We're made of sturdier stuff."

As I opened the door, Natasha straightened her spine to even more erectness, and her attorney smirked in our direction. He stood up, extended a hand and said, "Marty Vanderbilt and this is my client, Natasha Jones."

"Sergeant Spencer." I extended my right hand, then gestured towards my companion. "Assistant Commonwealth Attorney, Ms. Striker. Good morning, Miss Jones. I assume you know why you're here."

"Not really," Natasha said. "I borrowed your car because mine wouldn't start, and suddenly everyone was chasing me."

"Why don't you enlighten me, Sergeant?" Vanderbilt asked.

"Of course. Currently in Virginia, your client is facing charges of car theft, two counts of abduction, and two charges of assault or perhaps even attempted murder. And, I do believe, Tennessee is pressing charges on resisting arrest and two counts of assaulting an officer while in custody."

"For that, you chase her across the whole length of Tennessee?"

Danielle blew out her exasperation through her lips and said, "We are also interested in the possibility of charging her with triple murder."

"No one saw my client administer poison to that sweet old couple. No one saw her shoot the father of the child she is carrying," Vanderbilt objected.

"No," Danielle snapped back, "but we do have evidence of the drug that poisoned them in her home, and we do have a witness who saw her on the premises of the crime scene. And obviously, Martin Vanderbilt, Esquire, you know far more about your client's actions than you indicated."

I saw a bristle of irritation dance across Vanderbilt's expression before he forced a smile.

"No formalities, please. Marty is sufficient. That so-called evidence is certainly not enough to convict, and you know it."

Tired of the lawyer-on-lawyer squabble, I interrupted, "Miss Jones, I would like to ask you a few questions. What about the grains of Fentanyl found on the mortar and pestle in your closet?"

"I answered that already."

"Humor me."

"Asked and answered, Sergeant," the lawyer said, sounding bored.

"Oh, for heaven's sake," Natasha said. "Hank borrowed my mortar and pestle to grind up some pills for his mother. I had no idea what was in them. If I had, I would have stopped him."

"Are you saying he killed his parents?"

"I suppose it's possible. I didn't see him do that. If I had, I would have told you so."

"Really? Did you guess that he poisoned his parents and shoot him in anger over what he had done?"

"How dare you even suggest that. He's the father of my baby." She rubbed a palm across her stomach. "I needed him alive to help me care for our child. Besides, with his parents dead, I was exactly where I wanted to be. Hank said he wanted to leave his wife and marry me. But his parents adored Mary Alice. If he divorced her, they might cut him out of their will. With his parents out of the way, I'd be a fool to kill Hank."

"Are you confessing to the murder of the elderly couple?" I asked.

"Sergeant, that's uncalled for," Vanderbilt said.

"Besides, that is not what I was saying." Natasha grimaced and tossed her long hair over her shoulders. "I was just saying that their death was coincidentally good luck for me. The serendipity of karma, if you will."

"So, you think Hank killed his parents, and you were okay with him being a murderer as long as he took care of you and the child?"

"I did not say that. I do not know that he killed his parents. All I know is that I saw them dead on the bed, and I saw him in the bedroom. I have no idea if the two are connected."

Her smug look made me want to reach across the table and smack it off her face. I swallowed hard and resisted temptation. "What were you doing in the farmhouse that night?"

"I went to get help from Hank's parents."

"Help?"

"Yes. Hank was pushing me to get an abortion. I thought they would want to help me save their grandchild."

"Was Hank's insistence on an abortion the reason you killed him?"

"I did not kill him." Tears slid down her face. "I loved him."

Real emotion? Or faked? I didn't know.

Vanderbilt interjected. "This questioning is out of line. My client is pregnant, and you are upsetting her. Look at her—she's crying."

On cue, Natasha sobbed, and her shoulders shook.

"You should be ashamed of yourself, Sergeant," Vanderbilt added.

I rolled my eyes. Before I could make the crocodile tears accusation that was on the tip of my tongue, Danielle entered the fray.

"You should know, Mr. Vanderbilt, that we are assembling the evidence to charge your client with triple murder. When that happens, I will seek the death penalty."

Natasha gasped and paled.

"I call that intimidation of a witness, counselor," Vanderbilt barked.

"She's a person of interest, Mr. Vanderbilt. Time and her level of cooperation will tell if we charge her or treat her as a witness."

"I call that a threat," Vanderbilt retorted.

Danielle pulled her chin back to her neck as her lips curled in distaste. "Jeez, where did you go to law school? I call it an incentive to be honest."

"I call it harassment."

"Look at it from my point of view, Martin. I think she poisoned Mr. and Mrs. Monroe and then put them into their bed and covered them up. When Hank Monroe arrived, she shot him to cover up her crime. That is clearly within the realm of the death penalty. You're a Tennessee lawyer—not a Massachusetts attorney—you should be able to see those grounds readily."

"Only through the eyes of an over-eager, barely ethical prosecutor does that make any sense. The judge would throw you out of the courtroom."

"Excuse me," Natasha said as she lurched to her feet. "You are talking about me. I am not a trophy. Once I'm disposed of, neither one of you will care. So, shut up. I want to talk to Sergeant Spencer alone."

"I cannot condone that without counsel present," Vanderbilt objected.

"Fine. But sit there and keep your pie hole shut. And you, too," she said, pointing at Danielle.

For a few moments, no one spoke. Natasha slid down onto her chair, squirmed into a comfortable position, and replaced the haughtiness in her expression with a smarmy sweetness.

"Sergeant Spencer, you've always spoken the truth to me, and I believe that is a character trait of yours. So, give me a straight, honest answer. Is that woman serious about the death penalty?"

"Yes, Miss Jones. I'm sure she is. The death penalty is always considered in a triple murder. She does not have total control over the outcome, but I suspect she will push hard to get it."

"Thank you. Would you say that about a double murder?"

"Not necessarily. It would depend on the individual situation. For instance, were the two murders committed as a single act or not?"

"Okay. If you and the other woman will excuse me for a bit, I will confer with my attorney."

"Certainly," I said. "Let's leave them to it, Ms. Striker."

Out in the hall, Danielle asked, "Is she ready to break?"

"I don't know. I don't trust her. She could be playing us."

"I think she wants to confess."

"We'll see. Hush, now, I want to watch them."

At first, Natasha did all the talking. Vanderbilt sat across from her, and rested his forearms on the table, and turned his body towards her, his expression intent. Without warning, he jolted up from his seat and threw both arms up in the air. He paced from one side of the room to the other, rapidly gesticulating.

Natasha interrupted him, speaking for a minute or two. Her lawyer leaned over the table, rested one palm on the surface, and with the other banged hard on the tabletop three times. Natasha shook her head.

Vanderbilt's shoulders collapsed. He eased back into the chair and cradled both her hands in his. I was dying to know what they were saying to each other, but knew I'd have to wait.

"This could take a while," Danielle said. "I'll see if I can scare us up a cup of coffee."

I leaned against the window frame and watched the two heads bent close together, like any good co-conspirators would do. I might get some truth from Natasha, but I knew, regardless of what she told her attorney, all I would get was partial honesty—a story distorted by self-preservation.

After Danielle returned with two hot mugs, I barely had time to sip before Vanderbilt motioned to us to return. I studied their faces. Natasha would not meet my eyes, and Vanderbilt had an obvious expression of loathing on his face—I didn't know whether it was directed at me, Danielle, or his client.

"My client wants a plea bargain agreement," he said.

"I'm sure she does," Danielle said.

Vanderbilt's body tensed as if it took all his strength to suppress a volcano of rage. I wondered if he hated bargaining with a woman. Danielle had said in the past that she'd faced a lot of that from male defense attorneys.

Vanderbilt said, "Miss Jones has valuable information involving the murder of all three people in that farmhouse. We want all the pending charges dropped in exchange for cooperating with the prosecution of the crimes."

"Is she willing to testify in court?"

"Absolutely."

"And you believe that the information she has is so exclusive to her that it is worth dropping a charge of abduction?" Danielle asked.

"Come on. You know that is only a technical charge. She abducted no one. Sergeant Spencer was brought into Miss Jones' cabin at gunpoint. My client didn't do that. Dylan Flagg did."

"There are also two attempted murder charges. I find it difficult to believe that she possesses knowledge of a great enough magnitude to whitewash that."

"Oh, for pity's sake. She didn't throw them nude and bound out in the woods."

"No. But she turned off the heat and hoped they would freeze to death."

"But they didn't."

"I'll drop the car theft charge in exchange for information."

"That's not sufficient."

"What about seven years for each of the remaining charges?" Danielle suggested.

"Concurrent?"

"No. Consecutive."

"That's still twenty-one years. Not acceptable."

While they stared at each other, I felt like a pawn. How much was my life worth? I wanted answers, but Danielle sounded as if she was willing to overlook my ordeal and give Natasha nothing more than a slap on the wrist.

"All right. Concurrent."

"If her cooperation and testimony lead to successful prosecution, how about probation?" Vanderbilt pushed.

"Successful prosecution of all involved parties?"

"Of course."

"All contingent on the fact that she tells the truth. We catch her in a lie, and the deal is off."

"Not a problem. May I have a minute to confer with my client?"

I was dumbfounded. Out in the hall, I turned on Danielle. "What have you done? How could you let her off the hook so easily? Am I nothing?" Danielle laughed in my face. I was outraged. "Don't ever talk to me again," I said and turned to walk away.

Before I got two steps, she grabbed my arm and said, "Silly girl. I'm taking a risk, but I think I've got Natasha's number. She can't help but tell a lie. I am certain she killed Mr. and Mrs. Monroe. She's going to point the finger at someone else, and you are going to uncover her dishonesty. You know she's guilty, right? Honey, Natasha Jones is going away for a long time."

"Call me a skeptic, Danielle. I don't have your confidence about the outcome."

"Don't worry. I'll prove it to you. Look, Vanderbilt is ready for our return."

We were barely through the door when Vanderbilt said, "My client is ready to speak now. Go ahead, Miss Jones."

Natasha sat with her head bowed and her hands folded in a demure arrangement on the table. She raised her downcast eyes and smiled at her lawyer. Turning toward Danielle, she said, "Thank you, Ms. Striker." She cleared her throat and looked at me. "Sergeant, this has been a very difficult situation for me. I hope you will accept my apology for the treatment I gave you at the cabin. I was in shock and was not thinking clearly. I was thinking about my baby and not myself." She looked at me with great expectation of a positive response.

I squeezed my eyes tight to keep them from rolling and said, "Of course."

Natasha smiled with all the sweetness she could muster. "I was terrified that night," she began. "I went out to the farmhouse to solicit support from

Hank's parents, as I said. But Hank was already there. The front door was wide open, so I thought something must be wrong. I rushed in and saw Hank dragging his father down the hall and putting him in the bed. I asked him what was wrong with his parents, and he said, 'They're dead at last.' I said, 'Hank, what happened?' He said, 'They won't be standing in our way now, Natasha. We can get married and make a home for our baby.' I asked, 'Did you kill them, Hank?' Then, he said, 'Ask me after we're married.' I didn't know what to do. It looked like he was responsible, and if he was, did I want to marry a man who was capable of killing his own parents?" She sniffled.

I pushed a box of tissues across the table, wondering if she realized she was contradicting her previous response. She gave me a weak smile, blew her nose, and dabbed at her eyes.

I asked, "What happened, then, Miss Jones?"

"A man burst through the basement door and pushed past me—"

"Do you know who that man was?"

"I think so. He looked like Hank, so it must have been his brother, Chuck. And he said, 'You son of a bitch.' And a gun went off." She gasped and wiped at her eyes again.

"What did you do then, Miss Jones?"

"I turned and ran out of the house as fast as I could. I was afraid he would kill me next."

Danielle put a hand on my forearm. I turned to her and saw the question in her face. I nodded my agreement that she speak. "Miss Jones, do you know Marvin Givens?

Tasha shook her head. "No."

"On the street, he's known as Mo' Money."

Vanderbilt leaned forward. "For heaven's sake, Striker. My client is a middle school guidance counselor. Street names aren't exactly her forte. How could she know something like that?"

Danielle ignored the defense attorney. "How about Bobby Lee Hunter, Miss Jones?"

"The name sounds vaguely familiar, but I don't think I know him personally. It could be a student's name. I don't know for sure."

Danielle turned to me with a huge I-told-you-so grin. "Thank you, Miss Jones."

"Are you satisfied, Sergeant?" Vanderbilt asked.

"No. Not yet. I have a couple more questions. Natasha, when you left the farmhouse, did you go to your car?"

"Yes, ma'am."

"Where was it parked?"

"At the edge of the next driveway up the road."

"Why did you park there?"

"I saw Hank's truck in his parents' driveway, and I didn't want to give him a heads up on my arrival."

"Really? He's the father of your baby. Why would you be concerned about that?"

"Well, I figured if he saw me coming up the drive, he would know I was there to talk to his parents about their grandchild. I didn't want him to say something to get them on his side before I had a chance to speak my piece."

"Just to satisfy my curiosity, Miss Jones, I'd like to ask a question about Dylan Flagg."

Natasha rolled her eyes. "Yeah, go ahead. What do you want to know about that loser?"

"Were you two ever really engaged to be married?"

"Oh, Good Lord, no."

"He said he proposed, and you accepted."

"Only an idiot would have believed I was serious. I didn't realize then that Dylan was as brain-dead as roadkill. Look. We were at a wedding. We were both drinking. He was staggering drunk. He proposed. I didn't take him seriously. I squeezed his face in one hand and said, 'Yes. Of course, I'll marry you, little man.' I explained later I didn't mean it, but he wouldn't listen."

"Why did you tell me at the cabin that you thought Dylan Flagg killed the elder Monroes?"

Natasha sighed. "I must be honest with you, ma'am. I lied because I wanted your assistance tying up the little son of a bitch. I was afraid of him, and I needed your help."

"Until you didn't," I snapped back.

"I said I was sorry. I was so mixed up and distraught that night. I shouldn't have done that to you. Won't you please accept my apology?"

Natasha's eyes were wide open, and her lashes were batting as if in rhythm to some song running through her head.

"I see. I have no more questions at this time."

"Can I take my client home now?"

"No. She will be held in custody here in Tennessee. They've filed for car theft, assault, and resisting arrest."

"But she's cooperated—"

"Yes. But I do have to verify her version of events."

"You doubt them?"

Danielle could keep quiet no longer. "Counselor, please. She pinned the blame for two murders on a dead man and one on a missing man. We have two witnesses who place her there and who contradict her story in some regards. I will be preparing extradition papers when I return."

"Two witnesses?" Natasha said. "Chuck and who?"

"You think about that, sweetheart," Danielle said.

We both left and drove over to trooper headquarters to speak with the arresting officers before we headed home.

Chapter Forty

The ride back was more grueling and boring in two vehicles. Danielle and I coordinated our stops for gas, restrooms, and food. All in all, it was a long, lonely experience. I had a lot of time to think. If Chuck had told us what really happened, Natasha murdered all three people. If Dylan spoke the truth, Natasha killed Mr. and Mrs. Monroe, and either she or Chuck shot Hank. If Natasha's story were true, Hank Monroe killed his parents and was murdered by his brother. And I had no idea which scenario was true. Probably, every single one was wrapped around a lie. Somehow, I had to disentangle each knotty deception and dispose of the deception. Otherwise, a jury would find reasonable doubt, and I would've failed everyone again.

I was crossing the Virginia line in Bristol when my cell rang—Jack was on the line.

"We found Chuck Monroe."

"Is he at the justice center?"

"He's on his way."

"Hold him there. I should be back in three hours or so. I've made it just inside Virginia. Can you get Dylan Flagg over from the jail? Miss Jones contradicted some of his testimony. I want to nail this all down as quick as I can."

"Alrighty. See you soon."

I called Danielle. She answered with a question. "You need to pee again already?"

I laughed and assured her a stop was not needed. "I have good news.

Chuck's in custody. I'll see what he has to say about Natasha's version of events."

"I betcha every last one of these guys has a lie or two in their stories."

"That's usually true. I wanted a homicide case, so I'm the lucky girl who gets to separate the b.s. from the facts."

* * *

When we got back to town, Danielle exited the highway first, heading for home. It was well past dark before I pulled up to the justice center. Jack greeted me at the elevator.

"Hey, Chuck is fidgety but quiet. Dylan is throwing a fit, hollering about harassment. I told him you had a few questions to ask him, but he still won't settle down."

"I'll get to him first. I need to review his statement again, but you can tell him I'll only be a few minutes."

I arrived at his interview room at the promised time.

"It's about damned time," he said as I entered the door.

I ignored his surly attitude. "Good evening, Dylan. So nice to see you again. I want to go over your statement and make sure you left nothing out of it that matters and straighten out some contradictions in the story that I got when I talked to Miss Jones."

"Well, she's a liar. Always has been."

"Okay, Dylan, let's stick to facts. Now you told me that when you arrived at the farm, the only person there with Mr. and Mrs. Monroe was Natasha Jones, correct?"

"Yep."

"No one else was there?"

"Nope. Not then. Hank's truck didn't arrive until later."

"Okay. You said that you couldn't hear all the conversation, but you did hear some of it when Natasha was shouting at Hank. You said that she said, 'I did it for you. I did it for us.' Is that correct?"

"Yeah, something like that."

"Something like that?"

"Well, yeah, exactly like that."

"Now, I want you to think really hard. At first, you said that when you heard the gunshot, Natasha was outside. Then you said you weren't sure. I need you to focus on that one little moment in the timeline. Inside or out? Think."

"I—" Dylan began, shaking his head.

"Try," I urged.

He bowed his head and closed his eyes. I sat still, hoping he was thinking and not taking a power nap. After three minutes, he looked up. "I can't swear that she was inside when the shot fired, but I am certain that I did not see her outside until after the gun went off."

"You're certain about that?"

He nodded his head.

"Are you positive that you didn't see the person you thought was Hank Monroe until after you saw Miss Jones running towards her car?"

"Oh, yeah. I'm sure about that."

"Okay, Dylan. Thank you. I'll get you taken back to lock-up as quick as I can."

* * *

I leaned my back against the wall. Who had the most to gain from the deaths? At first, I thought Mary Alice did it, based on what she would gain financially from the will, but she was no longer a viable suspect unless I'd misread everything—a possibility I could not afford to entertain at this time. I'd let it disrupt my sleep later.

Natasha had a vested interest in the deaths of the elder Monroes, but why would she kill Hank, except, maybe, in a fit of anger? Did Hank tell her that he still had no intention of leaving his wife and threw Natasha into an irrational rage?

I believed Chuck wanted his parents alive because he yearned for reconciliation. But what about Hank? If Chuck wanted his brother to own up to his lie, he would want him alive, wouldn't he?

And Dylan—an admitted stalker, willing to force me under his control at gunpoint—what did he have to gain from any of the murders? He had jealousy as a reason to kill Hank—one of the oldest motives in the world. Was there something else I couldn't see? Or was he the most credible one in the bunch? Now that was a scary thought.

I pushed away from the wall and went down the hall to the interview room where Chuck waited. He was the most pathetic guy in the bunch. I didn't want him to be guilty, but his fingerprint was the only one on the gun that killed Hank.

Chuck was bent over in his chair with his head resting on the tabletop. Sound asleep, he didn't move when I entered the room. I laid a palm on his back and said his name. He sat up, confusion on his face. He shook his head and looked up at me.

"Sergeant Spencer?" he said.

"Yes, Chuck. We need to have a conversation. I've talked to a couple of people whose statements are not consistent with yours, and we found evidence that you did not tell me the whole truth."

"What does that mean?"

"Chuck, we found a gun hidden in Hank's truck."

"You did? Hank always liked guns. I'm surprised that you found only one."

"Someone had wiped all the prints off the weapon but missed one."

Chuck stared down at the surface of the table.

"It was your print, Chuck."

"Okay. I left something out of my story. It seemed like a good idea at the time."

"What didn't you tell me, Chuck?"

"Well, before I went upstairs that night at the farmhouse, I went out to the truck hoping the keys would be in the ignition. They weren't, but there was a gun in the glove box. I took it to get Hank to give me the keys to his truck. I went back into the basement and crept up the stairs. I opened the door and went into the hall. Just as I got to the bedroom entryway, that woman jumped out and grabbed the gun. She was waving it around, and I ran out of the house."

"How did you get the keys to the truck, Mr. Monroe?"

"Oh, right, I left that out. They were in the ignition the whole time. Don't know why I didn't see them when I first went into the truck."

"Uh, huh. What else haven't you told me?"

"Umm. Oh, I heard a gunshot as I opened the door of the truck."

"Did you see anyone else at the farmhouse? In the house or in the yard?"

"No," he said with a shrug.

"There was someone else there, Mr. Monroe. He was hiding on the side of the house. He saw you. He thought you were Hank."

"Maybe it was Hank," Chuck said.

"No, Mr. Monroe. The witness heard a gunshot before he saw you exit the house."

"He must be mistaken. Or, maybe, maybe, he shot Hank. Maybe he poisoned my parents."

"It's more likely that Natasha Jones murdered your parents. The witness who saw you leave also observed Miss Jones dragging their bodies into the bedroom. He wasn't sure who fired the shot that killed Hank. He knew it had to be you or Miss Jones because you both fled *after* the shot fired."

"It was the Jones woman who shot Hank."

"But, Mr. Monroe, we found your fingerprint on the murder weapon. Not a single one belonging to another person. Why did you kill your brother?"

"I didn't. I didn't. I didn't," Chuck said, thrashing his head from side to side, causing tears to splash around the room. He grew still, and for a minute, then he asked, "Are you saying that Hank didn't kill Momma and Pops?"

"No, Chuck, he didn't."

"That woman did?"

"It appears that way."

Chuck squeezed his eyes shut and threw a hand over his mouth. "Oh my God! Oh my God! I should have shot her."

"What are you telling me, Mr. Monroe?"

"Oh my God! Oh my God! Oh my God!" he said, with his head thrashing back and forth again.

I switched to his given name. "Chuck! Chuck, look at me."

He raised his head and wiped his eyes. "I'm so sorry. Oh God, I'm so sorry."

"Why, Chuck?"

"I only did it because I thought he killed my parents. I thought he did it so that I could never talk to them."

"Chuck, are you saying that you fired the shot that killed Hank Monroe?"

"I think I need a lawyer," he said. He threw his head on the table and sobbed.

Part of me wanted to put an arm around his shoulders and comfort him. He was such a sad case. Instead, I stood and said, "Charles Monroe, I am charging you with the murder of your brother Hank Monroe. Deputies will be in here in a few minutes to take you to lock-up where you will be processed once again.

Chapter Forty-One

Eight months after that sad interview with Chuck, I watched the crowd in my dad's condo overlooking the James River. Smiling faces, hands clutching glasses filled with wine or martinis. The room was filled with rented, round, chest-high tables surrounded by groups of people and filled with plates piled with shrimp, meatballs, and a host of other mundane and exotic edibles. A lot of laughter and joking; here and there, a serious conversation.

Most jubilant were the bride and groom, holding hands, exchanging glances, beaming like floodlights. Every time I looked at the newlyweds, I had to smile. At times, I had wondered if Dad would ever get past Mom's murder. It did a daughter's heart good to see his joy today. I still could not understand why Ruby refused to celebrate Dad's happiness. I kept expecting her to change her mind, but yesterday, if anything, she was angrier than ever. First, she accused me of betraying Mom for attending the wedding. Then, she switched to claiming that I had stabbed Lucinda in the back by not stopping Dad from marrying "that other woman." Basically, Ruby lived in a bubble of confusion and immaturity. I hoped that time would reshape her perspective.

Most of the people at the reception were strangers to me—family and friends of the bride, medical professionals Emily and Dad worked with at their respective hospitals, or through their missions with Doctors Without Borders. Here and there were friends of mine. I looked out at the outdoor space, which was glorious in October with the red, gold, and orange trees lining the river. Many were out there enjoying the view on what the developers had called a riverfront balcony—the name balcony seemed odd since it's so expansive, running the full length of the living space and wrapping around the corner to the French doors off the master bedroom. Out there, I saw Jack chatting with a pretty, blonde nurse. He'd agreed to come to the wedding as my escort once I promised him free food, booze, and lots of smart, pretty, young women.

At the kitchen island, my mentor, Lieutenant Lucinda Pierce, sat on a stool talking intently with the hospital pathologist. She had, once again, been a great support as I struggled through the aftermath of my first homicide case. The media kept trying to make me the star of their stories in the newspaper and on television. Lucinda helped me to navigate the onslaught and to keep the focus where I wanted it—on the victims and on justice.

I'd seen Mary Alice Monroe several times after the arrests. In the summer, she'd moved out of her cute little Cape Cod and put it up for sale. She asked if I thought she should adopt Natasha's baby since it was her husband's, too. I warned her that it could be a big mistake that kept her tied to the past. Mary Alice took my advice. She was in Williamsburg now, a freshman at William and Mary. She wanted to get her degree and then attend graduate school to become a social worker or a legal aid attorney in the Domestic Violence field. Neither one paid the big bucks, but, with her inheritance, she certainly didn't need the money.

Kent Howard took on Chuck Monroe's case pro bono. Chuck agreed to testify against Natasha Jones and pled guilty to a lesser charge. He was now serving seven years for manslaughter. Mary Alice visited his lawyer after the case was closed and left a substantial amount of money with Howard to hold in escrow for Chuck until his release.

"I know he killed my husband," Mary Alice said, "but Hank cheated him. I want to do something to balance the scales."

Dylan Flagg asked me out to dinner and a movie several times, and my increasingly forceful refusal never dimmed his enthusiasm. His mother offered me one hundred thousand dollars to get the charges dropped against her son. She portrayed him as an innocent victim of the manipulative Natasha Jones. I turned her down, too. Dylan was a dangerous man in need of psychological help. After I saw him lurking around my apartment on three occasions, I spoke to the Commonwealth Attorney, who had his bail revoked. Dylan was sitting behind bars awaiting trial.

Natasha Jones gave birth in jail to an eight-pound, seven-ounce baby girl. The infant was in foster care while Natasha took her time deciding whether to relinquish her parental rights and allow the baby to be adopted. In a recent television interview, she still spouted venom about me, Dylan, Hank, and the justice system, saying we all took advantage of her fragile state as an expectant mother. Even thinking about it made my eyes roll. Her attorneys were bargaining with the prosecutors, hoping to get a good deal. Danielle assured me that they were willing to drop the death penalty but were determined to get life without parole in the plea agreement.

When Emily and Dad planned the wedding reception, they asked for my input. My typical response was "whatever makes you happy" or "whatever you do, I'll be there." I knew it was frustrating for Emily. She wanted to please me, and I wasn't helping with my non-answers. I think Ruby made her skittish about a relationship with either of us. Then, one day, she asked me about the food that would be served. Her eyes were intense, she bit her lower lip, and I realized at that moment how much it mattered to her that something at the party would be special to me.

"Soft, warm chocolate chip cookies," I said.

"Really?" she said with her head tilted at an angle.

"Really. Any chance you could bake them yourself?"

Emily had looked at my dad with a furrowed brow and a puckered mouth. I could tell she sensed something was going over her head. Still, she'd looked back at me and nodded.

"Sure, I can do that."

Dad had squeezed my arm and planted a kiss on the top of my forehead. "Emily, I'll explain later. For now, let's just say you don't need to worry about Charley accepting you ever again."

I rose from the sofa, grabbed a glass of wine at the bar, and walked over to the buffet. At the far end of the table, a warming tray waited. Loaded with chocolate chip cookies. I grabbed one. Making sure I was in Dad's line of vision, I sank my teeth into it, letting the gooey goodness fill my mouth. Dad poked Emily, and she turned towards me. She raised her champagne glass in the air and gave me a smile.

About the Author

Diane Fanning is the Edgar Finalist, bestselling author of fifteen true crime books and thirteen works of crime fiction, and a recipient of the Defender of Innocence award from the Innocence Project. She lives in Bedford, Virginia.

AUTHOR WEBSITE:

  http://dianefanning.com

SOCIAL MEDIA HANDLES:

  https://www.facebook.com/diane.fanning/
  twitter.com/dianefanning
  https://bsky.app/dianefanning
  https://www.instagram.com/dianefanning

Also by Diane Fanning

Lizzie

The Trophy Exchange

Punish the Deed

Mistaken Identity

Twisted Reason

False Front

Wrong Turn

Chain Reaction

Scandal in the Secret City

Treason in the Secret City

Sabotage in the Secret City

Bite the Moon

Through the Window

Into the Water

Written in Blood

Gone Forever

The Pastor's Wife

Out There

Under the Knife

Baby Be Mine

Her Deadly Web

Sleep My Darlings

Mommy's Little Girl

A Poisoned Passion

Under Cover of the Night

Bitter Remains

Death on the River